Acclaim for the Songbird Series

ACCLAIM FOR
Love Lifted Me

"Country singer and songwriter Evans and novelist Hauck (*Dining with Joy*, 2010) have proven to be a winning team. [*Love Lifted Me*] . . . carries [an] emotional wallop . . ."

—*Booklist*, starred review

"[T]ouching and emotive . . . sizzles with passion . . . a beautiful story of hope tackling betrayal and love manning up to win the game."

—USAToday.com

"The third installment of Evans' Christ-centered drama about a woman who is redeemed through submitting to God and forgiving her husband . . . Feel-good fare."

—*Kirkus Reviews*

CLAIM FOR

nd Tenderly

r family stories will love this southern-
"

—Lisa Wingate, best-selling author of
Tending Roses and *Larkspur Cove*

ACCLAIM FOR
The Sweet By and By

"A heartwarming collaborative debut."

—*Publishers Weekly*

"Enter the magic of Whisper Hollow and open your heart. Like Sara Evans's bittersweet songs, the notes and melody of Jade Fitzgerald's past sing a new future. In a world of wounded souls, forgiveness and redemption are the lyrics of this enchanting story."

—Patti Callahan Henry, *New York Times* best-selling author of *Driftwood Summer*

"*The Sweet By and By* is the flowing story of a family struggling across the generations for redemption and reconciliation. The women in this novel are sometimes funny, sometimes serious, but always interesting. I was hooked from page one."

—Homer Hickam, best-selling author of *Rocket Boys* and *The Red Helmet*

". . . witty dialogue, believable characters, and a page-turner of a plot. Just what I look for in a good book!"

—Cassandra King, author of *The Same Sweet Girls*

Love Lifted Me

Love Lifted Me

SARA EVANS
WITH RACHEL HAUCK

THOMAS NELSON
Since 1798

NASHVILLE   DALLAS   MEXICO CITY   RIO DE JANEIRO

Published in Nashville, Tennessee, by Thomas Nelson. Thomas Nelson is a registered trademark of Thomas Nelson, Inc.

Thomas Nelson, Inc., titles may be purchased in bulk for educational, business, fund-raising, or sales promotional use. For information, please e-mail SpecialMarkets@ThomasNelson.com.

Scripture quotations are taken from the NEW KING JAMES VERSION, © 1982 by Thomas Nelson, Inc. Used by permission. All rights reserved.

Published in association with the literary agency of Alive Communications, Inc., 7680 Goddard Street, Suite 200, Colorado Springs, CO 80920.

Publisher's Note: This novel is a work of fiction. Any references to real events, businesses, organizations, and locales are intended only to give the fiction a sense of reality and authenticity. Any resemblance to actual persons, living or dead, is entirely coincidental.

ISBN 978-1-4016-8721-2 (trade paper)

Library of Congress Cataloging-in-Publication Data

Evans, Sara, 1971-

Love lifted me / Sara Evans with Rachel Hauck.
p. cm. -- (A songbird novel ; 3)
ISBN 978-1-59554-491-9 (hardcover)
1. Married people--Fiction. 2. Betrayal--Fiction. 3. Forgiveness--Fiction. 4. Career changes--Fiction. 5. Tennessee--Fiction. 6. Texas--Fiction. 7. Domestic fiction. I. Hauck, Rachel, 1960- II. Title.
PS3605.V3765L68 2012
813'.6--dc22
2011038299

Printed in the United States of America
12 13 14 15 16 17 QG 6 5 4 3 2 1

One

By the time July's heat settled over the Appalachians, Jade Benson was getting a little bit stronger. As she unlocked the front door of her riverfront Chattanooga shop, the Blue Two, she knew what she had to do.

The hollow sound of her footsteps in the empty shop echoed in her soul and back again.

Jade dropped her keys on the sales counter, a lovely antique case once belonging to Woolworth's, and peered in the Walmart bag swinging from her fingertips.

For Sale.

If she'd learned anything from the spring, it was that sometimes a girl had to let things go—the past, fears, hurts, dreams—and start over.

You are here. Chart a new course.

Jade wadded up the plastic bag as she pulled out the For Sale sign and considered her options.

Should she sell? Surveying the shop, she considered the remodeled walls, the new windows and door. The fragrance of lumber and fresh paint lingered in the air.

When a racing F350 had crashed through the Blue Two in the wee hours of a March morning, she never dreamed it would symbolize her life.

But, ho boy, and boy howdy. Jade tapped the sign against her palm. Yeah, sell. She never wanted a second vintage shop anyway. The venture had been her mother-in-law's brainchild. Not for herself, of course, but for Jade.

She'd resisted until the second miscarriage. But then busyness proved to be the drug she'd needed to get through the days.

A lot had changed since she opened this store over a year ago. She wasn't *just* Jade Benson, business owner and Maxwell Benson's wife. She was a mother. At least that's what her heart told her every morning when she woke up with Max's son sleeping down the hall.

Asa. The twenty-two-month-old with expressive brown eyes and bow lips called her *Mama*. He was the beautiful silver lining amid Max's betrayal and Jade's mama's death. The mama who forced her to take command of her life and stop being led where she didn't want to go.

All this time she thought she was in control. But fear had ruled her from her core out.

Asa was a complete and utter wonder. Jade never tired of him and each time his pulpy little hand slipped into hers, she changed. It was the most magical feeling on earth. Possibly in heaven.

Oh Max, you broke my heart, then healed it with your son.

Except things with the little charmer's father weren't settled. Their Saturday calls were charged with feelings waiting to be spoken face-to-face. Jade expected Max home any day now, but when she asked for a specific date, he'd answered with a vague, "Next week."

Believe it or not, she understood him. He was nervous. Not quite ready to face his mess. Neither was she.

Jade leaned against the window and stared toward the Tennessee River and the downtown park. She missed springtime—the festivals and the flow of vintage-hunting customers. She missed the bloom of the magnolias. With the remodel, this shop could—no, *would*—take off. But her heart belonged somewhere else.

Do it.

Why did doing the right thing prove challenging? Jade crossed the barren shop with a determined thump of her heels and snatched the Scotch tape off the top of her desk.

Tearing off two strips, she returned to the front pane and stuck the sign to the glass.

For Sale.

She stepped back, testing her decision. The Blue Two was for sale. Closing. Going away. This part of her life would be over.

Jade exhaled. Relief. The shop had served its purpose. Now it was time to move on.

She didn't have time to linger—she needed to pick up Asa from school. Jade had him in Ritterhouse Academy from eleven to two every day. While he played, she ran errands and took care of shop business.

She might be selling the Blue Two, but she still had the Blue Umbrella up the mountain in Whisper Hollow. *That* shop would never go away.

Jade tossed the tape onto the sales counter and snatched up her keys and the Walmart bag. Tomorrow, she'd call a Realtor. Make it official.

It felt good to decide. She was getting a little bit stronger every day.

As Jade headed for the door, a woman—a svelte and toned brunette in designer clothes and sun-kissed hair—walked in.

"Can I help you?"

The woman returned Jade's query with brilliant blue eyes. "Are you Jade Benson?" Her voice was low and unsure.

"Who would like to know?" Jade rattled her keys, crunching the Walmart bag with her fingers.

"Taylor Branch." She approached Jade with her hand outstretched. "I hope I'm not disturbing you."

"Actually, I'm on my way out." Jade matched Taylor's firm grip. "I need to pick up my son."

"Asa?"

Jade stepped back. How'd she know? "Is there something specific I can help you—"

"I'm a friend of Rice McClure's. I'm a paralegal at the law firm where she worked. I was in Nashville visiting family and decided to drive over to see you."

"How did you know where to find me?"

"I called your other shop. The girl there said you were here."

Lillabeth. Trustworthy girl Friday. Always faithful—but a bit loose-lipped.

"Rice was more my husband's friend." Jade tugged her phone from her pocket and checked the time, making a point. "If you want to talk about her, you might want to drive up the mountain to Whisper Hollow and see her parents. I don't believe they've left for Europe just yet."

"I came to see you."

"Me? Why?" A warm rush under Jade's skin. A familiar sensation, one stirred by her heart when she braced for unexpected news. But how many more surprises could this year bring?

The warm air of the shop hovered close. Jade wished for a cool drink and a river breeze.

"Selfish reasons, I assure you." Taylor inched farther inside the shop, confident and poised. "Rice talked about you. She respected you even though she never regretted what happened with your husband."

"Max said she did. They both did."

Taylor smiled. "Rice knows how to say the right things to the right people."

"Why are you telling me this?" For claiming to be Rice's friend, this Taylor painted a darker picture of the woman Jade knew. A childhood friend of her husband's. His former fiancée. The mother of Asa. "What are your selfish reasons for being here?"

"Rice left Whisper Hollow because she felt bad for you, yes, but once she had the baby, she hoped Max would follow her to California." Taylor peered at the floor, skipping the toe of her leather shoe over the painted cement. "She was a brilliant lawyer, but a bit of a dreamer when it came to everyday life."

"Manipulative would be a good word."

"It's what made her a great lawyer. In the courtroom she was solid, grounded, levelheaded. In her personal life, she was more of a romantic with her head in the clouds."

"So . . . you drove from Nashville to tell me Rice loved my husband?" After this spring, such a confession merely bounced off Jade. Worse had happened.

"Not exactly." Taylor shifted her stance. "Holding out for Max was the one thing I never got about Rice. I mean, the man of her dreams was married. And from what I could tell, he wasn't giving up his marriage to you for Rice. Even after Asa was born. He came to see him, but—"

"He flew to California?" Jade fielded the small confession, then tossed it from her heart. She wasn't really surprised. Max did try to do right by his son, even if he had betrayed Jade by not confessing his bachelor-weekend encounter with Rice.

"He came to see him for a day, signed the birth certificate, and held him for a while. Then flew home. His company has a jet, I guess?"

"Yes, Benson Law has a jet." Pieces of Max's confession surfaced. "Max said Rice wanted to raise Asa alone. She didn't want him in her life."

"Bluffing. Another thing she was really good at. Did you ever play poker with her?" Taylor closed her eyes, shaking her head. "Anyway, Rice figured Max couldn't resist the lure of a son. After all, he is a third or fourth generation lawyer, heir to a big legal dynasty. What prince doesn't want an heir? A son? I told Rice to move on, you know? California is a bastion for good-looking, savvy, smart, wealthy men. She could've had anyone she wanted. But she had her mind set on Max. He was the one that got away. Maybe convincing herself one day she'd get him back, especially since they were bonded by a son, was her way of coping."

"Coping with the fact that Max was married to me or that she seduced a man before his wedding?" Jade checked the time on her phone again. "I'm sorry, but I need to go pick Asa up from school. We have a playdate in the park with some friends." Jade took an affirming step toward the door but Taylor didn't move. Jade sighed. "Is there anything else?"

"Rice wanted what she couldn't have and the more she couldn't have it, the more she wanted it. That woman loved a challenge. I drilled her a hundred different ways. Why Max? Of all the men in the world, why some old boy-friend from high school? Why the man she could've married but didn't? For crying out loud, if she really wanted him, why didn't she marry him when she had the chance? I swear she only wanted him because you had him."

"Wouldn't surprise me. So, Taylor, do you have a point somewhere in this story?" Jade kept a slight irritation in her tone, hoping to prod Taylor along.

"I'm getting to it. This is where it gets sticky. Where Rice went too far and why I'm standing here."

Now she had Jade's attention. Her heart waited. Wide open. The mood between them shifted. Friendly fire fixing to hit.

"Asa was Rice's ultimate coup. It's how she figured to keep Max in her life forever." Taylor paced to the sales counter and propped against it, her confidence fading. "She created an unbreakable bond by having his child."

"His first, I know. And a son." Those two facts visited Jade at night and demanded her attention. Max had a son. But she was not his mother. She'd cried out for peace and wisdom from her Lord in those times.

"Right, right, of course, you've thought of that." Taylor fell silent.

"Is that all?"

Taylor shook her head. When she peered at Jade, her eyes glistened. "I thought this would be easier." She exhaled, pinching the bridge of her nose, squeezing her eyes shut. "It just makes no sense, but—?" She tossed her hair over her shoulder. The blue light of her eyes dimmed. "Rice lied, Jade."

"She lied? About what?"

"She lied about Asa. Max is not his father."

Two

Under a blaze of Texas sun, Max rolled left, arm cocked for the pass, looking for his receiver. A teen named Calvin Blue.

When the kid broke through a pack of defenders and slanted across the meadow, Max spiraled the football toward him, hitting the young would-be tailback in the hands. Calvin tucked the ball away and raced for the orange pylons.

Touchdown. Calvin juked and jived in the makeshift end zone. "Can't touch this. Can't touch this." He spiked the ball into the mowed grass, then strutted past his opponents, taunting, "Sorry to make y'all eat my dirt."

"All right, Calvin, bring it back. Nice play. We're all amazed." Max had been around football his whole life. It was his passion next to Jesus, Jade, and the law, and he'd never seen a sixteen-year-old cut and run the ball like Calvin.

The boys gulped water from the cooler. Max reached for his shirt tossed on the ground. Today was a shirts and skins game. The last.

Taking a long drink from his own water bottle, Max dumped the rest over his sweaty head. The cool wetness ran down his hot face and into the collar of the T-shirt that swung loose about his waist. Between fasting before the Lord, ranch work, and afternoon football, Max's lawyer physique had been whittled down and chiseled.

He whistled for them to huddle up. Calvin arrived first and propped his arm on Max's shoulder, sweating and panting, his dark skin glistening.

"Good job today, everyone. I'm proud of you. Dale, nice crab block on Sam here." Max jutted his elbow into big Sam's ribs. He was what, fifteen, sixteen, and twice Dale's size. "And Tucker? You created the hole for Calvin's touchdown." The shy sandy-blond boy kicked at a clump of grass. He was lean and built, with undisciplined athletic prowess because he lacked the confidence to develop his skill.

"And you." Max turned to the cocky star player leaning on his shoulder, then bounced the ball against his head. "Remember, every great player needs a team."

"Coach." Calvin clapped his hand to his chest. "You think I don't appreciate my homeboys?"

"Just keep it in mind." Max took a few more minutes to encourage the rest of the players in the huddle. He'd practiced what he wanted to say next—his good-bye speech—but emotion gummed up his words. "This is the last day of camp because it's my last day at the ranch."

He exhaled, fighting the tears behind his eyes. Why was this moment so hard? Something had happened in his heart when he started working with these Colby, Texas, teens. They were good kids, but adrift, looking for a safe place to land.

"I'm going to miss y'all. Thanks for coming. You've . . . you've impacted me." Max patted his hand over his heart.

Every afternoon for six weeks, a Randall County rec center bus drove the kids to the ranch. Forty minutes out, forty minutes back. Not one boy ever missed a day.

The bus driver said he'd never seen kids stay so committed to a program.

Maybe, Max decided, it was because he needed them as much as they needed him.

Axel Crowder, the man who ran the Outpost Rehab Ranch, suggested the camp one evening after he and Max had talked football, and since Max had hours in his day to fill, he agreed. Besides, it was football. Say no more.

He watched his team file onto the bus, a missing-them sensation traveling across his chest. When the last one got on, Calvin hopped off.

"Got something on your mind, Calvin?" Max started gathering the gear.

"So, no more ball, Coach?" Calvin said. "They're letting you out of this nut farm?"

"It's risky, but they have to cut me from the herd." After three months and a lot of face-to-the-ground time, Max knew he had to face Jade and the dirge he'd left playing in her heart. "I miss my wife and my son." He stuffed footballs into a duffel bag.

"You got a kid? No fooling." Calvin picked up a ball and tossed it between his hands. The bus driver tooted the horn, but he waved it off.

"He's almost two." Max didn't admit he'd only held his son once in his young life before March rolled around. Then all the buried lies surfaced when Rice McClure died.

"Think he'll play football?"

"If he has any talent. If he wants to play."

"I got talent for it."

Max tossed the duffel into the bed of the Outpost pickup. "About as much as any kid I've ever seen."

"Really? Who've you seen? Ain't you a lawyer or something?"

"Yeah, I'm a lawyer, but I played in high school, a year in college. Used to coach youth league, sort of what we did here this summer."

"I thought so, I thought so. Seemed you knew what you was doing."

The bus beeped. "Calvin, the bus is leaving." The driver inched forward.

Calvin gazed over his shoulder but didn't flinch. "Our football here stinks. Can't keep a coach. Five in six years."

"Yeah, I know." The Outpost was just on the edge of Colby, Texas, a panhandle city that once reveled in state football championships. But in the last decade, something fierce went wrong with Colby High football and no one knew how to fix it. "I hear the coaches quit or get fired."

"Yep. The more we lose, Coach, the worse the coaches. Who wants a job with the Colby Warriors? It'll kill a guy's career." Calvin squinted at Max. "My brother got recruited to Texas from here. Got his college paid for, but there ain't no chance for me."

"I'm sorry, Calvin. What about academics?"

He laughed, pressing his fist to his lips. "I can run. That's what I do. Run and catch footballs. I got grades that'll get me in, but nothing so high and mighty as a academic scholarship." At sixteen, the muscled, quick Calvin stood eye to eye with Max, caught somewhere between boyhood and the man he was to become. "Scouts don't even bother coming our way these days. Why should they? All the good players transfer to Amarillo or Canyon."

"Why don't you?" Max crossed his arms and leaned against the side of the truck. From his position he could see the rec center bus inching down the winding Outpost driveway.

"Don't got no kin or 'cousin' in those districts whose address I can use." Calvin air-quoted "cousin" and backed away. "Best go catch my bus."

Calvin cut across the field, sprinting low, using his arms and legs to pump up speed. He caught the bus just as it turned onto the highway toward town. Max grinned, shaking his head. Incredible.

Then he gathered the pylons and flags, broke down the water table, and loaded up the truck. He'd come to love this place—the space, the miles of blue sky unfurling overhead, the fragrance of a storm rolling in off the prairie.

Fifteen men had started the program the first of April with Max. Men like him with wealth and privilege. Athletes, lawyers, CEOs, entertainment professionals, and one senator. A month later, ten remained. By the end of May, Max was one of six.

Climbing in behind the Dodge's wheel, Max fired up the old beast, as Axel called it, and followed a rutted path to the Big House—a high and wide two-story ranch nestled between barns and bunkhouses.

He arrived at the Outpost pain-pill addicted, gritted up, ready to work, primed to face his weaknesses. He wanted to understand why he used and why he slept with another woman a week before marrying the love of his life.

He'd prepared for anything and everything Axel Crowder might throw at him. Except one. The love and mercy of Jesus.

Max gunned the gas, firing the truck across the pasture. Yeah, how did a man respond to mercy and grace when he knew in his deepest parts he deserved none of it?

Parking alongside the house, he unloaded the gear into the shed, a fresh gust of manure hitting his nose. He was going to miss that smell.

He locked the shed and started for the house, his heart fixed on a shower before dinner, when he spotted Axel riding the corral rails. The lanky pony-tailed cowboy-counselor waved him over.

That's how Axel did most of his counseling—sitting on the rail. Listening was his specialty, next to pulling scripture to combat a man's sorrows.

Max hopped up next to him, hooking his heels on the middle rung, gazing toward the meadow where the cattle roamed.

"Last night," Axel said.

"Last night." Max looked east when a truck rumbled up the driveway, gravel crunching beneath the tires. A blue Suburban floating on a cloud of white dust. "But I'm ready."

"Sure you are. Never seen a fellow work so hard. You got a lot of Texas sun on your Tennessee shoulders, Max. I'm proud. You cowboyed up. God's got good things for you." Axel jutted out his chin, watching the Suburban, waving when the driver and another man hopped out. "Go on inside," Axel called to them. "I'll be along. See what Cook's set out."

Speaking of Cook, and dinner, Max's stomach rolled with a bass rumble.

"You'll do all right if you lean into Him."

"He can have it all."

"How you think Jade's doing in all of this?"

Max couldn't calculate the hours he and Axel had sat on the rail talking about Jade, marriage, and the responsibilities of love.

"She's been doing a lot of her own counseling and praying. She sounds good. Dubious. Don't blame her but I think—" What? What did he think? That he'd go home tomorrow and be welcomed in her heart and in her bed?

No, the Outpost was prep. The real work would begin when he went home and started winning back his wife after knifing her with his finely honed selfishness.

"Carry on the way you have been. Ain't nothing special about the ranch other than outside distractions. Prayer works here. Prayer works at home. Deal with your marriage and your mistakes like you done all spring. Humble, facedown, bathed in prayer."

Axel was devoted to prayer, and Max was confident that's why the ground shook beneath the man's feet. Prayer, he said, fueled the Big *L*s. The Lord, love, and life.

"I'm sure you're looking forward to lawyering again."

Max peeked at his mentor. He was fishing. "You want to ask me a question?"

Axel made a face, meshing his lips toward his lean nose. "Just checking in with you. I'm your counselor, you know. How are those back pains?"

"Not a one since that one night. Two months now. Pain-free, med-free." When the wind blew east, Max stared toward the dimming horizon. He'd be winging toward that thin black line tomorrow. "I'm going to miss this place, the boys, and our talks, but I have a gorgeous, kind, patient wife at home and a son to raise. God help us glue all the broken pieces together."

"He didn't bring you this far without a plan, Max. He'll not let you down. Just keep that 'Yes' in your heart."

"Question is, yes to what?" Max said. "Taking over the family's seventy-five-year-old firm? Benson Law is a great tradition. One of the best firms in the country. But, I don't know, doesn't feel like me anymore. It doesn't feel as important."

"The ranch has a way of fixing a man's priorities." Axel hopped off the rail, his boots rustling up a bit of dust. "Come on." He started for the house. "I got a couple of fellas from town waiting to talk to you."

"Talk to me?" Max hopped down, suspicious now of the blue Suburban. Who'd want to talk to him? He didn't know anyone from town. He only went to Colby once a week to check e-mail and call Jade. "Do you want to tell me what this is all about, Ax?"

"Not particularly." Axel shoved through the short, white gate. Dirt and pebbles crunched under his feet. He took the porch steps with a long, angular leap. "I'll let the boys speak for themselves."

Three

"Lillabeth." Jade exited the Blue Umbrella's office, scanning her iPad calendar. She couldn't find the date the reporter and photographer were scheduled to come. "Do you remember when *Southern Life* is supposed to be here? I'm telling you, these electronic things do not work for me. I need sticky notes. Why fix what's not broke?"

"I'll buy you a case of them."

Definitely not Lillabeth's voice. Jade looked up, bobbling her iPad. "Max." He stood in the golden circle of sun falling through the shop's main window.

"Hey, Jade."

"Y-you're here." His presence stole her breath. Forever handsome, Max stood before her lean and tan, poured into a pair of jeans. Leather boots replaced his leather loafers. The breadth of his chest filled the white oxford and tapered to his trim waist.

Locks of his silky dark hair curved down his neck, into his collar, and a light brown beard barely dusted his cheeks.

"You look good, Jade." He dropped his duffel to the floor, the sound covering the timidity in his voice.

"So do you." Jade cradled her iPad against her chest. "Did you just get here? I didn't realize—"

"I came straight from the airport." Max motioned the bag by his foot. "I wanted to see you. If you're busy, we can catch up later." He bent for his duffel.

"No, no, I'm not busy. Just trying to remember when *Southern Life* will be here."

"The sixteenth? Didn't you mention it on our last call?"

"Right, I did. The sixteenth." She scanned her iPad calendar. Sure enough. "Right in front of me."

"Max!" Lillabeth breezed in from the storeroom. "You're back." She embraced him freely, openly. The way Jade wanted to but couldn't because her wounded heart refused to yield. "Great hair. You look like a real cowboy."

Great hair, great face, gorgeous cowboy. But liar and betrayer. *Don't forget those, Lillabeth.* Jade had trusted before. She'd believed Daddy when he said he'd be there for her.

"Jade, you called?" Lillabeth said.

"I—what? Oh yeah, right." Her heart beat so fast. "I couldn't find the date of the *Southern Life* shoot." Why was the shop so *hot*? Perspiration sprinkled the back of Jade's neck.

"July sixteenth?"

"Yep." Jade held up her iPad. "Max remembered."

Lillabeth slapped him a high five. "And he wasn't even here when you set it up. Keep him around, Jade. Aaron never remembers dates or details."

"Well, he *is* fighting a war." Lillabeth's husband flew F-18s and was deployed to the Middle East.

The bells on the shop door clanged as a customer entered. Lillabeth moved to assist. "Glad you're back, Max. We missed you around here," she said softly.

"She knows more about this place than I do," Jade said, eyes on Lillabeth who spoke with two twentysomethings, instantly identifying, directing them to a display of '70s tops.

Max angled toward Jade. "I really missed you." His eyes searched hers.

"Max—" Jade hugged the iPad to her chest, trembling. She felt exposed and raw under his clarion gaze. He'd changed. Not just his hair or his form, but— could it be true?—his heart.

He stepped back. "I think we were less awkward on our first date."

They met right here in this shop. The beginning of beginnings. In a way, they were there again. Starting over—with an honest marriage or an honest divorce.

"We didn't know then what we know now," she said.

"No, but this time the truth is on the table. No secrets. Right?" He dipped his head to see her face. "Is there anything you need to tell me? Any hometown, Prairie City, Iowa, lovers capture your heart?"

"No," Jade said rapid and low. The customers passed behind her, barely skirting the edge of this private conversation.

"I guess we can talk later."

Yes, later. About so many things. About truth and lies. Secrets. Forget her ex-husband in Iowa. Jade had wrestled two days over Taylor Branch and her news. If she told him, he'd be crushed. Would it send him tumbling back to his old ways of phantom back pains and pain pill addiction?

Secrets had all but destroyed their marriage. How could she keep this one to herself? She was sitting on a potential time bomb.

Jade had no proof to corroborate Taylor's claim. She could be lying for some hideous, bizarre reason.

Either way, she wasn't willing to blurt, "Asa's not your son," without some evidence. Without giving Max a chance to move home and consider a shave.

"Jade, are you okay?" Max curved his hand over her shoulder. "You sighed really heavy."

"Did I?" She moved behind the sales counter, meeting his eyes for a fleeting second. "Just, you know, taking it all in." She stacked the disheveled pile of sales flyers, then straightened the business cards. "So . . . here you are."

"Yeah, here I am." Max brushed his hair back so it layered like ripples on the surface of still waters. "How's Asa?"

"Brilliant." Finally—safe, common ground. "Yes, he's brilliant."

Max grinned. "You've been watching Hugh Grant movies again."

Jade made a wry face. "*About a Boy* was on last night."

"One of your favorites."

He remembered. "I love all the imagery and symbolism. I love how Hugh Grant's character changes." Jade peered at Max until he started playing her heart with his hazel eyes. "But it's just a movie."

The strange route of their conversation, the bumpy reintroduction, actually calmed her. But they couldn't stand in the middle of the Blue Umbrella forever—or until she could trust him. Love or not, sexy cowboy husband or not, the bridge of trust was blown to smithereens.

She couldn't just let him waltz back into her heart and into her bed without some proof of change. Looking fabulous in those stupid Levi's and speaking to her in tender tones merely skimmed the surface.

"Listen," he said. "I came home under the radar so we could have some time together. No one knows I'm home but you and Lillabeth. And those two tourists over there."

"Not even your mom?" Jade whispered.

"Especially not Mom, queen of parties and parades. I wanted time with you and Asa, if that's all right with you. Uncomplicated and quiet. Dad and Mom and the rest of Whisper Hollow will see me soon enough. You and I need to talk."

If he talked, she'd have to talk. Recount how he hurt her and how she wanted to smash her fist into his face when she found out about Rice and the evil night in Vegas. But deep down she dreaded bringing it all up again, rehashing her hurt, his explanation, *blah, blah, blah*. She wasn't in the mood to hear what he'd learned at the Outpost. She didn't want to hear that she'd always be inadequate for him.

Oh, she just wanted to move on before the cement at her feet hardened and she'd never be free. Could she simply hang a For Sale sign on this past year?

"Asa's at school." Jade motioned toward the back of the shop, moving away from the intimate, uncomfortable tones of the conversation. "I have to pick him up in a few minutes."

"Yeah, I guess we don't have to deal with *us* right now. I didn't mean to come in and disrupt your day."

Or my heart? My mind? My strength? The longer he stood there, the more he consumed her.

"We knew this day was coming," she said, moving away from the register for Lillabeth to ring up the customers' sale. The twentysomethings chose tunics and bell-bottoms. One of the girls also had a pair of Candie's platforms Jade loved. "You may be confident and together, Max, but—"

"Confident? Together? I'm a mess." Max drew Jade back to her office, eased the door closed, then took her hand and pressed it over his heart. "It's like wild mustangs in there. I can barely breathe. When I walked into the shop, I didn't know if you were going to welcome me or shoot me."

"Shooting might have been appropriate. But not my style." She pulled her hand away, the vibration of his heart still tingling on her palm.

"I'd deserve it." He dropped into the rickety metal chair she kept beside the desk. "I'm sorry, Jade." He peered at her. "You are the last person in the world I'd ever want to hurt. In fact, I was trying not to hurt you. Instead, I caused the worst kind of damage."

"It's okay." Jade ran her hands over her jeans. "Believe it or not, I do understand. For what it's worth, I shouldn't have run off like I did. I should've . . ." She paused to let her emotions clear. "I should've stayed. Given you a chance." Her heart knew he was remorseful. Knew he'd been faithful to her since their wedding. But hiding the existence of Asa cut far deeper than the affair with Rice.

"Do you think Asa will remember me?"

"Sure, Max. I show him your picture—every night."

"You show him my picture?" Max rose up, reaching for her, taking hold of her arm and palming the curve of her cheek. "Thank you for taking care of him. For loving him, Jade."

"How could I resist? The little booger is all charm and sweetness." Max's touch ignited fiery shivers. "I . . . I'm in love with . . . him . . . already." She couldn't think. Only feel. If Max didn't stop stroking his thumb across her cheek she'd collapse into a quivering puddle at any moment.

He'd told himself the whole flight home to go slow. Gentle his way back into Jade's heart and mind. Not go all *husband* on her.

But alone with her in her office, all bets were off. He pulled her to him and her curvy soft body started a consuming blaze. He ached to kiss her, carry her upstairs to the shop's loft, and make love.

He wanted to show her the old Max was dead. The new and improved Max stood before her, a solid and trustworthy man. Faithful as the rising sun. But he couldn't *tell* her; he had to show her. Going for sex within thirty minutes of his homecoming wasn't his best first move.

Besides, the loft? Too fraternity. And his hands all sweaty from nerves. So, he let go. One thing he'd learned at the ranch was to let go. He backed toward the door.

"I thought I'd bunk in Beryl's old room until we work things out. We are going to work things out, aren't we, Jade?"

She nodded. "We'd kick ourselves if we didn't try." She moved toward him and brushed her hand over his cheek, her mountain-flower fragrance filling his senses. "Cowboy stubble."

"Should I shave?" Max cleared his throat. Nothing like stoking his passion fire just when he'd doused the flame. "Too Marlboro Man?"

"No, not at all." She tipped her head to one side. Even the swing of her ponytail was sexy. "Max Benson, the Marlboro Man lawyer."

"There you go." He grinned. "See you at home?" He nearly bent to kiss her cheek, but backed up, opening the door.

"Sure. Asa will be happy to see you, Max. He will." Jade led the way back into the shop, passing through the shower of sun drops falling through the back window. "I can order Mario's. Didn't you say you missed his pizza?"

"I did, yeah." But was he hungry? He was starving. But not for Mario's. Max hoisted his duffel bag to his shoulder. "See you soon."

"Okay." She exhaled, shyly digging her hands in her pockets. It was her go-to move and it endeared her to Max even more. If possible. "See you at . . . home."

He wanted to kiss her, darn it. Lillabeth shuffled around the shop, passing between and around them. *Forget it.* Max dropped his duffel bag to the hardwood floor and crossed to Jade in a few quick strides, scooping her into his arms. "I'm going to kiss you, Jade." His pulse thundered in his ears.

"Who's stopping you?"

Max traced his fingertips along the base of her neck, slipping his hand into her hair. Gooseflesh rose on his skin as he whispered a kiss to her lips as if casually saying hello. Then he sank into her fragrance and taste, wrapping her tighter and losing himself in the moment. Jade yielded, molding into him. When she ran her hands over his back they were like hot coals.

As he released her, she pressed out of his arms, trembling, resting her fingers over her lips. "I'll"—she inhaled—"see you at home."

"Yeah, see you at home." What happened? It was the perfect kiss until it ended. Her yes morphed to a no.

Retrieving his duffel, Max exited the Blue Umbrella, reminding himself again to be cool, go slow.

He dashed across Main Street, aiming toward Laurel Park and the side roads that led to Begonia Valley Lane.

Breaking into a light jog, Max cut through the fresh, cool air of the Hollow. The dewy texture was a welcomed contrast to the hot, arid air of Texas. Home. It was good to be home. And close to the arms of his wife again.

Four

Sometime after ten, Jade made her way through the house, turning off lights. With Max home, the atmosphere had changed. Felt fuller. Complicated. Maybe balanced was the word. Definitely a combination of joy and sorrow.

Over pizza, he shared the things God had taught him while at the Outpost. Jade envied his journey a bit. Painful, yes, but glorious. She could see in his eyes and hear in his voice how he'd changed. How encountering Jesus healed his self-inflicted wounds and removed his shame.

Her heart pulsed for him. The man she fell in love with had returned. Only more so. She felt as if she'd found a polished, gleaming gem.

But it was all surreal. Too good to be true.

"Max?" With the last light out, Jade jogged up the stairs. When she hit the second-floor landing, she caught a soft glow coming from Asa's room.

"Max?" she whispered, pausing outside the door.

"Yeah, in here."

Jade slipped inside and settled on the floor by Asa's bed. "What are you doing?"

Max rested against the opposite wall, in the glow of the night-light, his arms propped on his raised knees. A lock of his glossy, loose hair slipped over his cheek.

"He's not moved since I tucked him in."

"I'm not surprised. You wore him out tonight."

"Me? I'm beat. And I just spent three months on a working ranch and coaching football camp."

"He does play hard. Sleeps like a rock too." Remembering this, Jade raised her voice from a whisper. She straightened Asa's legs and fixed his covers.

"He remembered me."

"I told you he would."

"I owe you, Jade."

"Stop. You don't."

"I asked you to raise my secret son while I knocked the kinks out of my life. You embraced the challenge when you could've walked."

"Asa's won my heart, Max. I did it for him." *And yes, you.* Which was so hard to confess. His humility confronted her. She wanted a defensive, partly broken Max to return to home. Not this . . . cowboy hero.

Jade stood. "I think I need a Diet Coke." From the corner of her eyes, she could see Max pushing up off the floor, following.

A Diet Coke would taste good, but what Jade really wanted was to break away from Max's steady gaze and gentle confessions.

But now he was following her downstairs.

She'd expected to duke out their relationship over months, slowly letting go of her hurt and anger. Gently releasing her hold on the affair and lies. She wanted to punish him. Hadn't she earned that guilty pleasure?

But how could she when he readily spoke of his failures and owned his mistakes? Maybe he could handle the news about Rice.

She'd imagined telling him several times tonight but couldn't bring herself to do it. She needed proof. Max would ask a hundred questions once she unfurled the news and her answer had to be more than, "Taylor said."

If not for Max, then for herself.

Max's footsteps tapped on the marble foyer floor in time with hers. In the kitchen, Jade jerked opened the fridge door and reached for a soda can.

"Do you want one?" She peered back at Max standing on the other side of the island.

"Yeah, sure." He took the can from her with the same piercing look he'd worn in Asa's room.

Jade leaned against the sink as she popped open her drink. If she wanted more space between them, she'd have to go out to the porch. And he'd just follow her.

"I already loved you, Jade, but coming home and seeing how you love Asa as your own . . . it makes me want you even more."

Max's tone and inflection swirled a warm bevy of her emotions against her cold heart.

Jade took a long sip of her soda.

"He'll be two soon," she said, moderating her tone to between casual and cool. "I researched potty training for boys who sleep deep. Did you know we can buy an alarm to wake him up at the first drop of urine?"

Max shot her a sleepy grin. "What deep psychological ramifications will that have on the poor kid?"

"I know, right?" Jade swallowed, fighting the power of his pull. How was a girl to resist when a man kept looking at her like he could get lost in her charms? Jade had standards to keep. A litmus test for establishing trust. "Hey, baby, I want you," just wasn't going to cut it.

But deep down she yearned to wrap in his arms and burrow into his chest. Live in the moment.

"Tell me about you, Jade. How are you doing, really? Any more episodes of panic, the depersonalizing?"

Right. Those. Last time Max saw her, she was running freaked-out down the road after Mama's funeral. She had been diagnosed with severe anxiety and depersonalization disorder, but she'd been on her own healing journey. Not as intense as Max's, but focused on God's truth.

"I saw the counselor in Des Moines all spring. Met with Carla Colter's pastor twice a week. All we did was pray, but those times were the ones where I left changed." She paused. She'd never assessed her time in Iowa verbally before—not in those terms. A breeze of relief cooled her heart. Prayer worked. "No attacks since Mama's funeral."

He smiled. "I prayed for you, a lot. Axel's big on prayer. 'What is the counsel of men compared to the counsel of God?'"

"I prayed for you too."

"So maybe we start there, Jade. The first stepping-stone toward healing us is prayer."

She nodded. "And we'll see where it leads." It seemed like a safe place. Prayer with Max, and God sitting in between. "Oh, I'm selling the Blue Two."

"Yeah? You never were sure about that place anyway."

"For a while, it was a necessary burden. But not anymore." *So, I met this woman, Taylor Branch . . .*

She breathed in, ready to speak.

"I'm sorry about the kiss in the shop."

Jade stared at him. See, there was never the right segue. "It was a good kiss." A toe-curling, heart-caressing kiss.

"It was a great kiss," Max said.

His sleepy-sexy was about to do her in. It would be so easy to surrender. Jade felt suddenly weary of flashing her palm and telling life to stand back, she didn't want to get hurt. But if she waved Max back into her bed, would she regret her late-night impulse in the morning? Oh wow, what if he said no? She'd not even considered that.

"Jade." Max got her attention. "Do you want to be married to me?"

Million-dollar question. She'd like to phone a friend.

"Remember when you asked me to marry you?"

"Which time? The first? The second? Or the third? I liked my first time best. Kind of raw and impulsive."

"And on the streets of Manhattan with hot dog mustard all over our lips."

"But it was sincere, Jade."

"I felt it then. I wanted to go running down Broadway screaming yes."

He stood straight, shoulders squaring back. "Faker! Why'd you say no then? Sting my heart that-a-way?"

"Because, dude, I'd been married once to a romantic, passionate guy who promised me forever. I got five months."

"I didn't know about Dustin then."

"See, this is why we need to be forthcoming in our relationship, tell each other things."

He laughed and toasted her with his soda can. "I'm not the one who said 'let the skeletons stay in the closet.'"

"No, but you quickly agreed."

"Jade, don't you know, I'd have walked across hot coals up Signal Mountain if you'd have asked me to."

"But you couldn't stay out of Rice's bed?"

He deflated, sipping his drink. "You got me there. I can't . . . I don't know what . . . it happened. Not enough wishing and praying can undo it."

"So ask me your question again."

"Jade, do you want to be married to me?"

"Do you want to be married to me?"

He laughed. "You've learned too many legal tricks. Yes, babe, yes. More than breathing I want to be married to you."

"I'm scared."

"But I'm not, Jade." Max scooted over to her. "I believe in us. I believe in God keeping us. I *know* we can do this."

His intensity flared and challenged her to believe too. "You're so persuasive, Max. I hear you. I feel what you're saying. My heart is shouting *believe, trust.* But my head is saying *don't you dare.* You have a way of making me feel so safe, Max. Like I can do anything with you by my side. But then you do something so stupid as forge prescription drugs and get addicted. Or cover up a very large secret."

"Help me fix that image you have of me, Jade. Give me a chance. Do you want to be married to me?"

She sighed. She had to speak her heart. She had to continue to kick fear to the curb. "Yes, Max, I want to be married to you."

Five

Monday morning Max sat on the back porch drinking his coffee, staring out at the summer grass. The breeze coming down from the ridge blew cool and clean.

After his intense talk with Jade Thursday night, Max had suggested they just have fun on the weekend. Play. Laugh. Forget about lies and infidelity, death and panic.

Jade jumped in with both feet. It was the first real hope he had for them. She even remembered to stand on their first stepping-stone—prayer.

They were loaded into Max's car when she smacked her hand on his and said, "Pray first."

He grinned at the memory. They played hard three straight days with Asa. At Laurel Park, Asa showed Max his routine on the playground. What was it?

First the slide, then the horses. After that, the sandbox and finally the swing. Something like that.

Asa was a routine kid. Smart Jade had picked up on that and established Asa's days so he knew what to expect and when.

He was in love with his son. In love with his wife. In love with his life. The only thing this weekend lacked was an intimate encounter with Jade.

Give her time, Max. Go slow.

He did manage to steal a peck on Jade's forehead—but nothing more.

He sipped his coffee, surprised when his phone pinged from his pocket. Chevy Buchholz, the man he met his last night in Texas, was texting him.

Still interested in u coming out, Max.

Yeah, well, the man was crazy.

"There you are," Jade said, stepping onto the porch. Max's heart jumped. Her summer skirt flitted about her knees and the scoop in her top accented all the right parts.

"You look gorgeous," he said.

"Thank you." She smiled. At him. "I'm heading to the Blue. Do you want me to take Asa or leave him here with you?"

Oh, right. Dad duty. Max stood. "I guess . . . leave him. Yeah. What time does he go to school?"

"Eleven, but Max, I can take him with me. I've been doing it since I got home from Prairie City. What are you doing today?"

"I thought I'd run down to the office, talk to Clarence, get back into it. Maybe start full-time next week. Now that I'm home, I realize how long I've been away." Not a bad thing, in the big picture, but his dereliction of duty was weighing on him.

It was his family's law firm. And leading it would be his responsibility now that his dad sat on the state supreme court.

"Are you ready to go back?"

"As I'll ever be, yeah." He walked toward the kitchen. His coffee had gotten cold. "I'll take Asa to school, then go down to the city."

"You sure?"

"Don't make it sound like I'm doing you a favor or that I'm being put out. I'm home and I'll parent-up." He'd planned to talk to Jade about adoption when the time was right.

She briefed Max on Asa's morning routine and left for the Blue without kissing him good-bye. Max watched her go down the walk and disappear around the edge of the garage.

Fun was one thing. Intimate trust another.

The clock rounded toward noon by the time Max entered Benson Law and rode the elevator up ten floors to Clarence Clemmons's office.

The senior and managing partner of the firm resided in the office once occupied by Max's dad, Rebel: the office Max would soon occupy.

"Ah, the prodigal comes home." Clarence rose when Max entered his office unannounced and shook his hand with a firm grip. "Didn't expect to see you today. You remember Bradford Trusdale." Clarence motioned to the man reclining in the wingback chair.

Max ignored Clarence's little daggers. *The prodigal comes home. Does he remember?*

Max shook Brad's hand. "Good to see you. How are things at Trusdale Industries?" Bradford Trusdale's business alone was a line item in the firm's annual budget.

"Great, thanks to Benson Law. Keeping our heads above water in this economy." Brad commanded the room when he spoke. "I should be asking how things are with you."

"Good, thanks." Early on, Max had developed a policy to keep his personal life separate from his business. Brad didn't need any more details.

"Max, Brad and I were in a meeting," Clarence said. "Can I get with you later today? We can check my schedule with Gina."

"Don't put off Max on my account, Clarence. We have nothing pressing here." Bradford stood, tucking his fine-weave dress shirt into the waist of his tailored slacks.

"If you're sure." Clarence walked the CEO of Trusdale Industries to the door, sealing their conversation in murmured tones.

"So, Max, how are you?" Clarence said, his cordial tone gone. "Rehab treat you right?"

"It was good, Clarence. Successful." Max took a seat. The room's hot, stale air clung to his skin. In Texas, his work space had been the open plains. It made the opulent, high-rise office feel like a sweatbox. "Everything okay with Bradford?"

"Yeah, nothing we can't work out over drinks." Clarence displayed his capped smile as he walked to the back of his desk. "Bradford's got a couple of stockholders giving him some trouble."

"Brad isn't used to trouble. His way or the highway."

"He does have a way of getting what he wants." Clarence sat down and leaned back in his seat. "Firm's doing great, Max. Profits per partner were up another 2 percent. The associates . . ."

He prattled. Max listened. Mostly he picked through his conflicting feelings. Being in the office felt like home. He was in familiar territory. He was good at the law. He knew the law.

But there was an opportunity . . . a wild, crazy opportunity that he found himself considering more and more. Would Jade go for it? Could he even do the job? It was one thing to head up junior football; it was another to take on a high school team.

". . . which brings me to you."

"Me?" Max sat forward, a blip of *somethin's-up* on his radar.

"I'm putting you on probation," Clarence said without hesitation.

"Probation?" Max slid to the edge of his seat, the fine threads of his Armani slacks gripping around his knees. The fabric felt odd against his skin. He'd grown accustomed to the tough rub of denim. "What are you talking about?"

"The executive partners and I think you need time to prove yourself. After all, we've seen the results of your rehab before." He got up and walked around to the front of the desk. "It didn't stick."

"Executive partners? I'm an executive partner." Max stood. "What are you up to, Clarence?"

"Guarding this firm. You're an executive partner on hiatus, off to rehab. The rest of us—Don, Seamus, Larry, and I—decided it was best for the firm if you had a probationary period. We're not willing to risk our careers again for your habit."

"Clarence, I've *been* on probation. Self-imposed. What do you think the Outpost trek was about? To get free. To figure out why I popped pills. I'm not going to go down that road again." The execs had tried and condemned him without a chance to plead his case.

"Maybe you did well out in the middle of nowhere, miles from anyone, experts watching over you. But you're home. Back on familiar territory with all your drug suppliers a mere phone call away."

"You do know Dad and I can outvote the partners."

"You used to, yes. But with Rebel on the state supreme court, divested of all his interest, and you on leave, the execs pull rank. You know that, Max."

Yeah, he did. Funny, he'd anticipated resistance from Jade, but not from Clarence and Benson Law.

"If you were in my shoes, Max, you'd do the same thing. Besides, every time you fall off the wagon, the rest of us have to scramble. I had to placate some of the partners this time. If you don't stay clean, the firm will suffer. Can't have resentful partners. I'm not going to let you loose in this firm until I'm convinced you're not shopping docs and popping pills."

So it boiled down to this. He'd put his life on hold—career, marriage, and fatherhood—to confront his demons, enduring hard days and lonely nights with only the stench of cow manure and his own soul to keep him company.

Axel had warned him. Restitution came with a heavy price tag.

"Never known you to be silent in a fight, Max." Clarence's low laugh didn't disguise his callous tone.

"Just thinking," Max said. "I wrote the Code of Conduct policy. Wrote the partner agreement and I've violated my own rules. Forging prescriptions is a class D felony. Grounds for dismissal."

"I wanted Reb to put you on probation years ago." Clarence crossed his ankles in a relaxed manner. He'd bested the boss's son. "Fire you, even. You broke the law, Max, and when the heir to the firm screws up, the whole firm is implicated. Reb stood for it because you were his son."

Max waited for Clarence to end his speech with, "There's a new sheriff in town and I'm cleaning up this place."

"It's a little late to pull the ace out of your sleeve, Clarence. If you wanted me out of the way, you should've done it when I was addicted and actually forging prescriptions."

"I'm looking out for this firm, its tradition, and its reputation."

"How long is probation?" Max made his way to the door.

"Ninety days. Three short months. You can still come to work, help research, advise the associates. Some clients have missed you on the golf course."

"I'll see you in ninety days, Clarence."

"Suit yourself."

At the elevator, Max punched the Down button, glancing back at Clarence's office. What was he supposed to do with this? He fumed at Clarence's arrogance. But he was right, Max would've done the same thing. Dad should've fired or suspended him on his first offense. But he didn't, and all roads led to where Max stood now.

The elevator doors opened and Max stepped in. The only question he had about this journey was which direction to take now.

Six

"Yes, may I speak to Taylor Branch, please?" Jade doodled on the sticky note where she'd jotted Taylor's work number.

Between the shock of Taylor's news and being in a hurry to pick up Asa that day, Jade had forgotten to get the woman's number. So this morning she'd Googled Rice's obituary for the name of her California firm.

"This is Taylor Branch."

"Taylor, it's Jade Benson." Silence. "Hello?"

"Why'd you call me?" she whispered tight and low into the phone.

"Because I need proof. Your word is not enough."

Taylor exhaled. "I don't have any proof, Jade. Just what I know. Trust me, it's true."

"Trust you? I don't even know you. I need proof that Rice actually told you this, or better yet, proof of who Asa's father really is. I can't go to Max with, 'Hey, a friend of Rice's said so.'"

"Look, I don't care if you tell your husband. I just wanted someone else to know."

"What about the biological father? Where's he?"

"I told you, he lives in Denver. Rice met him skiing and they had a long-distance thing for six months."

"You're sure he wanted nothing to do with Asa?"

"When Rice first got pregnant, he walked. I didn't know her then, but she told me all of this after she had Asa. We'd become pretty good friends and I think she needed someone to talk to, you know?"

"So, the father doesn't know that Rice . . . passed away?"

"I don't know. He came around after Asa was born, got all mushy for a day or two, took a paternity test to prove his devotion to Rice and Asa, but he didn't stick around long enough for the results. Rice said there was no way she was letting that deadbeat's name go on her son's birth certificate, so she named Max as the father. Rice checked the paternity results a few months later and sure enough, deadbeat was the dad. But by then he was long gone. She called him and told him Max was the father and that was that."

Jade pressed her fingers against her forehead. She didn't need a headache today. "So the father—what's his name?"

"Landon."

"He never requested the lab results?"

"I have no idea, Jade. When Rice told him Max was on the birth certificate, she said he was relieved. Glad to be off the hook. Landon was young, like twenty-six, good-looking, cocky, just starting a career in finance. Traveled a lot. He wasn't ready to move to California and be Asa's daddy."

"So where are the paternity results? Do you have the name of the lab?" Jade reached for a pen and her yellow sticky pad.

"No, I don't know, maybe . . ." Taylor sighed. "Even if I knew the lab, they're not going to give the results to you. But Rice's parents asked me to go through her things after the funeral. I have a file cabinet of bills and receipts, tax forms, stuff like that. I thought Asa might like to have them some day. A part of his mom's life he'll never know otherwise. I haven't gone through them but I can."

"Taylor, you have to look for me. You brought me this bomb, now tell me how or *if* I should use it. I'm not going to tell Max Rice lied without proof. It'd break his heart. So, until I know more, it's not true. Max is the father. Rice said he was, he believed her, signed the birth certificate, and there is no other man."

"But there is, Jade. Landon Harcourt. I'll find the paternity results."

Jade ended the call and dropped her forehead to her desk. Why, why, why? She did not want this burden. Why had Taylor chosen to unburden herself to Jade? Rice's parents lived just up on the ridge. What about Landon? Or Max even?

Lillabeth came in the office wrapping her mass of blond locks in a ponytail. "Well, how was your weekend?" She wiggled her eyebrows.

Jade grinned. "Stop wiggling your eyebrows. It wasn't that kind of weekend. We're taking things *slow*. But we did decide to have fun, forget all the gunk. We went to the park and the Tennessee Aquarium. Asa had a blast. Max and I have some hard conversations ahead of us, but this weekend it was about fun."

"You look happy."

Jade buttoned her lips. Except for Taylor . . . "I am." She wrinkled her nose. "It almost feels too easy. I can't trust him, Lillabeth. I can't."

"Yet."

"We'll see. I hope it's just a matter of time."

Jade walked Lillabeth through the shop, gave her an update on business, and talked about how to balance their schedules—Jade's as mom, Lillabeth's as UT Chattanooga student.

Then she collected Asa from school, sped through The Market for lasagna fixings, brownie mix, and ice cream. Max must have mentioned lasagna and brownies three or four times this weekend. Jade figured building a bridge of trust between them began at both ends.

By the time she pulled into the garage behind the house, rain clouds capped Whisper Hollow's Appalachian peaks. Jade loved the idea of a good, soaking rain. The Hollow needed refreshing. *She* needed refreshing.

In his car seat on the passenger side of the truck, Asa dozed. Krista said he'd played hard at school today. Even he had changed since Max came home. He was . . . confident. She smiled at the thought of Asa needing more confidence for his twenty-two-month-old self.

Looping her hand through the grocery bags on the floorboard, Jade balanced her load before hoisting Asa out of his seat and cradling him on her shoulder.

Asa wove his fingers through her hair. He'd been doing that since the first night he crawled into her arms.

"You need a nap, buddy."

"I not tired." His wee voice bloomed a large love in her heart.

Jade made her way up the back walk to the house, but stopped with a jitter as a booming *thwack* ricocheted across the yard. She whirled toward the wooded area just beyond the garage and squinted into the leafy green shade. The sound resounded and hovered again.

Then a rain-scented breeze parted the branches, exposing a glint of steel and a tan, broad back, bare and glistening.

"Max?" Jade cut across the lawn as he brought down the ax again. "What are you doing?" The muscles in his back rolled as he took another swing at a thick block of cut-up tree. "Max!"

He spun around. "Hey, sorry, I didn't hear you." He pulled out a pair of ear buds. "Chopping to some Jesus Culture." Wedging the ax in a stump, Max shoved through the branches and kissed his tired, sleepy boy. "Here, give me the groceries."

Ah, relief. Jade shook the blood flow back to her arms. "Where's your car? It's not in the garage. And why are you chopping wood? Is this some Outpost therapy?"

"Not exactly. But it's one way to deal with stress. I've been wanting to cut up those pieces for firewood since we moved in, and today seemed like a good day. I parked my car out front."

Jade regarded him. "What happened today?" She walked with him to the house.

"Clarence put me on probation. Says I'm not trustworthy. I need to prove myself."

"What have you been doing if not proving yourself?" Jade shoved the kitchen door closed with her foot, covering Asa's back with her hand.

"That's what I said. But the Outpost wasn't real-world enough for Clarence. He got the partners to side with him and I'm on extended vacay." Disappointment played on his face. Jade figured this to be his first setback. "Truth is, I'm not sure I blame him."

"So you came home to chop wood?" Was he stressed already?

"I came home to think and pray. I was going to go for a run when I saw the wood."

Jade wanted to talk this through with Max, but Asa was heavy. "I'll be right back." She carried him around the corner into the media room, took Max's Duke blanket from the couch, and spread it on the floor. What a blessing that Asa slept well anywhere.

Back in the kitchen, she started unloading the groceries. Max leaned against the sink with a large glass of water.

"I can't know for sure, but I think Clarence has an ulterior motive. He's always wanted Benson Law. Man, by the time I get back, I'll be gone from the firm six months. It has an impact on our finances. My cut from the profits will be significantly less."

"We already have more money than most people earn in a lifetime." Jade retrieved a skillet from the drawer under the stove.

"Clients will lose confidence in me." Max reached around Jade to refill his water from the fridge dispenser. Jade bent beneath him to retrieve an onion.

Max paced to the other side of the island and as Jade chopped the onion, she peeked at him. He was shirtless, lean, and chiseled. His shorts bagged around his hips. *Chop, chop, chop. Focus on the onion, Jade. Don't leap too soon.* Max was just now facing his first test. His pride, his identity, his career, and finances were being threatened.

"What will you do in the meantime?" she asked.

"Clarence wants me to play golf and be an advisor to the associates. Do research—which *is* being an associate. It's like he wants to knock me down a few pegs."

"So what? How's that going to change your life, Max? At the end of the day, Benson Law still belongs to you." Jade dumped the onions into the skillet. They sizzled on the hot surface.

"Funny thing, I'm not sure I care."

She whirled around. "What?"

He shrugged. "Just doesn't mean as much to me as it used to."

She unwrapped the hamburger meat and crumbled it into the skillet with the onions. Max not caring about Benson Law? His confession, his tone, rattled her core. For all his flaws, she counted on Max to be Max. Rooted. Stable. Safe.

"So, you don't want to be a lawyer?"

"Yeah, I do, Jade. I'm just—" He stared out the back door's window. "Restless." He opened the door. "I'm going to clean up the mess out back. Do you have more groceries in the truck?"

"No. I'm making lasagna for dinner. It'll be ready in an hour or so."

"Lasagna?" Max paused with his hand on the door. "You heard me? I thought I was talking to myself."

"Out loud?" Jade said, smiling.

"New thing I picked up in Texas. Cows don't really care if you talk about lasagna or not."

"Max, is being restless good or bad?" She had to ask. The notion started sinking deeper and taunting her fear.

"Hey, babe." Max walked over to her and swept her into his arms. "It's not a bad thing. Just a thing. Makes me go to God to figure out what's next. He didn't bring me this far to put me on the bench."

She relaxed against him. "You'll tell me if you start feeling pain or cravings, right?"

"Yes, but I'm not going there again, Jade. I don't know that guy. He's a foreigner to me now." Max lifted his chin from her head. Without a word, he bent to kiss her. First her forehead, then her cheek.

Jade submitted to his soft caress, eyes closed, heart peeking out from behind the curtain.

"My stars." The screen door slammed. "Max, it's true. You're home." June Benson barged in on the intimate husband and wife moment.

Max looked sideways at his mother. "Hey, Mom."

Jade ran her tongue over her lips. She was so thirsty. "Afternoon, June. How are you?"

"I'm right as rain except my son is home from Texas and I didn't know. Why didn't you call? And what in the world? You're a sweaty mess—oh goodness, I didn't interrupt anything, did I?"

"He was out back chopping wood," Jade said. *And yes, you interrupted. Probably for the best.*

"Well, get cleaned up. Rebel's on his way and we're going out for a celebration dinner." June wore a navy blouse and white slacks with low-heeled sandals. The blunt ends of her bottle-blond hair aligned with the lean edge of her jaw. She looked like she'd stepped out of a spa—tanned and refreshed.

"June, I've got lasagna started," Jade said.

"Mom, how'd you find out I was home?"

"Gina called." June shifted her Birkin bag from one arm to the other. "Naturally, I pretended I knew all about your homecoming, but land sakes, my heart was bottomed out like a Florida sinkhole by the time I hung up. Why did you go into Benson Law without telling me you were home?"

"I wanted time with Jade and Asa before all of Whisper Hollow knew, *Mom*."

"What are you saying—I have a big mouth?" Even she couldn't keep a straight face.

"I'm saying you're proud of your son and you'd want people to know he was home."

"Can you blame me? That's why I want to celebrate. Jade, you can make lasagna anytime. Now, where's my grandson?" June peered out of the kitchen. All of the downstairs room orbited the large foyer. "Asa?"

"He's asleep, June."

"Mom," Max said. "Jade's making lasagna. We can go to dinner another night."

"Nonsense. She's been working all day. A nice dinner out is every mother's dream. Besides, your dad and I want to see you, catch up on the news."

"Mom, Jade is cooking here tonight." Max remained resolute.

"June, why don't you and Reb join us? I'm making brownies for dessert. Reb's favorite."

"Or how about we have dinner later in the week?" Max arched his brow at Jade.

"Fine." June shifted her brown eyes—so like Max's—between her son and daughter-in-law. "How about tomorrow night at the house? I'll have Reb grill steaks." She headed for the door with a backward glance. "You look good, son. Jade, kiss Asa for me."

Jade watched June *swish-swish* down the sidewalk. She was tennis-four-days-a-week fit, beautiful, and youthful for sixty-two but with a bundle of secrets and scars inside. Reb's years of infidelity had left a permanent wound. She'd started to heal in the spring when she went with Jade and Mama to Prairie City, but once she returned to Whisper Hollow, all forward progress seemed to have stopped. It was life as usual.

"We could've gone to dinner with them, Max."

"We'll have lots of dinners ahead with Mom and Dad. I want to be with you tonight. It means a lot to me that you're making lasagna." He gently brushed his hand over her hair. "So how are ol' June and the Reb doing? Whenever I called them, Mom gave me the sunny skies weather report."

"She does the same to me. They counseled with Reverend Girden for a while, but then your dad got busy and your mom stopped talking about it."

Jade loved her father-in-law, but she'd never forget the evening she and June discovered him with another woman.

"Hey." Max lifted her chin. "I see what you're thinking, and I'm not my father."

"Yeah, and I'm not your mother."

"Oh, trust me, babe, I know." Max planted a slow kiss on her forehead. "Do we continue where we left off or—" His intonation filled her with liquid fire.

"Max, we should give ourselves time."

"I was afraid you'd say that." He backed toward the door, giving her a wink, letting her know it was okay. "You're just so darn gorgeous. And it's been a long time."

"Am I wrong?"

"If your heart's not ready to trust me, then no, you're not wrong."

When he left, Jade turned back to her browning meat and onions. That tangy aroma filled the kitchen and made it feel like home, the place to be.

Yeah, she wanted to know in the core of her heart that she trusted this man. She looked out the kitchen window. Max was dragging branches across the yard, his arms taut and golden brown in the sun. She smiled, her whole body yielding to the joy of discovering Max and love again.

Seven

The colors of the Thursday morning dawn drifting through the second-floor skylights filled the hall with a pink emollient light. Any other time, Max might have appreciated the gentle effect, but he was distracted and wanted to talk to Jade.

The restless tug in his spirit refused to yield to reason or prayer.

As he approached her room, he inhaled the faint scent of water lilies and knew she was up. He'd wanted to come to her room every night for two weeks, but not for this.

He thought the restlessness in his bones was from Clarence putting him on probation. From feeling suddenly free to go anywhere and do anything the Lord willed. Surely God would give him something worthwhile to do in Whisper Hollow besides golf with elite clients. Then Chevy Buchholz had called again Wednesday afternoon.

"Jade? It's me." He knocked, eyes fixed on the floor.

"It best be or I'm in trouble. Some strange man broke into our house." She eased the door open with her bare foot and headed back for the bathroom, a towel turban balancing on her head, her short robe swishing around her toned legs. "Is everything all right? Is Asa awake? I thought he was still sleeping."

"Yeah, everything's fine. He's still dead to the world. I'm glad you're awake though. Could you could join me on the porch? I want to run something by you."

Before Rice and his secret son, he and Jade used to sit in the rockers and talk about anything and everything until the night birds sang their lullabies from the trees. Looking back, it amazed him he'd kept Asa a secret at all.

Jade regarded him as she untangled the towel from her head. "You sound serious." Her dark, damp hair fell around her shoulders in shiny rings. Max drank in the sleek contours of her face and the curves of her form.

"It's a little serious. I need your insight." Max valued Jade's counsel. It's why he should've told her about Asa from the beginning.

"If you think I can help. I'll be down in a minute." She eased the bathroom door closed.

In case he was wondering about the *other thing*, there was his answer. *Not yet, cowboy.*

Max checked on Asa, then headed to the kitchen to get the coffee brewing and rustle up some grub. Hadn't he seen some Grands cinnamon rolls in the fridge?

Until Clarence's probation, Chevy's offer to make him head coach of Colby High's football team made no sense. Max had a career and responsibilities. His wife owned a business in Whisper Hollow. They had friends and family here. Never mind Max had absolutely no experience coaching high school ball, let alone heading an entire program.

Chevy assured him that he and the boosters, as well as the athletic director and assistant coaches, would support him fully.

Max shook his head. It made no sense. Who gave a greenhorn a head coaching job? By the time Jade came down—in jeans and a top that did Max no good—he'd run every scenario in his head over and over and come up with one illogical, ridiculous response. *Yes. Go to Texas. Take the job.*

"Smells good." Jade inhaled, smoothing her hand along his shoulders as she passed him for a cup. "Cinnamon rolls." She whirled to face him. "Uh-oh, what's up?"

He leaned against the kitchen island and sipped his doctored coffee. "Save it for the porch."

The cinnamon rolls came out of the oven hot and fragrant. Jade smoothed on the icing before the buns cooled. On the porch, facing the sunrise, they rocked and sipped coffee, eating cinnamon, sticky goodness.

"All right, Max, you've been plied with breakfast. What's going on?" Jade set her plate down and wiped her hands on her napkin. A scented gust stirred the trees.

"Jade," he said. "You know I ran a football camp at the ranch for the parks and rec department. Part of my rehab."

"Yeah, the boys really responded to you."

"Apparently, so did their parents. One of them is a big-time booster, and he got with the high school principal and well, they made me a job offer."

"What kind of job offer?"

"Head football coach."

"What? Head football coach?" She started to laugh, then clapped her hand over her mouth. "You're serious."

"Very. Colby's had a lot of trouble finding a good coach. They've hired the best in the biz, but they leave after a season or get fired for violations or butt heads with the athletic director. They've had five coaches in six years. The principal decided to take the reins and find a man he believed in. Didn't matter if he could coach right off. The coach could grow with the program. They're already losing every game." The more he talked, the more he knew his answer. "Jade, they used to be one of the best programs in Texas. Two or three state championships a decade. Now they have the worst program."

"And you're supposed to fix it? Max, you're a brilliant man and I believe you can do anything you want, but coach football? In Texas? It's crazy."

Max rocked to his feet, pacing the length of the porch. "What am I going to do here for three months? Golf? Advise associates on stuff they can find on their own or get from any one of the partners?"

"How about raise Asa? Be with me?"

He peered at her. "That's a given."

"So, you dink around here for three months. It'll go by fast." She wasn't biting on his excitement to coach. "Max, why do you want to do this?"

"That's the crazy part, Jade. I just do. I've already turned them down three times, but they keep calling back. Last time was yesterday when their recent hire backed out last-minute for another job."

"Have you prayed about it?"

"Yes, all day, every day since they asked me. The desire to go gets stronger."

"You believe God is leading you to Texas?" Jade's tone and posture conveyed her doubt.

"Okay, I know it sounds *woowee*, nut job Christian. Like I'm using the ol' 'I heard from God to justify my own will,' but let's just look at the facts. One, the principal came to me based on my little camp's success. Two, Clarence put me on probation. Did not expect that. I'm suddenly available. Three, I've turned Chevy down three times and three times he's come back to me. Four, I pray and the desire to go only increases."

Jade rocked in silence. Considering. "Max, it just seems so out there. Of all the coaches in this country and I'm sure in Texas, this Chevy wants you?"

"Seems that way."

"Aren't there assistant coaches who can do the job?"

"Chevy doesn't want them. Says they don't have the leadership qualities he wants."

Jade regarded him, pursing her lips and squinting dubiously. "Doesn't it seem too good to be true? What's the catch?"

"As far as I can tell, no catch. Like I said, they're looking for a man, not a coach. They want to build up the program and the kids. They've had some good coaches in the past and Chevy decided to find one who had more character than experience."

Max's heart brewed, ready to explode. He *had* to take this opportunity. He had to go to Texas.

"You're seriously considering this?" Jade rocked forward to see his face. As she did the breeze swirled through the ends of her hair. "What about Benson Law? You've been planning to head up the firm since you were a kid."

"I know, Jade. But it just doesn't seem so important anymore. To be honest, I never even asked God if I should take over the firm. I assumed it was my destiny. But three months at the Outpost shook loose all my preconceived ideas about my life."

She paled. "How do I fit into this new revelation? Did you pray about marrying me?"

"As a matter of fact, I did." Max smiled. "I dreamed about marrying you not long after I met you. I knew you were God's gift to me."

"You never said you had a dream." Jade's countenance softened.

"I tucked it away as one of those things. Maybe I dreamed it because I wanted to marry you, but I know now God was speaking to me."

She sat back, folded her arms, and stared toward the backyard. "I like being a lawyer's wife." Jade shifted her gaze back to him. "Why can't you do pro bono work during your hiatus? There're plenty of deserving people who can't afford a Benson lawyer otherwise."

"You're right, I could do pro bono." Max ran his hand through his hair. "But that's not on the table. Coaching is, Jade. This is a real offer. Such a unique, incredible opportunity."

"Do you *want* to coach high school football?"

He laughed. "I never confessed this out loud but coaching was my hip-pocket dream. The one I'd pull out if I didn't get into law school or pass the bar."

"Max, really? You've never said a word about it."

"I am now, Jade." He slipped out of his rocker and bent to one knee in front of her. "I want to do this. What do you say?"

"What about firm profits and money . . . all your yammering when Clarence first put you on probation?"

"What about 'we already have more money than most people earn in a lifetime'?"

"I'm fine with that, but are you? Does this coaching job pay?"

"Yeah, not much, a teacher's salary, but you know money is not an issue, Jade. Why not take some Benson Law bonus dollars and invest in our future, a different future? And invest in the lives of the kids?"

She stared at him for a long moment. "Do you have to teach? It's a lot of work to prep for teaching, Max. And what will you teach? Your undergrad was in history but that was a long time ago."

"I'll only have coaching responsibilities, but I'll need some certifications, which is why—" Here came the hard part. "I need to decide and get moving on this. Two-a-days start in August. I know I can do this, babe. I can help those kids, make a difference."

"What about me and Asa?"

"I was thinking you'd come with me." He treaded tenderly.

"And the Blue Umbrella? *Southern Life* is coming next week. They expect their feature business to still be open when the issue hits the stands."

"More good points, more good points." Max rose off his knee and paced in a small circle, thinking. He'd been so focused on figuring out his heart he didn't have time to ponder solutions for Jade. "Okay, how about Lillabeth? She's been running the shop. Doing a great job. We can hire her to be manager. Hire part-time help for when she's in school. Worse comes to worse, Mom could run the shop for a while." Max's spirit sparked. Something divine was happening in his heart.

"Worse comes to worse?" *Oooh, bad choice of words, Max.* He knew *that* tone and inflection. "The Blue Umbrella is not a hobby. I've worked hard to build that business. Your mom doesn't know how to run a vintage shop."

"She's raised millions of dollars for charity, Jade. I think she can run the Blue for a few months." He reared back when the steel glint in her eyes flared hot. "Babe, you're a great businesswoman. What you've done with the Blue Umbrella deserves every respect, but I'm just saying between Mom and Lillabeth, the Blue Umbrella would be fine."

"Let's say we do this crazy thing. For one season? Then what? I thought the purpose was to hire someone to build a program. Not to keep having a new coach every year."

"Yes, that's the intent. I'd have the option to leave, and they'd have the option to fire me but, yeah, the idea is to be permanent. Listen, we don't have to pack up the house. We'll rent a place out there while we see if we like it. Get new furniture. That'll be fun. A bit of a splurge. Shopping, you like shopping, right?"

She snort-laughed. "Don't use lawyer tricks on me. Yes, I like shopping but this is uprooting. Max, you're talking moving permanently to Texas. Are you seriously considering leaving the law?"

"Do you think you could learn to love being a coach's wife?"

"And the Blue?"

"Move it to Colby. I bet there's fun vintage in Texas. Or sell it. Stay home with Asa."

She rocked out of her chair and stared out over the lawn, arms folded, saying nothing for several weighty seconds. Max stopped pacing and stood alongside her.

"I remember when you brought me here right before we were married," she said, low and slow. "Before you'd gone on the bachelor trip. When you told me this house was mine, I couldn't believe it. Somehow all the stars aligned to make my dreams come true. My amazing fiancé just gifted me with a sprawling Victorian home with hand-carved moldings and imported marble floors. It was too much for a poor girl from Prairie City." She looked up at him. "Was I right? Too much for a poor girl like me? The dream was only a façade?"

"The façade is believing those things make us happy, make us a couple." Max took her arms and gently turned her to him. "This right here, Jade, you and me discussing our lives, our future, is what makes us a couple. Building a life together, building our marriage around each other and who God's called us to be. That's the dream. Not living in buildings, running mad after careers and calling it a life. That's the façade."

"I want to grow old in the Hollow, Max." She stepped out of his light grip. "Walking in Laurel Park under the summer sunsets with you, talking about our grandchildren. I want to raise Asa here. I don't want to live temporarily in Colby, Texas. It's in the middle of nowhere. Asa's finally settled after a tough year for such a little guy. Did you see him at the park? He's all about routine. He's only been with us for four months. Before that, it was just him and Rice. And technically, you can take him without me. I'm not his mom."

"You are his mom and if you don't want to do this, then we don't." Max surrendered, raising his hands, then letting them fall to his sides.

"No, Max, you can't put this on me. I won't have you resent me on top of everything else we're going through. You can go without me, you know."

"Not an option, Jade. Not an option." He'd anticipated resistance. After all, this idea came out of the blue for him too. Max had hoped to persuade Jade, but she remained as solid as the mountain ridge.

"We're at a stalemate then. You want to go. I don't."

"Then we pray. You pray, I'll pray. Can you do that much for me? There's a solution in here somewhere, Jade. But whatever we do, we do it together."

"All right, I can agree to prayer." Finally, she melted a little, softened her stance. "Max, why does it mean so much to you? Is it more than just a chance to live out your hip-pocket dream?"

"I've asked myself the same thing a hundred times." He returned to his rocker and eased against the ladder back, setting it into motion. "The firm, our clients, they don't need me, Jade. They *like* me for what I can do for them, but there are plenty of lawyers to fill the bill. But those boys at Colby High have no one to believe in them. Since I can remember, people have believed in me, encouraged me. I want to give that back to boys who need it. Their fathers and grandfathers played for a winning program. If I don't go, there might not be a football program this year. First time in a hundred years. Since the school was founded."

"No one? Surely an assistant coach, a booster, the parents—"

"Chevy said he'd just as soon shut it down than to get the wrong coach again. There's politics going on but he's not forthcoming."

"Then you can't go. Walk into a firestorm? It's crazy."

"Not if God's calling, Jade. Remember the girl who came to speak at church last fall? She was, what, twenty-one? Spent six months in Africa working with boys rescued from guerilla armies. One day she called her missions supervisors and said, 'God's telling me to speak to the leader of the boys' army.' They thought she was crazy at first, remember? But agreed it was God and let her go. She traveled all night on a bus alone and when she got there, the man agreed to speak with her. A little blond, blue-eyed girl. If she could step up, why can't we? She won over that army lord. Why can't I, we, win over forty high school boys?" The emotion in his voice surprised him. He batted the moisture from his eyes, then bent forward with his face in his hands, his heart churning.

After a moment, Jade returned to her rocker. "I said I'd pray, Max. And I will."

So it wasn't up to him anymore. It was up to the God of heaven and earth. Only He could change Jade's heart.

Eight

Liz Carlton, one of Jade's regular consigners, popped her head into the Blue Umbrella. "Jade, sugar, you'll want to see this."

"What? The coon dogs running?" July Days in Whisper Hollow meant anything goes. Yesterday afternoon, two rival bakers had celebrated Pie Fight Day. Main Street was littered with piecrust, berries, and whipped cream. Today was Coon Dog Day.

"You'll wish it was the coon dogs." Liz tipped her head toward Main Street. "Hurry."

She followed Liz out. *This better be good.* Business was slow today so Jade spent the quiet moments praying, asking God to align her heart with Max's. Or his with hers. Football. Texas. It just never, ever entered her mind as a life they'd lead. Even though she did love the game.

How many hours of Midnight Football had she played in Prairie City?

A crowd gathered on the sidewalk outside the Blue Umbrella. Mae Plumb, the owner of Sugar Plumbs, glanced at Jade and squinted through the trail of smoke rising from her cigarette.

"She's gone plum wild, Jade."

"Who?"

An air horn blasted the air and knocked Jade's lulled heart awake. The crowd leaned back in unison, ooohing and ahhing.

"Jade," Mae called again. "You best do something, shug."

"Me? Why me?" Jade cut through the crowd and stepped into the street. The air horn blasted again. Jade spotted a golf cart at the top of the hill.

"Get your Rebel Benson gear, folks." The horn blasted. The cart drifted forward. Clothes flew out of the side and hit the pavement.

Oh no. June. Jade started up the hill, easy, careful not to spook her prey. More clothes flitted from the cart, hung in the air, then sank to the street.

"Golf clubs, shoes, balls, and towels. Platinum cuff links." Two shiny bobbles arched out of the cart. A hiker raced into the street. "Good for you, boy." June blasted the air horn. "I got Armani. Ralph Lauren. Hand-stitched leather loafers all the way from It'ly." The shoes clunked against the street.

June blasted the horn again. And again. The crowded thickened. Cars pulled over and tourists unloaded.

"Come one, come all, get your Rebel Benson souvenirs right here." Blast-blast of the horn. More clothes littering the street. The golf cart eased over the yellow line. A cluster of onlookers scrambled out of the way.

"Whisper Hollow mistresses of the not-so-honorable Judge Rebel Benson, come out, come out wherever you are. Heck, maybe even a tourist or two has had a tryst with the noble judge. Get your Rebel Benson souvenirs."

Shirts fluttered in the air.

Jade met the cart in the middle of Main. "June, what are you doing?" She looked sane. Jade sniffed. She wasn't drunk.

"Mind your own, Jade." June blasted the air horn in her face. Jade winced, leaning away. "Look there, my old bridge buddy Pollyann Markham. Admit it, I know you had a little crush on my husband, Pollyann. Didn't you have a weekend at your sick aunt's a few years back? The same weekend Reb had an emergency lawyers' convention. There's no such thing as emergency lawyers' conventions."

Blast. Clothes. Another blast. Pollyann Markham disappeared in the crowd.

"June." Jade walked alongside the cart. "Why don't you hit the brake and let me climb behind the wheel?"

Blast. "No."

"June, you've lost your mind." A man called from deep in the crowd, "Go home."

"Forget it, Bob Zimmer. I've earned this, don't you think?" June tossed another bundle of clothes from the cart. A watch. Rebel's new Cartier. Ties. "Get your Judge Rebel Benson souvenir."

"Pull over, let me drive." Jade tried to get in, but June pressed the gas.

"You're not the police, Jade." June gunned the gas again so Jade lost her hold on the side and barely kept herself from crashing to the pavement. Okay, she saw how June wanted to play.

"June!" She pulled over. Finally. And stepped out, raising a megaphone to her lips.

"Listen to me, Whisper Hollow. You marry the man you love with bright, blinding, I mean *blinding* stars in your eyes, believing true love has chosen you. On your wedding day, you walk down the aisle toward your handsome groom, tall and resplendent in his hand-tailored tux, heart exploding with so much joy, love, and excitement you can barely draw a deep breath."

"June, give me the megaphone." Jade tried to snatch it but her tennis-playing mother-in-law was too quick. She ran around to the other side of the cart. The crowd shifted with her.

"Then it happens. Kaboom. Lies, cheating, lust; the destroyers of all dreams. I'm here to tell you, ladies and gentlemen"—June pointed to the crowd, an evangelist for the lovelorn—"there is no such thing as true love, or fidelity. No such thing as 'til death do you part. Oh no, *parting* is the death. Only trouble is, the man still lives, kicking and breathing, reminding you every day that forty-one years of your life were given to the wrong man. What then? Some of y'all know what I'm talking about. Liam Lowe, you been married, what, four times? And you, Beth Trout, you must have had two, maybe three affairs. Was your marriage worth a dalliance into adultery?"

Several onlookers gasped. Some laughed.

"That's right. It's shocking. It happened to my own daughter-in-law, right, Jade? Thought she married a faithful man, a true man."

"June, stop." Embarrassment burned down Jade's middle. "Why are you doing this?"

June lowered the megaphone. "Because I'm sick and tired of lies and secrets."

"You've lived with them for forty years. What's changed?"

"Me."

June had caught Rebel with another woman back in the spring, about the same time Jade discovered Max had a son. Together, the two of them drove Mama back to Prairie City in a '66 convertible Cadillac. Pink. A few days later Reb flew to see her in the company jet and pledged to change his ways.

"June, you're a classy, cultured lady. This is beneath you."

June eyed Jade with a hard optic rebuttal and jammed the megaphone to her lips. "It's time to take life by the reins. Don't let life rein you."

Jade flattened her hand over the megaphone speaker. "So you're throwing his stuff in the streets and calling out his mistresses?" Not that Reb didn't deserve it.

"I'm sixty-four years old, Jade. I'm through with pretending. Everyone in this town is hurting, hiding, thinking no one knows the things they've done. Well I do and I'm putting it all out there." June jerked away from Jade and went back to the megaphone. "Did y'all know my son had a baby outside his marriage? Sure did. And Jade here had an abortion when she was sixteen. Now she can't get pregnant to save her—"

Jade lunged at her mother-in-law, shoving her into the golf cart, stumbling and tripping, and pinned her against the seat. "You blast your business if you want, but you don't blast mine." Hard, passionate words.

The woman had lost her mind. Lost. Her. Mind. Jade yanked the megaphone from June's tan, slender, bejeweled hand. "You're making a spectacle of yourself."

"Oh, Jade." Her laugh was weak. "I've been a spectacle for a long, long time. Only today, I'm in on it. Now let me up." June righted herself, fixing her hair and smoothing her hand over her tennis top. Her congregation started to dwindle.

Jade spotted Chandler Doolittle from the *Whisper Hollow News*, a weekly paper, creeping along the back of the crowd with his camera.

"Chandler's here, June."

"Oh good, he got my message." June stretched to see him, smiling when she did, and waved.

Jade ran around to the wheel and hopped into the cart before June got out. She released the brake and mashed the gas. "Hang on, June."

"Wait, did Chandler get my picture? Woohoo, Chandler, did you get it all down for your 'Hollow Happenings' column? Call me."

"June, stop. You don't want this on the Internet." Jade powered the cart down the hill, made a U-turn at the light, and headed back up toward the country club. She hollered at Mae as she passed, "Get Rebel's stuff."

What bothered Jade the most about June's Main Street confessional was the truth embedded in her words. The woman spoke from experience and from her heart. Embarrassment aside, Jade believed everyone within hearing distance of June went home convicted about examining their hearts. Even if for a moment.

You marry the man you love with bright, blinding stars in your eyes, believing true love has chosen you . . . Lies, cheating, lust; the destroyers of all dreams . . . There is no such thing as true love, or fidelity.

Despite the cordial culture of Whisper Hollow and the full church pews on Sunday mornings, the Hollow harbored secrets. Infidelity. Backstabbing. Gossip. Lost love. Destroyed dreams.

Standing at the sink peeling potatoes for dinner, Jade realized she'd already experienced a taste of the world June described, and it went down bitter.

After dropping off June and her borrowed cart at the club, Jade had closed the Blue Umbrella and driven up to Eventide Ridge to think and pray. For June. For Max. For the secret she knew about Asa. For her own heart and weak trust. It took a good hour to exhaust herself at the foot of the cross.

Then she came home and Googled a few things.

A car door slammed. Jade looked up, out the kitchen window. Max rounded the corner of the garage hoisting Asa on his shoulders. Against the green backdrop of their wooded yard and the golden trails of afternoon sun lacing through the treetops, her husband and son created a serene picture.

"Mama." Asa ran to her when Max set him down. "Look." He held up a toy car.

"Drugstore." Max set a small bag on the counter.

"Very nice, son."

"I thought we could watch a movie tonight so I picked up some snacks at Kidwell's." He held up a box of Milk Duds, rattling the contents. "But you have to eat your dinner first."

He could be so wonderfully goofy. "I'm fine with dinner first. You're the junk food junkie." Jade peeked into the bag. M&Ms, all varieties, chips, jelly beans, popcorn, and licorice. "Who else is watching this movie with us?"

"No one, but I wasn't sure what we wanted." Max kissed her forehead. "I heard some interesting whispers in Kidwell's."

"I bet you did." Jade quartered the potatoes and slipped them into the boiling water.

"Mom drove a golf cart down Main Street? Tossing out clothes, yelling things about Dad?"

"In rare June Benson form."

"Do you know why?" Max came around the island and leaned against the counter.

"She said she's had enough. Your dad canceled counseling, but other than that I don't know if anything happened between them." Jade twisted open a can of green beans. "She also blabbed our business to the crowd. I pushed her in the cart and drove away."

"Our business?" Max said. "You mean, mine."

"I mean ours. Your affair, my abortion. Chandler Doolittle heard it all. Can you get me the small saucepan?" Jade pointed to the island cupboard.

Max reached down and handed it to Jade. "If you didn't see it with your own eyes, I'd never believe it."

"I couldn't believe it, Max. Even though I chased her down Main Street. I thought she was drunk, or that something really bad happened that made her finally snap. But she seemed of sound mind. Sober."

He stared at the wall. Jade knew what he was thinking. How to avoid becoming like his parents. She'd been pondering the same thing all afternoon.

"I think I'll give her a call," Max said. "Check in with Dad too." Asa stood at Max's feet, offering up his Cheerios container. "Open, please." Max popped the top and handed it back to Asa. "Here you go, buddy."

Jade locked in on Asa's face. He looked so much like Rice. But didn't Jade see Max in his eyes? And the full pout of his lips?

She'd checked the mail and her e-mail when she came down from the ridge, in the middle of her Googling, and had received nothing from Taylor. But silence was golden at this point. It meant Jade didn't have to speak about this to Max.

Max leaned over her shoulder, the scent of his skin seeping into hers. "Smells good. What are you making?"

"Meat loaf, mashed potatoes, green beans."

Max lowered his head to see her face. "You're making all my favorite dishes."

"A man's gotta eat." Her gaze met his. She was tired of being in debt to fear and betrayal, driven by bitterness. Enough already.

"Thank you." He lifted her chin and kissed her, a teasing spark of passion buzzing across her lips. The soft ends of his hair brushed her cheeks. "I'm all in, Jade. I promise you." He pulled back and leaned against the counter. "By the way, I checked in with Tripp. He's a good friend as well as accountability partner. I can still see his face when I told him I'd do anything to get clean. Also I called Clarence and said I'd work with the associates, take pro bono cases. I'm golfing with the Rainwaters in the morning. Even though Gil Rainwater is about the most bleeping client on the face of the earth. Pray I don't smash him with my club instead of the ball. I won't be able to take Asa to school, though. And oh, I also talked to Reverend Girden. He can counsel with us if you want."

"What happened to Texas and football?" She felt a bit deflated. She'd spent all day praying. Googling. Thinking. Surrendering.

"Well, it's still there, but you really didn't seem to want to go, so I started figuring out what I'd do if we stay here. You're right, there's lots to do and the time will go by fast. What? Why are you looking at me like that?"

"Max." Jade grabbed the pale yellow collar of his oxford. His long bangs framed his temples, accenting his eyes. Everything about him made her want to love him. Trust him. "Look me in the eye. You *really* don't have any phantom back pains or desire for pills?"

His gaze held without a flinch. "No phantom pains, no desire for pills. At all. He whom the Son sets free is free indeed. Why be a prisoner when Jesus already paid the price? Granted, I have to do the work to stay free, but I have no craving or desire whatsoever to go back to my old ways. I don't even like that guy."

"I believe you." She released his collar. Max didn't move other than to rake his hair out of his eyes.

"Okay, now that I passed the test, what's going on in that pretty head of yours?"

"I've been praying . . . and don't give me that look. I told you I would. Spent an hour up on the ridge after I got your mom out of the street."

"And?"

"I came home and Googled Colby. It's not like the Hollow, but it seems like a nice little town. Yeah, it's in the middle of nowhere—but with a population of fifteen thousand, it's bigger than the Hollow." Jade flipped on the oven light to check the baking meat loaf. "I didn't realize it's only twenty-five minutes from Amarillo. I read a few articles and it does seem Colby High needs something good to happen for the football program."

"You're making my heart go pitter-patter."

"Maybe you are the man for the job, Max. Did you know they used to be state champs two or three times a decade all the way back to the teens?"

"Yeah, I know, I told you."

"I hate when traditions die. When old things are forgotten or tossed aside." She absently wiped her hands on the dish towel. "Max, what happened with your mom today scared me. In a good way. Could that be me thirty years from now? Driving down Main in a stolen golf cart, throwing your things or anyone's things into the street, blurting my guilt and shame?"

"No, that's not you thirty years from now. Or me. We're nothing like Mom and Dad."

"Not today, Max. But the Hollow has a way of lulling people to sleep. We think we're safe up here, cloistered away from the world, but we're just as evil and sinful as everyone else. We get comfortable. Lazy in life. Do you know how many affairs and secrets are in these hills?"

"Scary, I know. But there're good people too. Reverend Girden and his wife. Tripp and his family. Lillabeth and her parents are honorable, God-fearing people."

Asa ran into the room with his new car and opened his personal cupboard. "Drink, please." He offered up his cup. Jade tugged open the fridge and filled it with his apple juice.

"There you go, sweets." She kissed him, brushing his hair aside. And, she told herself, if they went to Colby, Jade might be able to bury Rice's secret in the Hollow. Where it belonged.

"Colby probably has just as many ruts and pitfalls as Whisper Hollow. We just don't know what they are yet, Jade."

"But we go in fresh, with new eyes." She came around the island to Max. "If we're starting over, then let's start *over*. Let's go someplace where the only person we know is each other. That'll make us or break us—fast."

Max narrowed his gaze and stepped back. "You're willing to trust me that much?"

"I'm going to trust God and pray hard. Max, it's time to be happy. To choose life. I want to try. Let's pull out my roots and transplant them in Texas. I don't want to be my mom, flying off and wild, but I don't want to be your mom either. Stuck in the Hollow, bitter and resentful."

"As long as you're with me, we can do anything."

Max grinned, then donned his cross-examination expression. "What about the Blue Umbrella?"

"Lillabeth agreed to take it. I can hire a few part-timers. The shop is solvent, takes care of itself. Lilla can take the profits. We won't earn any money, but the shop won't cost us either."

"You're serious then."

"Yeah, the more I prayed, the more I felt what I saw in your face this morning. I can't believe I'm saying this, but let's go to Texas. Coach football."

Max snatched her up and spun her around. "Thank you, thank you, thank you. Woot!" When he set her down, he grabbed her face with his hands and kissed her forehead, her cheek, her nose, her lips, her forehead again.

"Call them." She tapped his pocket where he kept his phone. "See what they say." Excitement swirled low in her soul at first, growing larger, wider.

Max pressed his touch screen a couple of times and put the phone to his ear. "Chevy, hey, Max Benson. Good, good, listen—I was wondering if the coaching . . ."

Jade paced, her belly roiling. This was insane. *Oh, Mama, can you believe I'm doing this? Leaping out, catching the current in the wind?* Baby sister Willow had been Mama's kite in the breeze. Jade had been her roots in the ground.

"Yeah, that's good. Certainly, I understand. Okay . . . thanks, Chevy, talk to you soon." Max hung up, his expression dour and drawn. "Jade, listen, don't be disappointed but—"

"Oh, Max, no, they hired someone already? I thought they wanted you. You're the one for the job. *You.*"

"Yeah, they hired someone." Max slipped his phone in his pocket. A glint flashed in his eye. He walked toward the doorway. "How long until dinner? I'm going to call Mom, see what's up with her."

"What? Max, what else did he say? What?" Jade grabbed his arms, arresting his forward motion.

"Hey, don't make dessert." Max smacked his abs. "I just chiseled out this six pack and—"

"Maxwell Charles Benson."

"Oooh, the lady breaks out the middle name."

"Okay, fine, don't tell me." Jade released him with a large gesture. "I was going to make chocolate cake." She sashayed toward the pantry. "Isn't that your favorite?"

"Give, give, you win." Max's smile purchased the very last bit of her qualms. "He wants me there next week. Sooner than I thought. Will you be ready to go? I need to get started on certifications to coach."

"Next week?" Jade pulled up a mental picture of her sticky notes to-do list. "I don't know."

"We'll work together. Get it done."

"Then let's do it. Yeah." Jade opened the pantry for the cake mix. "We're moving to Texas."

Max dashed over and kissed her—long, wild, and exuberant.

Nine

Forget sleeping. A million thoughts ran through Max's head at a million miles an hour. From doubts about his decision to his speech on the first day of practice.

What am I thinking? I'm a lawyer, not a coach.

Jade doesn't really want to go, she's just being nice and I don't deserve it.

Need to call Coach Bonham tomorrow and set up a meeting.

One season, just commit to one season . . . you can always come back to Benson Law. Sure, easy. This will be a fun adventure. You and Jade can focus on being together, a team against the world.

Boys, I'll say on our first day, this is a football. *And hold up the ball. Yeah, and what if they don't know about Vince Lombardi?*

Max kicked off his covers and stretched long on top of the sheets, willing a cool blast from the air conditioner. But his thudding heart and careening thoughts made it impossible to cool down. Rolling out of bed, he walked down the hall to check on Asa. The clock flashed 3:16.

When he open Asa's bedroom door, the hinges creaked. Max made a mental note to oil them tomorrow. Along with the eight hundred other details he'd been logging.

Perching on the edge of Asa's bed, he squared away the cover and rested his hand on the boy's back. This kid inspired him. His son. So small, yet so bold and brave, tackling his little world—the playground at Laurel Park—as if he were Indiana Jones on a mission. Fearless.

Asa slept, lullabied by his own deep breathing. "We're moving to Texas, Ace. You'll be a baby Warrior. What do you think?"

Max had scheduled a meeting with his dad and Clarence first thing in the morning to let them know he'd spend his probation on a football field in Colby, Texas.

After the meeting, he'd get going on a house hunt. Friday to Friday, that's all the time they had. He didn't want Jade to worry about Realtors and houses while dealing with the Blues—selling one, handing over the other.

Jade could pick the house she wanted, but a Realtor could narrow down the field. Colby had a lovely historic district with gabled Victorian homes and quaint '20s bungalows. Outside of town, there were century-old ranch houses dotting the ends of long dusty driveways, shaded by elms and cottonwoods.

Max felt sure he could find a new Benson associate to live in the house. Jade had already started furniture shopping online.

Her decision to move to Colby blew Max away. *God, only you.* But she still treated him like a friend she had a crush on and didn't want to *mess things up.*

Max smiled. He could appreciate that, but thinking of Jade did nothing to cool him down. He loved being her friend and he'd committed to protecting her heart. He owed her that much. Love was patient and kind. Love didn't seek its own desire. Axel had drilled that into him. So he'd wait.

Heading back down the hall, Max paused at the second-floor landing. A thin ghostly light created a white pond on the foyer's marble floor. The front door stood wide open.

Jade. He thundered down the stairs. Was she having a depersonalization moment? Changing her mind and panicking? "Jade?"

She sat on the porch steps, the breeze in her hair. Asa's baby monitor sat next to her.

"What's going on?" Max stood in the doorway, watching. Under the thin material of her pajamas, he could see her shivering. But the night was warm and dewy. "Are you okay?"

"I'm trying to imagine Texas." Jade pointed toward the Van Gogh sky. "It's somewhere beyond that dark line of trees but not as far as the stars in the horizon." She braced against a tremor.

Max eased down behind her and wrapped his arms around her. "Did you have a DP moment?"

"No, just its evil twin, anxiety. I was fine when I went to bed. But then I woke up startled, my heart racing and my thoughts so dark. What if I get to Colby and . . . I'm all alone? Then I started worrying, wondering if I'd made the worst decision of my life. What if I can't undo it? What if it's an experiment in love and life that goes really, really wrong?"

"Do you really think the Lord would send us to Colby and then leave us?" Max settled his chin on her head. "But babe, we don't have to go. One phone call and we're back on track for a Whisper Hollow life."

"No." She shivered. "I can't let fear win . . . I can't raise Asa afraid."

"Are you worried about me? That I'll mess up? Or leave you? Jade, it's not going to happen."

"I'm not afraid of you leaving me, Max. Messing up maybe." He felt the reverberation of her laugh against his arm. "If I've learned anything in the past three months it's that you're loyal. You stick to your word, even when you're messing up other areas of your life. You won't leave me." Jade tipped her head back. Max inhaled the subtle scent of flowers. "But there's no guarantee I won't leave you. I'm the one who grew up with parents leaving. Your parents endured years of infidelity, but they stayed married. When you told me about Asa, you fought to keep us together. I was the one who hightailed it to Iowa in a pink Cadillac. I'm the one who panicked at Mama's funeral and went running down a country road in high heels. As much as I'm a roots-in-the-ground kind of girl, I don't mind moving those roots to different ground."

"If you run, Jade, I'll chase you. I promised you that night in Prairie City when we went to the Boss or the Hoss, whatever the name of that place. If you wanted to go off with your ex, Dustin, or leave me, fine, but I'd come after you."

"Dustin is not an issue, Max. If I wanted him I'd not be here right now. He wanted to marry me. But I came home. Whatever we had as teenagers died when we were teenagers. And I married you." She shivered again.

Max stroked the smooth surface of her arm and she tucked her head against his shoulder. This, *right here*, was what Max had dreamed of for three months at the Outpost.

"I heard you in Asa's room over the baby monitor."

"Eavesdropper."

"I think he sort of saved my life, Max. For sure my heart." Jade nestled closer to Max, a sleepy melancholy in her words.

"Oh, Jade-o, he surely saved mine. He showed up and forced me to deal with everything. I think I'll always love him a little bit extra for that, if it's possible."

"Some days I can't remember life without him."

"Tomorrow when I go to Chattanooga, I'll get Cara to start filing adoption papers. We won't have time to finalize before moving to Texas, but we'll get it going. Is that okay with you?"

Jade turned in his arms and rose on her knees to face him. "More than okay, Max."

He brushed her hair back, watching her face, then cupped his hand against her cheek and kissed her. "I am so hopelessly in love with you, Jade."

"Keep talking." She leaned against him, breathing easy without tremors. "I'm listening."

When Jade awoke, the room was filled with light. She'd stretched, rolled, and burrowed into her pillow. She slept so good. So peacefully. Did she dream about sitting with Max on the . . .

She bolted upright, scrambling out of the covers, catching her foot in the sheets, stumbling forward, and landing on the floor with a thud.

She peered out the window. So much light. The bedside clock flashed 9:02. *Asa.*

"Max? Asa? Where are you? Why did you let me sleep? Asa?" She ran to his room, her heels awakening the hardwood. His room was neat and picked up. His bed, empty and made. "Asa? Max?" Jade ran down the hall. Max's room was also vacant, picked up, bed made. Did she wake up in the twilight zone? Jade leaned over the banister. "Max?"

Not a creature stirred. Thankfully, not even a mouse. At the end of the hall, Jade peered out the window into the yard. Two redbirds lighted on a grassy sunspot.

This was unacceptable. Leaving without telling her. Jade ran to her room, charged and hot, and snatched her phone from the bedside table.

"Hey, babe," Max answered, cheery. Too cheery.

"Where are you? Why did you let me sleep so long? Please tell me Asa is with you."

"Yeah . . . he's with me. Where else would he be? Is there a problem?"

"Yes, you left without telling me and you took my kid." Jade paced to the window, striking her heel hard against the floor, and peered onto Begonia Valley Lane.

"Okay," he said, tentative. "I hear you . . . I'm sorry."

"Why didn't you at least leave a note?"

"I left a note."

"Where?" Jade whirled around, scanning the bedroom's surfaces.

"In the kitchen. On the island. You can't miss it."

"In the kitchen? I didn't even go downstairs." Jade jammed the heel of her hand to her forehead. *Asa is fine. Calm down.* "Next time, just wake me, okay? Asa is used to seeing me in the morning. We snuggle and kiss and talk. It's our time."

"Okay, okay . . . got it." Max held his voice low. Tender. "I just thought you needed to sleep."

"Max, I'm a mom." Best three words in the English language. *I'm a mom.* "And a business owner. I don't have the luxury of sleep. Now that the Asa crisis is over, I'm late for work." Jade headed to the bathroom. "Where are you, anyway? Did Asa have breakfast? He's cranky without breakfast."

"I made pancakes."

"I slept through pancakes?"

"You were tired, Jade. Give yourself a break. You don't have to be super-mom all the time. You held down the fort for me while I was gone, so let me help you a bit. Besides, I needed to meet Coach Bonham at the school before he left on vacation."

"Just don't freak me out, again. Please." He was laughing. "What is so darn funny?"

"You, Mama. Official or not, Jade, you're Asa's mom. Speaking of moms, I left Asa with mine. After I met with the coach, I drove up to see Mom and tell her about the move. She asked if she could have her grandson for the morning so I said yes. She looked kind of down."

Mom. The word always touched her heart. "Did she tell you what's going on? When I asked she clammed up." Jade cradled the phone, tied her hair back, and brushed her teeth. If she hurried, she'd make it to the shop by nine thirty. She hated opening late. It was bad business.

"She clammed up with me too. Said she was just tired of all the lies and secrets."

Jade listened as Max recapped his stilted conversation with June. A thought hit her. She peered at her reflection, the green toothbrush jutting from her mouth.

"In the end, all I can conclude is she's trying to protect Dad's reputation with me."

"Yeah, yeah, right."

If Taylor Branch's paternity claim was true, it didn't just impact Max. It impacted Jade and the adoption. It impacted Max's parents. And the McClures, Rice's parents, who'd sued Max for custody after she died.

If Max wasn't his biological father, they'd have grounds to sue again. Other than a deadbeat dad, Gus and Lorelai would be Asa's only blood relatives.

The toothpaste burned Jade's mouth. She rinsed, tucking her toothbrush away. What if they'd known all along? What if that's why they sued? Surely they would've said something. *Gus and Lorelai don't . . . they can't.* But Rice was close to her parents. Would she keep Asa's dad a secret from them but blab to Taylor?

It made no sense. Taylor had to be lying. But why?

"Jade, you there? I hear swishing."

"Um, yeah, I was brushing my teeth. Sorry." And going wild with thought. "What were you saying?"

"I said I know you're running behind, but do you have breakfast plans?" Max said, a kind lilt in his voice. "I mean, after you brush your teeth?"

"Don't make fun of my multitasking." Jade turned on the shower, then noticed the bare towel rack. Ah, that's right, she'd used her towel last night to mop up after Asa's hurricane-force bath. She hurried to the bedroom linen closet. "Rain check on the breakfast. Unless you want to bring something by the Blue—"

Max stood in the bedroom door, phone to his ear, a brown bag bearing the swirly Sugar Plumbs logo in his hand. The aroma of cinnamon and bacon filled Jade's senses. Her stomach rumbled and her heart ignited.

"—Umbrella." Jade lowered her phone. On impulse, she gathered her pajama top close, watching Max watch her.

He remained stalwart, his phone still pressed to his ear. "I'll leave if you want," he said, his eyes surveying her. His hair fell in soft layers around his face and curled into his collar. He'd trimmed his beard close to his cheeks and the dark hairs accented the familiar contours of his face.

"I'm late, Max. Work . . ." She swallowed her emotion but found no passion to her rebuttal. "I should get going." Jade motioned toward the bathroom. "The water's running."

He glanced at the Sugar Plumbs bag. Cute, shy, like a boy. "Mae put in two of her large cinnamon rolls, hot from the oven. I guess I'll run these down to the kitchen." But he didn't move as he lifted his gaze to her. "It's taking every ounce of self-control not to drop this stuff to the floor and cross this room to scoop you up."

Jade heard thunder in her ears. Her shallow breath made her throat feel thick as cotton. Max's gaze drew her in, reflecting his love, speaking to Jade of her beauty and his desire. With each heartbeat, the walls she'd built crumbled. She'd missed her husband. In every way.

"Then you should stay." Jade walked toward him, around the end of the bed, and set the Sugar Plumbs bag on the dresser. "We can eat this later."

"What about the shop?" But Max already had her in his arms. "Jade, are you sure?"

"The shop can wait. I'm already late, what's a few more minutes?"

"Or hours." His words were warm as he kissed her cheek. Slowly, he slipped his hand around her waist and along the curve of her hip.

"Or days," she whispered. She missed him. Until now, she didn't know how much. Jade smoothed her hands along the top of his shoulders.

Max tentatively moved his face to hers, touching her cheek with his lips, then brushing them along her jaw.

She closed her eyes and breathed in his soapy clean skin, responding to every kiss and touch. "Max." Tears washed her eyes. "I love you. I've always loved you."

He rested his forehead against hers. "It's been a long time—"

"So why are you talking, cowboy? I mean, coach." She laughed as Max tumbled with her onto the bed. This was Max. Her Max.

He brushed his fingers along her hair line. He stretched out next to her. "Jade, I promise you—"

"Stop, Max, I know. I believe you. I'm choosing to believe you." She pressed her finger to his lips. "I saw the change in you the first day back. In your eyes, in your voice, in your manner. Two weeks later, I still see."

Max raised up on his elbows and held her face in his hands, his eyes searching hers. A grin twitched the edge of his lips. "I feel like it's the first time."

"In so many ways, it is." Jade said, letting go and trusting her heart, trusting her Max.

Ten

"Max, where have you been?" Jade met him at the Blue Umbrella's back door with Asa on her hip. "We've been waiting." He had his phone to his ear, where it'd been all week as they scrambled to move.

"Taking care of details, Jade. You do want a house to live in, don't you?" He'd cut his long, dark cowboy locks yesterday as part of his transformation into a head coach. Without his hair around his face, his brown and gold eyes were beautiful but intense. "Hey, buddy, how are you?"

Asa reached for Max's open arms. "Truck." He held up his favorite item from the office toy box.

"I see. An old milk truck."

"I called over an hour ago." Jade leaned toward him. She'd been scrambling to get ready for the move herself, as well as prep for the *Southern Life* feature.

74

To complicate matters, the reporter and photographer had arrived early. Not minutes—hours. Dressed in jeans and a T-shirt with her hair pulled back in a ponytail, and a modicum of makeup, Jade looked more like the after-hours cleaning lady than the chic owner of a trending vintage shop.

"I had to take care of a few things in the city and it took longer than I thought." Max slipped a legal folder into the black shoulder case. "Why don't you just tell them you need a few minutes to get ready. Send them over to Mae's. That ought to be worth an hour of good entertainment for them."

"I can't. They want to shoot now. I think they did this on purpose to surprise me, catch me off guard. Let's just get this done so I can get ready to leave." Her background in PR told Jade golden opportunities like this one didn't come often or easy.

Tomorrow afternoon, June would drive them to the airport and they were off to Colby by way of Amarillo.

"Okay, I'll entertain them while you change."

"Too late." Jade's heart sank. "They've already taken a bunch of pictures." Forget that Jade planned to wear the perfect vintage outfit. A Dior shirtwaist dress. Unfortunately, she hadn't picked it up from the cleaners yet.

Later, when they were *supposed* to be here, she'd look the perfect vintage part of the perfect vintage shop.

"Ah, forget it, babe. This is the real you."

"Nice . . . sloppy and plain."

"Just the way I like you." Max hooked his arm around her, but his calm and relaxed, trained lawyer confidence was irritating. "You're gorgeous," he whispered, then stepped into the shop where the couple from *Southern Life* stood. "Hi, I'm Max Benson, sorry to make you wait."

On top of being calm, he looked like a million bucks in his jeans and white button-down that accented his tan and the hue of his eyes. Jade felt like a muddy heifer next to him.

"Eric Potter." The photographer shook Max's hand. "This is Raven Winters."

"I've heard about you, Max Benson. My fiancé is a lawyer for Sloan & Mynheir."

"Out of Atlanta. I've gone up against them a few times."

"So I've been told." Raven tapped on her smartphone, her tone baiting. "I hear y'all work hard and play dirty."

When she looked up, she smirked as if she knew all Max's secrets. Dread washed over Jade. Was that what the interview was about? Getting at a southern lawyer instead of a southern vintage shop owner? Benson Law constantly declined requested interviews. Did Raven find an end around?

"Dirty? No, smart." Max nodded at her. "No need to play dirty when you've got the goods."

"I heard you just returned from rehab, Max. An affair, drug addiction." Raven shivered. "Ooh, it's a John Grisham novel."

"Aren't you here to talk to my wife? She has an incredible, unique business here."

"So she does. So she does." Raven exhaled a high saucy laugh. "Are we ready to shoot? Jade, why don't you show us around the shop. I can ask questions while we walk."

Jade shoved a wisp of her hair from her eyes with a glance up at Max. His eyes said, "Sorry."

"This is the main shop." Jade moved to the middle of the room where the sunbeams liked to collect.

Eric aimed his camera and Jade tried to smile with a lively flare, but she felt tiled, off balance.

"My editor said you and Max are moving?" Raven offered up her digital recorder.

"Not permanently, no." Jade had called to let them know she would be gone for five months. The editor wanted to go ahead with the story. Now Jade knew why. Southern law scandal was more interesting than old clothes and an Iowa girl. "Max accepted an opportunity in Texas. In here we—"

"Is the move to get away from his bad-boy reputation with drug addiction and women?"

"Excuse me?" Jade confronted Raven. "Bad-boy reputation? Women? I think this interview is over."

"Jade," Raven condescended with her tone. "I'm trying to get the full story. The readers want to know everything about you and your shop. Max is part of your story. It's interesting. Our readers will love it. An up-and-coming vintage expert married to a prestigious, scandalous southern lawyer? It's a soap opera. A Lifetime movie. The fairy tale of a single girl marrying into legal royalty only to face infidelity and drama. Just like the rest of us. Girl, it's a great angle. My editor loves it."

"So that's what your piece is about? Me and broken fairy tales. To make the rest of the world feel better?" Jade curled her fingers into her palm.

"It's about vintage and the people who wear it and sell it. So what if a bit of your backstory hits the pages. Now, what's back here?" Raven brushed around Jade for the storeroom.

Jade glanced at Max who stood watch over Asa as he drove his truck along the perimeter of the sun circles. He queried Jade with his expression. *What? How can I help?*

Change your last name.

Jade motioned for him to follow her but his phone rang and he answered, holding up his just-a-minute finger.

Jade went to the dark storeroom alone. With Raven. "This is our storeroom. I keep all the inventory here, plus upstairs in the loft."

"It's quite large. Where do you get your inventory? Estate sales? Consignment?"

"Both. I also have private contacts who are aware of clothes and other vintage items not available to the public."

"Ooh, and who might they be?"

"If I tell you, then I'd have to kill you." Jade grinned, holding on to the thought for a moment. Sigh . . . *let it go, Jade.* "Upstairs is the loft. Like I said, it's used for storage and staging." Jade pressed her hand lightly to Raven's back and moved her through the shop. "And here's my office."

"What do you mean staging? And what's your hurry? Afraid I'll discover a secret?"

"Staging is where I pick a theme for the week and set up clothes and jewelry from that era. Like Bobby Soxers or Jackie O Days."

"Fascinating." Raven headed back to the storeroom. "Eric, did you see those calendars on the back wall? What are those about, Jade? More vintage lore?"

"It's the wall of calendars."

"Eric, get a shot of this. Here's one from 1914 and one from 1920. Jade, are these real? Not reprints."

"They're real. They belonged to the family who owned this space before me. It was a five and dime." Jade crossed the storeroom to Raven and as she did, she spotted Lillabeth in the alley talking to a man—no one she knew or had seen in the Hollow before. "When I bought the place, the calendars were already on the wall with certain days circled or marked. It seemed like a sign. Vintage shop with vintage calendars. There are significant days circled. See? August twenty-first, 1914. Beginning of the First World War." Jade moved to the next calendar and flipped to October. "Black Friday, 1929."

"What about this calendar from three years ago?" Raven walked the wall. "Why did you circle December twenty-fourth? What happened that day?" She leaned to examine the dark, thick circle as she might find some hidden clue. "Did you get a great Christmas present? A marriage proposal?"

"We were already married. I circled it because it was a lovely evening. We had a party here with Max's colleagues and our friends. Around dusk, it started snowing and we all went for a walk in Laurel Park. It was quite lovely." Jade smoothed her hand over the slick page, wiping away a thin layer of dust. "Lovely and hopeful."

"Hopeful? Come on, Jade, give it up. What happened on the twenty-fourth?"

"A day I felt redeemed." She peered at Raven without another word. That day was definitely not her business. It was when she told Max about their honeymoon baby and the residue of aborting a baby at sixteen washed away. She'd found out a week before but had saved the news for Christmas Eve.

"Redeemed? From what? Do tell. Are you a woman of faith?"

"I am a woman of faith. Redeemed but weak." Jade tapped the calendar. She'd lost that baby six weeks later.

"I don't see any new calendars. Not last year's. Or this year."

"Well, Raven, this year isn't over yet."

"What's the criteria to get on the wall?" She held up her recorder.

"Special. It just has to be a special year."

Raven regarded Jade through narrowed eyes as if she didn't believe her. "Do I have this right, Jade? Asa is Max's son but not yours?"

She'd certainly done her homework. But where? How? "Raven, if you want to talk vintage, I'm all in. But if you want to talk personal, then maybe we should just forget this whole feature."

"Tell me, how did you and Max meet?" She talked into her recorder, linking her arm through Jade's.

"Right here, in the Blue Umbrella." This kind of questioning was more like it. Jade led the reporter back into the shop.

"Very romantic. Who saw who first?"

"I saw her first," Max said from his perch against the sales counter. "Fell in love first too." If he was trying to make up for leaving her alone with Raven, he was on the right track. When he winked at Jade, she warmed. He'd been doing a lot of things lately to make up for lost time.

"What about you, Jade? Did you fall in love at first sight?"

"Maybe second sight." Jade regarded her husband. "But falling in love with Max was easy." Working out their relationship presented a bigger challenge.

Raven asked the technical details of when and where they were married and for how long. Then, at last, she talked vintage. She was quite knowledgeable, which redeemed her a bit in Jade's mind.

"Why vintage, Jade?"

"Because"—Jade glanced around the shop—"to me, things have value. Each item in here represents a time in our history that we shouldn't forget. Clothes, jewelry, music, books, even furniture pieces, remind us. The calendars on the wall." She walked toward the hat display. "If I say pillbox hat, what do you think? Jacqueline Kennedy Onassis."

Raven asked a few more questions, then tucked her recorder into her purse. "Great interview, Jade." She motioned to Eric. "Let's get some shots of the family."

Gathered in the sunspot, Eric positioned Max and Jade with Asa in between. "All right, everyone watch the birdie."

Max's phone rang and the first shot had him looking down, reaching into his pocket. "Sorry, it's our Realtor. One second please." Max set Asa on the floor and backed away.

Raven smiled at Jade as if she pitied her. Eric snapped a few shots of Asa. "Great thing about digital," he said. "I can take as many shots as I want."

"Okay, I'm back. Jade, the boosters are planning a welcome party for us."

"I thought you were talking to the Realtor." Between prepping to move and dirt-seeking Raven, Jade teetered on the edge.

"She's also the head of the booster welcome committee." Max swung Asa up in his arms and stood next to Jade. "Now we're ready."

But they weren't. Max's phone rang three more times. He answered it three more times. The last time, Jade followed him to the back of the shop.

"Max, Eric and Raven are waiting. Why do people answer phones only to ignore the people standing in front of them? You're not the only one with things to do. Everyone's time is valuable."

He peered at her. "Chevy, I'm in the middle of something," Max said. "I'll call you back."

"Are we ready this time?" Eric raised his camera for the shot. Max tightened his hand on Jade's shoulder. "Jade, you don't look happy. How about a smile?" She obliged, tugging on her T-shirt and smoothing her hand over her hair. Eric looked up from the viewfinder. "You look great. How about a smile? Ready? On three. One, two—"

"Schmile." Asa shot his little arms into the air, bared his baby whites, and slurred out his favorite word.

Jade burst out laughing. Max's deep chuckle rolled underneath hers. Eric captured the moment. The Benson family's last moments in Whisper Hollow, gazing at one another, laughing.

After Raven and Eric left, Max and Jade took Asa for lunch at Sugar Plumbs, breathed out, and laughed over burgers and fries.

"We sure are going to miss y'all around here," Mae said, clearing away their plates. "I check for your Open sign every morning, Jade. I tell you, when you were gone those months, my whole routine was off." The narrow woman with Appalachian charm frowned. "What am I going to do for five, six months? I'll burn half the town's hands pouring coffee."

"Mae, you had Sugar Plumbs twenty years before I showed up. Besides, Lillabeth will be here, running the shop."

"Yeah, and it wasn't 'til you moved in that my business got really good and I found my *nice* bone. Gave up my mean one. It just won't be the same. I tell you, not the same." Shaking her head, Mae stepped off.

"Appalachian superstitions."

"Yeah, Jade, but you have a way of making people feel right about their world." Max reached inside his black attaché. "I was late this morning because I was picking this up." He slid the envelope across the table.

"Well, it's not a diamond necklace or a new car."

Max laughed. "You want a new car?"

"What do you think? I love my old truck." They'd shipped their vehicles to Texas three days ago, using one of Rebel's trucks until they flew out tomorrow. "What is this?" Jade pulled out a legal-looking form. The word *adoption* caught her breath.

"Fill out and sign where Cara's marked. We can finish when we come home. Either for Christmas or for good. Either way . . ."

Tears surfaced with a rush and trickled to the corner of Jades eyes, and she stretched over the table to kiss her husband. "I think I'll keep you, Max Benson."

"For better. We've had enough of worse."

"Are you excited, Max?"

He cracked a sporty grin. "Nervous like a cat, but yeah, excited. I love a challenge."

"Your back's okay?" Jade had decided she was going to ask him about it if she wondered. "No temptation to go off with another woman?"

"My back is fine." His light faded. "There is no one I want but you. Even that night—"

"Sometimes I'm going to ask, Max. I am."

"I suppose you've earned the right."

They chatted a bit more, then Max took Asa up to school for the last half of his school day and Jade hurried across to the Blue Umbrella. Max was working so hard to prove himself. She vowed to work harder to *see*.

"Lilla, I'm back. Do you want to go to lunch?"

Jade's faithful sidekick came out of the back, a feather duster in her hand. "What took you so long? I'm starved." She removed her apron and tossed it with the duster into the storeroom. "I'll get it when I come back." She dashed out the front door and across to Mae's.

Oh, Jade was going to miss that girl. But there was no one she trusted more than Lillabeth to run the shop. Jade had hired Lilla's younger sister and one of her friends to work part-time, and Lilla had trained them and worked out a schedule.

Jade stepped into her office to put the adoption form with her bag to take home later. A business card sat on the edge of her desk. Jade scanned the dark lettering.

Landon Harcourt

Financial Planner

Denver, CO

Landon from Denver. Jade's pulse pushed hot, causing prickles over her skin. Asa's supposed father.

Jade ran out of the shop and dashed across Main into Mae's. A blue Taurus swerved wide to miss her.

Lillabeth sat at the counter, talking to Gypsy and watching TV. Jade dropped to the stool next to her.

"Where'd you get this?" She flashed the business card.

Lillabeth sipped her soda. "Some man stopped me in the alley, asking about you. I knew you were with *Southern Life* so I told him you weren't available." She peered at Jade. "Why?"

"What did he say? Did he say what he wanted?"

"Just to give you his card."

"That's it?"

"That's it, Jade. He was cute, though. Charming." Lillabeth looked down when Gypsy set a grilled sandwich sided with fries in front of her. "Kind of full of himself, though."

I bet. "Did he say how long he'd be in town?" Thank goodness the McClures were out of the country.

"Hey, Jade, I have an idea. Why don't you call the number on his card and ask him." Lillabeth smothered her fries in ketchup. "Now, if you don't mind, my show is on and I hardly ever get to see it."

"Yeah, sure." Jade absently snatched one of Lillabeth's fries. "Take your time."

Back in her office, Jade searched her desk for the candlelighter and walked out back to the Dumpster. Call him? She didn't know what this man wanted, but whatever it was, it didn't start with her. He'd better man up and face Max if he wanted to talk about his *supposed* son.

Rice, why didn't you think about the web you weaved?

Jade touched the candlelighter flame to the tip of the card and held it between her thumb and forefinger, letting the flame build and consume Landon Harcourt's name.

"Jade?"

She dropped the card to the pavement and snapped around. "Max, what are you doing here?"

"I left my sunglasses in the shop. Are you burning things?" Max nodded to the small pile of charcoal. "Is this some kind of ritual?"

"No ritual." Jade shook her head. "Paper shredder is broken"—which was true—"so I thought I'd burn—"

"You know you don't have to burn them one at a time." Max grinned with a wink. "We have a paper shredder at home. Just bring the stuff you want to shred to the house."

"I think this is the last of it." Jade ground the embers of the card into the ground with her heel, leaving the link to the dead woman's deceit smoldering in the alley.

Eleven

On Monday morning the third week of July, Max cut through the sun blades of Colby, Texas. The yellow daggers sliced through cumulus clouds, dividing the light and shade.

Colby High, home of the Warriors, was located on the south end of town, a straight shot from the '30s bungalow he and Jade rented on three acres just northwest of town.

The fifteen-minute drive down 23rd Street took Max through pasture and farm territory, past trailer parks and public housing, into the quaint, historic downtown where ancient foliage lined the streets. Colby Grounds Coffee Shop sat on the corner of Jones Street and 23rd. Until now, that's all he knew of this Texas town.

South of town new developments popped up on the plains. Moneyed Texans built rambling houses behind gated golfing communities.

A bend in the road, and Max saw the high school rising on the horizon. He tightened his hands on the wheel of his Mercedes.

This is it. Your big experiment is about to launch. Too late to turn back now.

But as Max neared the field house, something seemed amiss. Where was the beaten down, battered school with a failing football program?

In his mind he'd pictured a dilapidated structure with wobbly bleachers and a shed for a field house.

Instead, a pristine, massive structure rose from the prairie. The football stands looked more like a small college stadium. Fifteen-foot letters, at least, lined the top and spelled out Warrior Country.

Turning into the parking lot, Max followed Chevy's instructions to the field house. How could he miss it? An enormous Warrior, fiery spear in hand, rode a painted pony, galloping along the side of a beautiful block structure.

Confidence, don't leave me now. Max cut the engine and stepped out, tucking his keys into his pocket. The sign over the door read Warriors Enter Here.

His footsteps echoed in the hall. His breath filled his ears. His heart strained against his ribs. Cold sweats gathered on his neck and arms. This was not the field house of a dying program. This was the field house of a faltering program looking to regain the crown. How'd they keep this thing going?

Boosters. Money. Expectation. The hall echoed with opulence. The tile glistened.

He stopped cold when he passed the room on his left. He pressed his forehead against the glass like a kid at a department store Christmas display.

Weight room. State of the art. Better than his gym back home. He scooted down to see through the window on the back wall door. Were those Jacuzzis? The signs above read Hot and Cold. When he'd played in high school, he went home after a football game and filled a baggie with ice from the freezer to rehab his tired muscles.

Next came the locker room. A wide, spacious room, white with red lockers and a gold floor. When he turned to his right, Max found the equipment room, organized, neat, and set up for fall play.

He was hyperventilating in the film center, complete with theater seating, when Chevy found him.

"Max, welcome, welcome." Chevy strode toward him, hand extended. He wore pressed business clothes—slacks and a button-down with an open collar. He looked to be in his midforties, though his hair was completely gray. Probably from the last six years of football casualties. "What do you think? Let's get you set up in your office."

"Chevy, this is the high school field house? Do you share it with a college? Like Texas Tech or A&M?"

The principal laughed as he opened a dark wood, windowed door and led Max into a square, spacious office that rivaled his digs at Benson Law. A glass wall gave him a full view of the field from the south end zone.

First glimpse he had of the field. Manicured. Green. Painted. Amazing like everything else.

"We hope you like it." Chevy tapped a light wood desk complete with an iMac computer. Behind the desk was a credenza. Suspended from the corner was a flat panel screen with a Blu-ray player. "In here's your conference room for coach's meetings."

Max peered through the door Chevy opened. Mahogany table, whiteboard, TV, Blu-ray, of course. Warrior carpeting.

Max's mind conflicted with his heart. This was . . . fantastic. This was . . . a disaster. What had he stepped into? This wasn't a poor man's program.

"Now over here"—Chevy crossed to the other side of the office, opened another dark wooden door, and flipped on a light—"is your private quarters. It's not much, but you have a bath and sofa, fridge and little reading area. One year we had a young, single coach and he just lived in here."

"Not much? Not much," Max finally spoke. "Chevy, this is incredible. Spectacular. I thought the program was broke, busted, on its last leg." In all the dialog about coaching Colby High School football, Max never imagined asking about the condition of the field house—run-down, or in this case, state of the art.

"It is. Coaching-wise. But we have some very loyal, rich boosters. The field house was built eight years ago as we were coming off our winning season. Coach Burke had retired. We had a new hotshot coach, Fin Ryan, who immediately broke every rule in the book. Out-of-season practices, practices lasting too long, cheating, lying, steroids. We got nabbed on that one by the state. Seems we never recovered. The athletic director's looked high and low for our next Coach Burke."

"Steroids?"

"Ryan wanted to best Coach Burke's legacy. I think he felt pressured by some of the boosters. Took things too far. Lost our bid in pre- and postseason games as part of our sanction for three years. Can't win a championship if you're not allowed to play."

"Chevy, this is not the picture you painted for me when you asked me to come."

"If I told you, would you have come?"

"I-I don't know. Maybe." Max moved to the middle of his office. A leather, L-shaped sofa hugged the far wall. He imagined briefly it being a fun place to chat with the boys or coaches after practice. "I thought I was coming to help a poor school, a financially broke program."

"Well, we are poor in some senses, Max. Poor in leadership. Poor in coaching. Poor in our program integrity and skill. Last coach we had fielded a bunch of brutes."

"W-what about the A.D.? Isn't it his or her job to keep the coaches in line?"

"He says he did. You'll meet him in a minute as well as your assistants and a few key boosters." Chevy took a leisurely seat on the sofa. "Well? Did you see the film room when you came in? You can get the whole team in there. All your keys are in your desk. Do you know how to use a Mac?"

"Yeah, yeah." Max stepped to his desk, opening the drawer to see the keys.

"You have four assistant coaches. And an equipment manager. The Warriors still have an excellent booster program. With the recent slump in our football program, a lot of dollars have gone over to basketball, softball, and baseball. But I have their commitment to support you, Max. If you need anything, you let me know." Chevy checked his watch. "Let's go to the film room. We're meeting everyone in there."

Stunned didn't quite describe how Max felt. Overwhelmed. Deceived. Terrified. Those were good descriptions. Chevy led Max across the hall. The film room reminded Max of the Benson Law media center with its mounted screen and plush seating.

This couldn't all be from generous boosters. Max remained in the back, knots pulling taut in his belly. *What's the real reason you haven't been able to keep a coach, Chevy?*

"Max, welcome to Texas football. Come on, sit down. Don't look so distressed."

Lord, what have I done? Max eased down the aisle. "Chevy, any coach with experience or ambition would walk across the prairie barefoot for a chance at a place like this."

"I'm not interested in coaches who are bedazzled by the facilities. That's why I didn't really bring it up. You were willing to come without knowing. Big points in my book." Chevy turned on another set of lights. "I'm working on making this a prep school, Max. I need kids with academics and athletics. I don't mind starting over a football program with a green coach. I started over basketball two years ago and we won our first regional this spring. The kids are excelling on and off the court. I want that from you for this football program. I read up on you. Tenth in your law class. Graduated with honors from Duke and Duke Law. Lots of pro bono work. Other than your . . . *problem*, which I talked with Axel about, you are the best candidate for what I want."

Chevy glanced toward the door as a group of men made their way into the room. He greeted them, asked about wives and children by name, made each man feel important. Using the same charm on them he used on Max.

"Max, this is Lars Martin, your offensive coordinator." Chevy moved to the next man as Max shook Lars's hand. "Kevin Carroll here runs a mean defense."

"Kevin, nice to meet you."

"Same here." His tone betrayed his words.

Chevy introduced the special teams coach, the strength coach, and the equipment manager. Then they sat in the first row, arms folded, glancing back as another group of men filed into the room.

"Here we go. Max, this is Colby High's athletic director, Bobby Molnar."

"Bobby, nice to meet you."

"Welcome." Flat. Cold. Attitude galore. He'd been left out of this selection process.

Take it up with Chevy. But Max felt the tension. "Thanks, it's good to be here." *Stay cool. Stay humble.*

"This is Rick Lundy, president of the boosters and all-around Warrior fanatic. Bobby quarterbacked the team for the 1980 national champs. Rick here starred on the 1985 team, rushing for, what, thirteen hundred yards that season?"

"Thirteen hundred and fifty-two."

"But who's counting, right?" Chevy laughed and slapped Rick on the back. "If you need anything, Max, Rick is your man. He owns half of Colby, I believe. Restaurants. Apartments. Auto parts stores. I can't keep up."

"A few mini-marts," Rick said, smiling, shaking Max's hand.

"He's on his way to owning all of Colby," Chevy said. "And here we have the lovely Brenda Karlin. Brenda is the vice president of the boosters, taking care of fund-raisers and pep rallies and what all. Brenda, meet our new coach."

"We've met, Chevy. I helped Max and his wife rent that place up off Route 60. How y'all doing? Did your furniture arrive yet?"

"Not yet. All we have is an air mattress in the master bedroom, but we're doing well."

"I'm sure the furniture will arrive soon. We are so thrilled to have you, Max. I hear good things about you from Chevy." Brenda wore a dark suit with a vivid orange blouse. Her straight blond hair was short and styled, and something about her eyes reminded Max of the pebbles he used to collect from the Hollow's creeks.

A few of the players drifted into the room, moving among the chairs and sitting in small clusters. They looked and felt nothing like a team.

The arrogant and wealthy boys wore dubious, bored expressions with smartphones glued to their hands.

Another group of boys, chisel-faced and sinewy, with eyes like polished marbles, wore eager yet tentative expressions, appearing edgy, as if they might be asked to leave at any moment.

A spattering of boys of various shapes, sizes, and backgrounds sat in groups of twos or threes. But then there was a cluster in the center of the chairs. Four in all. They eyed Max with steel criticism. He knew them instantly. *The talent. The skill players.*

"Warriors, I'd like you to meet your new coach, Maxwell Benson. He came all the way from Tennessee to help us out this year." Chevy started the applause as he backed away, making room for Max to face the team.

His heartbeat robbed his breath and his voice. It would not be cool to appear nervous. But he felt like a man condemned under the coaches' and the boys' somber, sharp scrutiny. Max counted twenty players in all. He stood before them like he stood before a jury. *Make your case.* For all practical purposes, weren't they his jury? The ones who would judge his coaching and his program?

"Good morning," Max began, steady, calm, his gaze scanning the faces in the room. "I just want you all to know I don't need any of you to uphold Warrior football tradition." The boys glared at him. The coaches shifted their stance, shoulders against the wall, arms folded over their chests. "I don't. Because I can go out on the field every Friday night all by myself. Well, shoot, for fun, let's let my wife and two-year-old son play too. My wife's a pretty solid athlete—I think we could complete a few passes, make a few tackles." Max paced the length of the room, passing in front of the chairs. "Yeah, I don't need any of you to carry on Warrior tradition."

The boys fidgeted in their seats, their jaws set, their eyes tracing Max as he walked. Over on the wall, the assistants shuffled their stances.

"Because Warrior tradition is losing. In your last five seasons, the best the Warriors have done is one and eleven. One year, the Warriors lost every game. I can lose on Friday nights with the best of them. Why do we need to put the school and the boosters to all the expense and heartache of paying for this lovely football facility if all we're going to do is lose from week to week? Y'all can stay home. My wife and I will play. Save the school a whole bunch of money."

The coaches stood away from the wall. The boys sat back, squaring their shoulders.

"Hold up, hold up." The big kid on the third row, right side, shifted forward, a haughty blaze in his eyes. He looked like a skill player—quarterback or running back. "Is it true you ain't never coached football? And you lecturing us?"

Max stretched across the rows to shake his hand. "And you are?"

"Carter Davis."

"Carter, good to meet you. Running back?"

"Ain't it obvious?" He snorted back at his friends, his grin revealing thick white teeth. "I told you he ain't no real coach. Can't even tell a good running back when he's standing in front of him."

"You run the forty in, what, four-six, maybe four-five, but you want to get to four-four?" Max slapped his hands together and raised one eyebrow.

"You think you smart? My granny can read a stat sheet. Mr. Buchholz, you said we was getting a real coach." Carter started up the aisle with a large attitude and grand gestures to his teammates. "This is bull and y'all know it." He kicked the chairs in the back by the door. "How are we going to win with a coach who don't know what he's doing?"

"Carter, sit down." Chevy stepped in front of Max. "Listen to the man."

"Listen to what? He's mocking us, Mr. Buchholz. Saying how he's going to lose football while playing with his wife and kid. That he don't need us." Carter stepped toward Max. "He don't need us 'cause he don't know what he's doing." Carter cocked his body with attitude, ready to fire off at any moment. "Why we keep hiring coaches who can't coach, got one foot out the door, or get us in trouble with the rules? First Mr. Molnar, now you, Mr. Buchholz. Listen, my Aunt Tee lives down in Canyon territory. I'm going to transfer there. Now *they* have a coach who's taking them places."

"It ain't all about you, Carter." A wiry, skinny boy rose to his feet. "The rest of us want to play too."

"Go ahead an' play, Gellar. I ain't stopping you. But I want to play college ball." Carter gave Max a visual once over, a snide curl on his lip. "*He* sure as heck ain't getting me there. He don't even have connections."

"Mr. Buchholz has contacts." The Gellar kid braved an argument.

"Then why don't he use them to get us a coach?"

The boys started to argue, their voices growing louder, their chests swelling. "Sit down," Max said, low, strong, in command. "Face forward." He moved up the center aisle. "I'd like you to stay, Carter, but I understand if you can't. My point is I don't want to keep up current Warrior tradition, but get back to the *winning* Warrior tradition. That"—Max looked hard at every man in the room—"I can't do by myself. You're right, Carter, I'm new. I don't know what I'm doing." Max grinned. "Well, I know a little bit of what I'm doing. But I need all of you. The first step to getting back to winning seasons and championships is . . . you. We work as a team and take it one day, one game at a time."

Carter dropped to the end seat in the last row.

"Why am I the head coach when I've never done this before? Because Principal Buchholz thought I was the best man for the job. I love football."

93

Max gestured toward Bobby and Rick, leaning against the wall. "We have two former state champs right over there. Football is the greatest game in the world. It requires skill and talent. Football can make ordinary men great. Or it can make great men ordinary. But football is about being a team. There are no wins, no victories for anyone without eleven men on the field. There's no glory without heart. All the talent in the world is wasted on a player who is self-focused. I can see why some of your coaches might have left if this is the way y'all greeted him."

The boys shifted in their seats. The coaches in the front remained stalwart but had let go of their crossed arms and reclined in the chairs.

"Heart trumps talent. A winning attitude earns my respect before speed or power. If you want to play on the Colby Warriors football team, all you need to do is show up tomorrow—"

"Tomorrow? Coach, we don't start camp until next month." Kevin stood, glancing at Bobby Molnar.

"Show up tomorrow. Together we'll start planning how to make a winning Warrior football team. You're right to be nervous about me. I am."

"Coach, you know we can't start practice until August. Regulations." Bobby raised up next to Kevin, sounding like the athletic director he was.

"This isn't practice. It's a team meeting. If you want to be on this team, show up, seven a.m. Help me figure out how to make this a winning program. If you can't get yourselves out of bed, then stay home. Sleep in." Max glared at each boy. "But don't bother showing up for practice next month. Do any of you boys know Calvin Blue and Tucker Walberg? Get them in here. Any student who can run and qualifies to enter the boys' locker room is welcome on the team. I'll see you tomorrow."

"Coach." Bobby's expression darkened. "You're going to cut players before the practice even starts?"

"Like I said, heart trumps talent." Max started out of the room. He had to act like he was in command even though he felt like a wet rag floating down the river. They'd run roughshod all over him this season if he didn't come in hard. Even ridiculously hard.

In his office, Max stood before the window wall and gazed out over the field. This was what he came to do. Where the rubber met the road. No room for doubt—even if the job would be hard or uncomfortable. *Lord, you brought me here. Now what?*

At the light knock on his door, Max turned around. Chevy smiled, nodding. "Good job, Max. Good job."

Twelve

Bobby Molnar paced his office, crossing back and forth across the Warrior flaming spear cut into the carpet pile. Rick Lundy leaned against the wall, arms folded.

"He seems all right, Bob. Give him a chance."

"When Chevy picked that yahoo from Tennessee," Bobby said, feeling the storm gathering in his chest, "I said, 'Merry Christmas to me,' this guy will either quit or get fired before the end of the year. I'll finally be able to end-run that dang Chevy and get in as head coach."

"So what's changed?"

"He didn't seem like a yahoo when he left the meeting. But now I know I need a new game plan."

Bobby had let Chevy cut him out of the head coach chase so he would look like a hero when the needle-nosed principal's choice failed. When he brought Max Benson, a former addict lawyer to the table, Bobby knew, *he knew*, his day had finally arrived.

"What's the plan, Bob?" Rick said.

"I don't know . . . I don't know. Find out what you can on him. See if we can maybe push his buttons harder and faster. Maybe get him out by homecoming."

Rick's chuckle fanned Bobby's flame. "You really do want that coaching job."

Bobby paused his pacing to gape at his friend. "What do you think I've been doing? I've tried to cut the budget so the A.D. and head football coach are the same job. I've tried to hire bad coaches. I've tried to—"

"Frame them?"

"No, now. Bobby pointed at Rick, shaking his finger. "Kirk did all that on his own. Messing with a high school girl? Even at twenty-four, he should've known better. I just let that one play out. But Benson, he's got something different going on. This is going to be tough."

"His zip experience ought to help."

"Yeah, yeah, that'll bring some media pressure. I can work that angle. Bump up the news stories. Send a press release about how excited we are for our new, never-ran-a-program-before coach. If we're not the joke of the night on Channel 13, I owe you a beer."

"I'd rather not enjoy that beer."

Bobby paced. This head coaching job belonged to him. To his family's legacy. Rick was being too cavalier.

"Benson was at the Outpost," Rick offered, still leaning against the wall. "That's where Chevy met him. Maybe there's something there."

Finally, the man contributes. "Find it. See what you can dig up." Bobby toed open his minifridge and took out a water. He offered one to Rick who waved him off.

He reached for the door. "This is the last time, Bobby. You want the coaching job, you get it fair and square. No more manipulation. You're starting to hurt the program permanently."

"Then let this be the last coach before me." Bobby twisted the top off his water. "You worry about keeping the boosters on my side. Find out about Benson. I'll do the rest."

"You pull another Plano stunt, you can forget about booster support and filling your daddy's big shoes. Really, Bob, you should see someone about that."

Bob laughed. "About my tough old man? Just do your job. I'll take care of me." Bobby swigged his water. "Davy Crockett from eastern Tennessee will fail. And I'll be there to pick up the pieces."

"As athletic director, I'd think you'd be a bit more concerned about the boys and their football future instead of your football past. This is their time, Bob. Let them have it."

"It's also *my* time." He'd lost Texas as a player. Plano as a coach. He wasn't going to lose his alma mater.

As Rick exited, Chevy bumbled in. An intellectual who couldn't tell the difference between the spread and the option.

"Well, Bob, what do you think? I know, I know, our new guy's a tenderfoot, but I thought he handled himself well in the meeting. Considering all that attitude from the crowd. I'm going to count on you to help him fold in with the coaches and players, with the boosters. Starting over with a new basketball coach worked well. I think it will for football."

Except no one cares about basketball. Football is Warrior tradition.

"He's great, Chevy." Bobby smoothed on his frosted smile. "I think we've finally hired the right man. But we've been disappointed before. Does he have all of his certifications?"

"Working on them. I bet my Phi Beta Kappa pin he'll pass the exams."

"All righty." Bobby chuckled, then took a hit of water to keep cool. "Rick and I were talking. What conditions did you put on his contract? I want to see some real improvement, if not a win by homecoming."

"Oh, I don't know." Chevy rocked back on his heels, hands dug deep into his pockets. "I reckon we can give him the whole season. If he's pulled the boys together and played as a team, I'll consider the venture a success. Give him another shot if he's willing to stay."

"Hold on, Chevy. I'll have to see some real football coaching out of him. No need to talk of second seasons when season one isn't even out of the box."

"All right." Chevy backed toward the door. "I'll trust you to give him all the support he needs. Your buddy Rick too. Let's make him feel welcomed." He patted Bobby on the shoulder. "Tell that wife of yours hello."

"I will."

The door closed behind Chevy and Bobby reached for his phone, dialing Lars, Kevin, and the other coaches. Time to get a feel for where they were and lay markers to keep them on his side.

⁓

Connected to Colby Grounds Wi-Fi and sharing a toasted bagel with Asa, Jade e-mailed her brother and sister, ending with a line directed at her big brother.

Aiden, call me. I need to talk to you about something.

"Drink." Asa wiggled his messy fingers at his cup. Jade handed it to him, helping with the straw. When he took control of the cup, she let go. If he spilled his milk, oh well.

Colby Grounds must have been an old '30s diner. Long and narrow with high-back wooden booths along a brick wall, it had the feel of old time cattlemen. At least that's what Jade saw in her mind. Not that she knew much about old time cattlemen.

Opposite the booths was the mirrored coffee bar that probably once served liquor. Patrons sat on bar stools with their laptops and iPads.

Jade had chosen a high top table in the front by the window, with Asa in a booster seat beside her. She wanted to gaze out at her new town.

First day here she expected to feel alone, homesick, maybe wrestling with pangs of regret. But excitement waved over her. Chin propped in her hand, she glanced at Asa.

She wondered if Max's first day was going well. He said he'd slept last night, but it couldn't have been well. Jade knew because his tossing and turning kept her awake.

"Jade, shug, hey there." Brenda Karlin's strong voice came through the glass as she stood outside the coffee shop, knocking on the window. "Asa, hey there." She scooted toward the door, along with another woman beside her. They wore matching dark suits and orange blouses.

"Morning, Brenda." Jade closed her laptop and rose to greet her.

"I see you're up and at 'em early. Good for you, good for you." She exhaled, tugging her jacket into place. "Get the lay of the land and all. Look at this one, Bit. Ain't he as cute as Christmas? Jade, this is my associate, Bit Wiley."

"Nice to meet you." Bit's shy smile tried to cover her teeth, and strands of her dark hair kept springing up and flying away. Brenda was lean and effervescent. Bit was round and reserved. A blond Lucy and demure Ethel. "Welcome to Colby."

"Back in the day, *waaay* back"—Brenda bent backward—"our boys played ball for the Warriors. Both were on championship teams, weren't they, Bit?"

"Sure enough."

"So, we're so excited to have your Max as coach. Axel Crowder spoke so highly of him." Jade sat back on her stool and listened. It was nice to have company and not be required to talk. *So, what do you do? How do you like it here? How long have you been married? Are your folks alive?* "We need to get this program going again. Get our boys playing football."

"Max will certainly give it everything he's got," Jade said. "Brenda, thank you for all your help on the house hunt. We love the bungalow."

"I've been trying to rent or sell that place for a year but I've just not found the right people. When Max called, I said to Bit, 'I think they are the ones. I got the feeling.' Didn't I, Bit?"

"Yes, you did, Brenda." Bit winked at Jade. Ah, so she was a *clever* Ethel. Not prone to being swept along with Lucy's shenanigans.

"Bit, we got to get going. Jade, you got my number? Here's my card anyway. Call me if you need anything, shug. And I do mean it." She jutted her finger in Jade's direction. "Don't be shy."

Brenda hugged Jade, then Bit leaned close. "She'll reroute the Pecos for you if you need it. She's a little much at first, but you'll get used to her. Do call if you need something."

"Bit, come on—hay to cut, dough to make."

Brenda stuck her head back in the door after Bit exited. "Go Warriors. Chop, chop." She motioned a chop in the air beside her head. In a Pavlovian response, the coffee house patrons all whooped and chopped right along with Brenda. Some of them didn't even look up from their Nooks and phones.

Jade grinned, scrunching her shoulders together, tucking her hands between her knees. Lots to learn, but Colby certainly was warm. Could be fun to be the coach's wife.

"Don't mind them. They're harmless." A woman with crystal blue eyes and an angular face walked toward Jade from the far side of the shop. Slender and poised, she wore blue slacks and a cream button-down blouse. "I'm Dr. Gelman." She offered her hand. "Julie."

"Jade Benson, coach's wife. Please sit down." Jade motioned to the chair next to her.

"Those two." Dr. Gelman waved toward the window. "They're Colby's answer to Lucy and Ethel."

Jade laughed. "I wasn't going to say it out loud, but wow, it's what I thought immediately."

"My mom went to school with Brenda and Bit. And I went to school with their sons. They've been best friends since probably fifth grade. Brenda got married and became a career woman who practically took over Colby real estate. Bit got married, had four kids, and after twenty years of marriage her husband decided he'd done his time and retired. From marriage. After their divorce, Brenda took Bit under her wing, hired her at her office, and between the two of them, I think they own half of Colby. And I'm sure they know everyone." Julie motioned to Asa. "He's a beautiful boy."

"We think so. Asa, can you say hi to Dr. Gelman?"

"How do you do, young man?" Julie tucked her finger under Asa's hand and gave it little shake. Asa stared at her, then suddenly pointed. "Pretty."

"Why, thank you very much." She pressed her hands to her cheeks. "I declare, he made a grown woman blush."

"It's a new thing with him. If he sees something he likes, he points and shouts, 'Pretty.'"

"How old is he?"

"Twenty-three months. He'll be two August twenty-fourth. If you tell me you're a pediatrician I'll hug you."

"Ob-gyn, actually. I love babies and want them to get into the world safe and healthy. Is he your only child?"

"Yes." Jade hesitated. "Actually, Doctor, he's my husband's son." Jade picked up a napkin and wiped cream cheese from Asa's hands. "His mom was killed in March. Small aircraft crash. Max and I were married before he was born. Long story. But he's mine now."

"I can tell—I noticed you with him. You're quite devoted."

"A miracle." If the doctor knew the whole story, she'd agree.

"I used to see your husband in here on Saturdays. Axel brings the residents in to e-mail and call home. He always looked so happy when he was talking to you."

"How do you know he was talking to me?"

"I heard him say your name once. Then if I saw him after that and he had the same expression, I knew he was talking to you."

"Are you always so kind to strangers?"

"Just the ones I like." She grinned.

"What about you? Do you have children?"

"I'm divorced. No children." Julie shifted forward in her seat, propping her elbow on the table and her chin in her hand. "He couldn't take the other lover in my life, medicine, so he left. I'm a fourth generation physician but the first woman. My dad and grandfather gave their lives to medicine but somehow tended to their families." Julie shook her head. "I thought I could too, but it's different for women. At least for me. I couldn't leave work at work. I'm envious of the way men can compartmentalize." Julie peeked at Jade with a rueful smile. "Look at me, dumping all my sorrows on the stranger in town."

"Sometimes it's easier to talk to a stranger."

"I know. Why is that?" Dr. Gelman made a face, then motioned to her left. "My office is right around the corner. Gelman Medical. If you need an OB while you're here."

"I'll call you." But Jade doubted she'd need an ob-gyn. Three miscarriages, the last one a year ago. Jade had not been pregnant since.

Dr. Gelman leaned close. "Pardon me, but I see a lot of women who want nothing more in life than to be pregnant. I can always tell when I meet one. Even if she's sitting in a coffee shop."

Jade busied herself gathering wadded-up, cream-cheesy napkins. "I'm content."

"Sure you are, but doesn't mean a baby wouldn't light up your life."

"Are you always so bold?"

"Yes." She touched Jade's hand. "But your secret is safe with me." Dr. Gelman sat back. "I'll tell you who to watch out for, Jade. Brenda. She can spot a pregnant woman a mile away. Practically the moment the sperm hits the egg. And she doesn't keep it quiet."

"That's some talent." Jade tipped her head with skepticism.

"Tell me. She's blurted out a few surprises." Dr. Gelman wiggled her eyebrows. "If you know what I mean."

"Really?"

"I'm just saying. By the way, I love your top. Vintage?"

"Yes, from the '70s. Good eye."

They chatted about vintage, the '80s, Cindy Lauper's "Girls Just Wanna Have Fun," and Warrior football until Asa announced with a rather loud, incomprehensible statement that he was tired of being strapped to a booster seat.

Gathering Asa and her bag, Jade walked with Dr. Gelman out of the shop and into the west Texas day.

A car horn blasted as a woman dashed across the road, barely missing the bumper of a turning car. The driver powered down his window. "Watch where you're going!"

The woman ran toward the coffee shop, looking weary and strung out, as if she'd gone too long without food or sleep. She stopped in front of Dr. Gelman.

"Mariah, what's going on?" Dr. Gelman's tone was kind. "Why aren't you at work?" The doctor gently ran her hand over the woman's shoulder.

"Oh, they don't know their butts from—"

"Have you met our new coach's wife?" Dr. Gelman cradled Mariah to her, one arm around her, almost holding her up. "This is Jade Benson."

"Another coach's wife?" Mariah twisted her lips, slurring her words. "That dang school is about as crazy as my bosses. Don't know nothing. Nothing."

"Mariah, you're not using, are you?"

She shook her head like a scolded girl, trying to hold her bloodshot eyes wide. But her thin, flyaway hair and colorless skin told another story. "But I do need some money. The kid ain't got no groceries."

"Come to my office. I'm going to check you out, then we can go to United for groceries. Is Tucker at home? Does he need food? You know with a new coach, maybe Tucker can finally play football."

"Oh, I hope not, the kid can't walk down the road without tripping. It's embarrassing to watch him try to play."

Dr. Gelman glanced back at Jade. "United Supermarkets is just a mile or so south on 23rd. A great place to grocery shop. See you around?"

"See you around." Jade watched the doctor walk Mariah down the sidewalk, under the waving flags and banners left over from a Fourth of July celebration. Asa stood at her feet, tugging on her hand.

"Mama, go."

"Yeah, okay, son." Jade opened the truck door and slipped Asa into his car seat, her thoughts on the morning. As she climbed in behind the wheel, her phone rang.

She hoped it was Max, but when Jade read the screen her heart filled with dread. Gus McClure.

"Hello?" She winced, listening.

"Jade, this is Gus McClure. We got back into town from our vacation to find Max had whisked you and our grandson to Texas. What's going on?" His mountain voice planed away Jade's patience with its sharp edge.

"Yes, we're in Texas. Max took a new job—he's coaching football." Jade fired up the truck. The rattling engine shimmied the old chassis.

Gus grumbled. How ridiculous. What did Max think he was doing? What about their grandson? Jade responded low and kind, explaining, but Gus would have none of it. He huffed and said something about "this won't do," then hung up.

Jade exhaled relief. Maybe it wouldn't do, but from what she could tell, he didn't know about Rice and Landon, or Taylor's burdensome secret.

Thirteen

When he got home, Max intended to persuade Jade to switch vehicles with him. The new football coach couldn't go cruising around Colby in a late-model Mercedes. Didn't seem right.

Besides, with the truck he could haul boys around in the bed if he needed. Was that allowed? Kids in the back? He had a book of regulations to study and memorize.

The list of things to do mounted and for an intense moment, he was entirely overwhelmed. He whispered prayers, grateful God had delivered him from his back spasms and phantom pains.

Cruising east on Route 60, Max scanned the endless fields off to his right until he spotted a flatbed truck loaded with hay bales not too far from the highway. Slowing his car, he pulled off the road. Hopefully, on the other side of the truck he'd find Calvin Blue. Max had called the rec center to see if Calvin was around there today. He wasn't, but one call led to another until Max found himself chasing down a hay-laden truck to recruit what he hoped would be his star tailback.

Max's car skidded along the gravel berm and he gazed out toward the flatbed, which followed behind a hay baler. Sure enough, Calvin walked alongside the truck, tossing a fresh bale up onto the flatbed.

Max powered down the passenger window. "Calvin." He honked the horn. "Calvin Blue."

The boy looked up, squinting, then staring, then popping wide his white grin. Sweat glistened on his dark skin.

"Coach! What you doing here? Didn't you go home?" Calvin jogged over to the edge of the field. He was fit, Max thought, ready to play. "Nice ride, Coach. Did you fall off the wagon already? Come back to the ranch?"

"I'm the new head coach at Colby High." Max stepped out and came around the car.

Calvin stared. Then laughed. "You kidding me. Man oh man, I took you for smarter than that, Coach."

"I thought you wanted a football program." Calvin shrugged. Max jumped the small ditch and stood in front of the boy. "Come play for me."

"Why? So you can set us up, make us think we might be going somewhere, only to quit or get fired? Naw, naw, Coach. I'm trying to get over to Canyon High. Carter Davis has an Aunt Tee." Calvin headed back toward the trucks and Max followed.

"I heard all about Aunt Tee. So you go over there. You want to play behind Carter all season? Maybe your high school career?"

Calvin frowned. "What do you know about it?"

"It's my job to know." He'd spent most of the afternoon reviewing files and stats. The sheer amount was daunting. First semester of law school all over again. Only worse because he wasn't cocky and invincible.

"Carter ain't as fast as me. Come on, Coach."

"Then come out and prove it. Win a starting position. We have a meeting in the morning, seven o'clock." The sun blazed and perspiration popped along Max's forehead.

"Is he playing for the Warriors?" Calvin paced alongside the slow-moving truck, reaching for another hay bale as it popped from the baler and tossing it into the flatbed.

"We'll see." Max kept stride with Calvin. "What I need is for you to make up your own mind."

Calvin laughed. "Carter and I said we'd play together, Coach. Go to Texas or A&M together."

"Okay, fine. Canyon's got a great tailback already. You go over there with Carter, I think you'd best plan on an academic scholarship for college, Calvin."

He laughed. "Don't use your lawyer talk on me, Coach. I see what you doing. I can beat out Carter. Don't tell him, but I ain't worried."

"So you beat out Carter. What about the other backs at Canyon? You going to beat them all?"

"Yeah, yeah, I am."

"You have to start to be seen by scouts."

"Don't worry, I'll start." Calvin hoisted the next bale with attitude.

Max nodded, jutting his chin. "All right. But if you change your mind, I could really use you."

"This is Texas high school football, Coach. Not a summer program you throwed together out on the ranch. This is serious."

Max squinted in the sun. "Do I look like I'm laughing?"

"Coach, I wish you all the best. But I got to consider my future and signing up for a losing football program ain't it." Calvin tossed another bale. "No offense."

"None taken." Max watched Calvin inch down the field for a minute. So this mission failed. *Don't let it get you down.* But he thought recruiting players was the one thing he *could* do as a coach. "Calvin, seven a.m. meeting tomorrow on the field. See you there."

Calvin waved and tossed the next bale.

~

By the time Max turned into his new, winding driveway, twilight was settling over the plains. He parked in the detached carport and stepped out of the car, hot and thirsty. His car, his clothes, and his heart were covered with Randall County dust.

Warrior football was a mess. And after a day of trying to find his potential players, he felt quite sure Chevy had hired the wrong man. He wanted to talk to Jade. But how could he confess he'd failed her on his first day? He'd moved her away from her home, her business, her friends—for this?

Worse, he had no idea where to begin to straighten it out. If he found a thread to pull, would it unravel the whole darn thing? Did he have the skills? The right tools? The right coaches?

The screen door eased open as he made his way across the yard of waving prairie grass. Another to-do popped into his head. Hire a lawn crew. Jade stepped off the porch, swinging Asa down the steps by his hands. "Hey, where have you been?"

"Working." Max bent down as Asa ran to him, his little legs trying to keep up with the churn of his elbows. Max scooped him up and tossed him over his shoulder. "How's my little man? You want to play football for me? Maybe inside linebacker." Max pinched Asa's baby bicep. "Looks to me like you've got a good pump going, buddy."

Asa tried to pop his muscle, a new trick he'd been learning, squeezing his fist, scrunching up his face with a growl. "I strong."

"Then I'm signing you up for my team." Jade met Max halfway. She was warm, soft, and kissable. He sighed. "And the evening and the morning were the first day."

"What's wrong? How bad is it?"

"Pretty bad." Max lowered himself to the grass and closed his eyes. He'd intended to enjoy his pretty bungalow and pretty wife this evening instead of talking about the rich school with a poor program. "If you don't mind, Jade, I'd like to swap vehicles with you. I can't drive the Mercedes around town. I need the truck for the back roads, hauling equipment, maybe even some of the team."

"S-sure." Jade sat next to him. "I drove by the school today. It looks amazing. The field house was incredible. I thought this program was on its last leg. I expected rusty equipment scattered on a bare field with lopsided goalposts."

"Yeah, you and me both." Max sat up, drawing in his knees, propping his arms on top. "The program is not broke. In fact, the facility is nicer than some colleges'. Apparently some deep-pocketed boosters have really deep Warrior loyalties."

"You really didn't know the program had money?"

"You think I'd have signed up to coach if I thought they could afford a real one?" Max brushed his hand over Asa's soft hair. Jade's inquiry simmered in his doubt. "I feel like a chump."

"You didn't vet the program? Ask around? Google? You have an entire law firm at your fingertips. Two weeks before our wedding you discovered I was still married to Dustin Colter when I didn't even know it myself."

"Sure, sort of. I didn't do a big in-depth because . . . look who Chevy was talking to! Me. Axel recommended him and the program. That was good enough for me."

"Did you call Axel?"

"He's on vacation." He peered at Jade. "I'm sorry. I really thought I was all they could get."

"I think you were all they wanted, Max."

He stared toward the fiery curve of the horizon where nothing blocked his view but a low-flying bird formation. He recounted his morning at the field house and his afternoon of searching out players. "So, we'll see who shows up in the morning. See if I have some interest. The beginnings of a team."

"Max, did we do this or did God?"

When their eyes met, a sick swirl soured Max's stomach. "Are you having second thoughts?"

"It's only been a day, Max. Are you?"

"It *has* only been a day, Jade. Let's give it two." Max pressed a smiling kiss to her temple and fell back in the grass, pulling her with him. "Did the furniture arrive?"

Jade pillowed her head on his shoulder. "The shipment got delayed. But I did go shopping. We have food. And I unpacked the stuff we shipped from home. Towels, sheets, plates, and kitchenware. Are you hungry?"

"A little." The heat and pressure from the day blocked his appetite. He needed a minute to cool down, relax, and think. Close his eyes, let go . . .

Asa dove on top of him. Max *oomph*ed and snatched up his son, lifting him over his head. "What are you doing? Arms out, Asa. Fly. You're Superman."

Asa elevated his arms and legs. Then Max flipped him over, landing him on the ground. "So what else did you do today?" he asked Jade as a laughing Asa ran around for another turn.

Jade moved to lay on the grass next to him. "Went to Colby Grounds." She told him about Brenda, Bit, Dr. Gelman, and Mariah. "And when I was leaving to go shopping, Gus McClure called. They were pretty upset to come home from vacation to find we'd moved with Asa."

Max turned to her. "I forgot all about them in the craziness." He sat up. "We should've left them a message."

"I tried to smooth it over, but Gus hung up on me."

"I'll call him later." Max exhaled, closing his eyes, listening to the wind fluttering the leaves. The burdens seemed to fall on him in layers. Layers and layers . . .

Just as a bit of peace started rising in his spirit, a horn blasted over the house from the driveway. Max bolted up. Jade jumped to her feet, swinging Asa up in her arms.

Around the side of the house, Max spotted the trail of cars coming down the road and turning into his driveway. Horns blasted intermittently. Cars, trucks, a few horses gathered and surrounded the house. Warrior fans and boosters swarmed the side yard.

"Here we are, y'all." Brenda quickstepped toward Max and Jade, large duffel bags in each hand. "Welcome to Warrior Country. Here's your Warrior gear. Hats, shirts, shorts, socks, flags, pennants, you name it. Max, here you go." Brenda dropped the bags at their feet, pulled out a cap, and pressed it on Max's head. It was stitched with *Coach*. Then she pulled one out for Jade. It was stitched with *Mrs. Coach*—and in smaller letters, *Don't Mess With My Man*.

Jade laughed. How Max loved that sound. "Oh, Brenda, that's awesome."

"And one for our little guy. His first Baby Warrior item." That's what Asa's hat said. Baby Warrior.

"Now, these bags are yours. If you think of some other fun Warrior item you want, let me know and I'll get it. Like maternity things, Jade."

Max snapped his gaze to her.

"Thanks, Brenda, but we don't need any maternity items." She whispered to Max as Brenda headed off to direct the party, "No, I'm not pregnant."

"Y'all, set up the band over there." Brenda made her way through the crowds still spilling from cars and trucks. Tables popped up on the side yard. Tablecloths cracked the air and floated down. The fragrance of barbecue scented the air.

"I could get used to this," Max said in Jade's ear.

"Makes me think of Mama and all the parties she had when I was young."

Folks filed by, introducing themselves, welcoming the new coach and his family to town.

A smiling Chevy made his way toward Max along with Bobby and the coaches.

"Jade." Brenda waved her over. "Come meet the other coaches' wives. Bit, darling, put the desserts on one table. That-a-girl."

The Warrior drum line started a rhythm. Bass drums chasing the rapid beat of the snares and tenors. The dust on Max's heart vibrated away. Yeah, he could really get used to this. Suddenly, he felt like a football coach. The bubble of doubt in his heart ceased to simmer.

Just when he was starting to wonder . . . God sent a booster party and a rocking band.

Fourteen

Jade jolted awake when her phone rang. She snatched it from the floor and rolled off the air mattress. Her brother. She pressed the phone to her chest and sneaked out of the bedroom.

Through the thin moonlight she could see Max asleep on his back, cradling a playbook to his chest. All the football talk tonight with the coaches and boosters fired him up.

"Aiden, hey." Jade opened the front door and slipped outside. The scent of barbecue lingered.

After the barbecue, potato salad, chips, pies, cookies, and cakes had been eaten, and the soda coolers had been emptied, and the pep band had played their final song as the cars exited the same way they came in—a caravan down the driveway, their taillights creating a red river toward Colby—Max had talked football.

While Jade bathed Asa. While she diapered him and tugged on his pajamas. While Asa brushed his teeth. While Jade kissed him good night and turned out the light.

"Ah, it's after midnight there, isn't it. Sorry, Jade-o."

"It's okay. I'm glad you called. Where are you, by the way?" Jade cut through the warm porch shadows and sat on the porch steps. It felt good to have alone time with her brother.

"Australia."

"Australia? Really! Since when?"

"Two days ago. Just like your mad decision to move to Texas, I made a mad decision to take a job in Australia. A photographer friend of mine needed some help. I'll be down here for a few weeks, maybe a month."

"Texas, Australia, Guatemala." Jade eased down onto the porch steps. The breeze rode low and strong over the prairie tonight. "The Beryl Hill children are all over the place."

"Mama would be proud of her adventurous offspring."

"Have you heard from Willow? She's not responding to my e-mails."

"She went on a medical trip to Cuba. As far as I know, she was fine as of two weeks ago. Still loving on Guatemalan orphans."

"Maybe she'll be the next Mother Teresa."

Aiden laughed. "Only less virginal. Hey, remember the time she wanted to live like Laura Ingalls Wilder? No electric, no running water?"

"Yeah, she was five and the little smarty was already reading the Little House books. She drove Mama and Granny crazy begging them to play *Little House on the Prairie*." Jade closed her eyes to see the images of the past clearer.

"Mama said, 'Willow, look around at this place, girl, we *are* a little house on the prairie.'" Aiden did a good Mama impression.

"Granny couldn't take it any longer so she agreed to a trial Little House week."

SARA EVANS *with* RACHEL HAUCK

"First day, Willow came downstairs in that bonnet." Aiden's laugh reminded Jade of their Paps, a good man, a Christian man. "She was all into the game until five thirty when she wanted to watch her *Full House* rerun."

"But Granny outsmarted her and hid the TV in the closet." Jade laughed, remembering. "Willow was so mad."

"And . . . the experiment was o-ver," Aiden said, his voice low, resolved, a bit sarcastic.

"We have to be together this Christmas. Please. Don't book a job over the holidays. I'll get Willow home."

"You may be onto something, Jade. Granny wouldn't want us to drift apart."

"Neither would Mama. For all her craziness, she loved for us to love each other."

"And if she didn't, we'll love each other to spite her. So, you said you needed to talk? What's going on? How's Max?"

"He's doing really well considering the past four months. The football job is not all he thought it would be. It's more." Jade explained the surprises of the Warrior football field house and lavish set up. "But he's really excited about this. After all we've both been through, it feels good to start something fresh, in a new place."

"What about you? Any more depersonalizing moments?"

"No, Aiden. God has . . ." Did she dare believe? "Done a good thing."

"I can hear it in your voice. You and Max are—"

"Putting the past behind us. Forgiving. Moving on. Starting over in a new place with a new commitment to *us*."

"If anyone deserves it, you do, Jade. You like being a mom?"

"Love it. Sometimes I lie in bed at night and think about the day with him, or what we're doing the next day, and my heart is so full I can barely breathe. I can't believe he's mine. Well, almost mine." Jade blew out a long breath. "Speaking of Asa, I need some big brother advice."

"You've come to the right place. I'm full of it."

Jade smiled. "Don't I know it. Anyway, about three weeks ago . . ." Jade spoke of her encounter with Taylor, the request for proof, and the lurking image of Landon in the Hollow the day before she left.

When Jade finished, Aiden said nothing but whistled low. "So what's your question to me?"

"Do I tell Max?"

"You still only have this Taylor chick's word?"

"Right."

"Jade-o, I don't know. Look, it's up to you, but if I were Max, I'd want to know. What happened to the new commitment to the relationship? Keeping secrets got you guys in trouble before."

"True, but I would tell him if I knew for sure, Aiden."

"Why does it have to be proved? He should know what you know, Jade."

"To what end? So I tell him. Then what?"

"Why does there have to be an end? You tell him because it's the right thing to do. Secrets like this have a way of coming out. It may hurt him now, but it'll hurt worse if it comes out next year, or in ten years. He'll wonder why you kept the secret. What about Asa? You and Max need to figure out together how to tell Asa he's adopted. Don't risk him finding out as an adult and make him second-guess his whole childhood."

Jade sighed, combing her fingers through her hair. "I knew you'd say that."

"Because you know I'm right. What if the birth father gets all sentimental and starts looking back at his life deciding he needs to make amends? Happened to a friend of mine. Thought he was Joe and Sue Donaldson's kid. Turns out his father had an affair and his mom is not his mom. She took him in and raised him as her own when the mistress bolted. He was pretty upset. Felt like his life was all a big lie. Tell Max. Do not shoulder this alone. He has a right to know."

"You make it sound so easy."

"It is. Do it. What's holding you back?"

"I don't know if I believe it. Who knows why Taylor told me that wild story? It may not be true. Asa turns two in a month. After that, the bio dad can't challenge the birth certificate—if there even *is* a different bio dad. Max will legally be Asa's father."

"Don't drag this out. *Tell* him. What is it with you? Where did you get this philosophy that keeping secrets from the man you love is the best way to have a relationship?" Aiden's words cut hard. "Think how hurt you were that Max didn't trust you enough to believe you'd love him through his big mess."

"This isn't my mess, Aiden. It's the continuing saga of his. Even though Rice did him wrong on this one. And I learned the keeping-secrets thing from growing up with our mother."

"Mama? You're crazy. She was the bare-it-all kind."

"Then this is my reaction to her. She told it all. I hide it." Aiden made a good point. Mama's baring it all—whether it was secrets or skin—embarrassed Jade on more than one occasion.

"You called for my advice and despite your stellar rebuttals, I remain standing on my 'tell him' soapbox. Tell him, tell him, *tell him.*"

Jade shoved the heel of her hand against her forehead. "I will—if and when I get the paternity from Taylor."

"Or, here's an idea, *tell him.*"

Jade held the phone from her ear. "You don't have to yell."

"I do if you're not listening."

A low breeze cooled the hot tears in Jade's eyes. "Every time I picture myself telling him, I see his face and it breaks my heart. Rice was one of his best friends growing up. They were engaged. He really cared for her and she paid back his kindness with deception. For her own gain. She didn't care if she hurt me or our marriage. Why should I allow her the last hurrah? Huh? Why let her charade continue? Let it end with me."

"It doesn't end with you and you know it." Underscoring Aiden's words was the power of truth. "Jade, got to run. It's teatime. Listen, let me tell you something about men. We're simple. Not complicated. Max is a big boy and he can handle the news. Don't assign him your fears."

"It just hurts." Jade smoothed the tears from her cheeks and lowered her forehead to her knees.

"I know, kid sister. But rip the Band-Aid off now. Quick jerk."

As she ended the call, the screen door groaned and Max stepped onto the porch. "Hey, what are you doing, babe?"

Had he heard? "Max, you're awake." She couldn't see his expression in the dark.

"Rolled over on my playbook." He sat on the step next to her, yawning, rubbing his eyes. "Are you okay? What are you doing out here?" He pressed his hand over the base of her neck and wove his fingers through her hair.

"Aiden called." She held up her phone. "He's in Australia."

"The man gets around." Max pointed toward the amber lights of Colby. "There's our new hometown. New opportunity. Fresh chances." He breathed in and glanced at her.

"Sounds like you're feeling better about things?"

"I am. We're where we're supposed to be. Did you have fun with the boosters?"

"The coaches' wives were fun. Sweet. Kathy Carroll invited me to a playdate next week. She said her nana's house is a vintage lover's candy store."

"See? Connections already."

"I hope so. I really liked her."

Max bumped her shoulder. "Did you see the redbirds tonight? In the trees."

"Perched on the limbs. Yeah, I saw them." She remembered seeing a redbird in the spring at Mama's last party. Mama had died a few hours later. But a little redbird flitted to the ground at Mama's feet and sang the sweetest song to her. Then chirped a message or warning or something to Jade.

"It's a good sign, those birds."

SARA EVANS *with* RACHEL HAUCK

"Max, all I ask is that if you start feeling the old stress—"

"I'm not going to feel the old stress."

She peered at him for a long second. The light from the single living room lamp stretched through the screen to halo his high smooth cheek. "How do you *know* you won't feel the old stress? What exactly happened when you were gone at that camp to make you so sure? And why haven't you ever talked to me about it?"

"I'd planned on telling you." Max drew his arm back and rested his elbows on his thighs. "I started to once, but I couldn't. It seemed private, between Jesus and me." When he peered at her she could see the glisten in his eyes. "You know how something cool happens and it feels so special you don't want to tell anyone in case they ruin it, or don't get it? Sort of like when a man falls in love with the right woman, he doesn't go into the locker room and talk about how many bases he covered."

"Did you think I'd make fun of you?"

"Not really, just maybe that I couldn't communicate what was so special to me." Emotion watered his voice. "I never knew God loved me so much."

"Remember when I finally told you about having an abortion? And how I finally confessed it to Jesus and He forgave me? I lay facedown in the backyard of Miss Linda's bed-and-breakfast while fireballs burned away every bit of shame."

"I remember."

"You responded with kindness and understanding. How would I not do the same for you?"

"Because since then you learned I was far from the stellar man I pretended to be." He smiled a slow smile.

"Tell me." Jade slipped her hand into his and rested her head on his shoulder.

Max said nothing for a long moment. Jade thought she could hear his whispered prayers. "I'd been at the Outpost for about a month. I was mad, cranky, giving Axel a hard time. His method of rehab was pointing ranch residents to Jesus and the cross. Every time we got offtrack, he'd turn us around to face the cross. 'All the help you need is right there.'

"My progress was slow. Then Axel called a fast. Three guys bolted that week and I almost went with them. But I thought of you and Asa, and I knew I was exactly where I was supposed to be. Axel had a crude cross on the property that I could see from my bunk. During the fast, I'd lie on my side and watch the moon pass over the cross. One night while my stomach was growling, I started praying, 'Lord, heal me. Fix me. I'm a wretch and a wreck.' I realized that was the point of the cross. To be free from myself. A man can't live free if he's in debt to sin, and I was up to my eyeballs in debt."

Jade listened, brushing away her tears.

"I started to cry. Just watery eyes at first, then sobs. I buried my face in the pillow to keep from waking the others. I wanted to slip out, but I couldn't move. I felt like I was lying in a bed of warm oil. The more I wept, the thicker and warmer it became. I swear I heard Jesus say to me, 'I have things for you to do. Come, follow me.' Then He poured more oil. I couldn't keep my eyes off the cross, weeping, soaking in that oily sensation. By morning, I thought it was all a dream. But over the weeks at the Outpost, I knew it was real. No more pains, real or phantom. No craving for meds. Love met me and lifted me out of my sin. I look back at the addicted Maxwell Benson and wonder, 'Who *was* that guy?'"

Jade lifted her chin to his shoulder and started to speak. To say she believed him, that she loved him, and that she had something to tell him.

But no . . . not tonight. Not while they had moonbeams in their hair and the hum of the stars in their hearts.

Fifteen

At five 'til seven Tuesday morning, Max left the field house for the field. Dawn had just broken with a clear blue sky and the promise of a warm day.

Max gripped the Warrior duffel bag in his right hand, ignoring the chilly wash of nervous tension in his veins. He resettled his Warrior cap. The confidence and excitement from last night's spontaneous booster party faded the closer he got to the field. Drifted away on the breeze with the last scent of spicy barbecue.

Max broke into a jog as he passed through the gate, anticipating a handful of boys on the field. He came around the south end of the home side bleachers. His coaches should be on the field. He crossed the running track. A ping of excitement trumped the nervous twist in his gut. He stepped onto the field. And stopped.

Max was the first to arrive.

I can do this, Lord. I can do this.

He ran to the fifty yard line, dropped his duffel with an exhale, and waited. Seven o'clock and he remained alone.

Seven-o-five.

Seven ten.

Seven fifteen.

Max jogged across the field to the parking lot. Nothing. He ran the other way and surveyed the field house. He caught no movement.

Seven twenty.

He glanced down at the duffel bag. He'd planned to get the boys' names and positions. Talk about goals and what it meant to really win. He was going to pass out the Warrior T-shirts he'd found in his office closet. That little room was a treasure of Warrior gear.

Seven thirty. Max reached down for the duffel, his heavy heart crashing against the walls of his chest. Did he really expect the boys to come? New coach, second day in town?

Yeah, he really did.

He expected his coaches to show up. Even Bobby Molnar, who'd yammered on and on last night over a plate of tangy pulled pork about how he expected Max to do great things.

As he turned for the field house, an abrupt, "Coach," arrested his next step. A stout man wearing a worn Aggies hat jogged onto the field, huffing and puffing, and when he got to Max, he dropped to one knee, gulping for his next breath, his massive chest swelling.

"Sorry I'm late, Coach. It won't happen again."

"Late? You saved me from complete humiliation." Max offered his hand. "Max Benson. And you are?"

"Coach Howard Hines. But folks call me Hines. Or Coach. I'm here to help, do whatever you need me to do." An African American man, dressed for a day of coaching, approaching sixty-five or seventy, was the first ray of hope in Max's short football coaching career.

"How'd you know about this?"

"Word's out. New coach is in town. I'm the chief volunteer." Hines rose to his feet. "I retired from coaching four years ago myself and the wife wanted to return to Colby. We grew up here." He gestured toward the stands. "I was a Warrior back in the day. Played on two state championship teams. Fullback. '59 and '60. Course we didn't have nothing near as grand as all this." Hines propped his hands on his hips as he gazed around. "We used to run the cow pastures for PT. Lifted hay bales, tossed bags of feed. We were tough as nails. The field turned to a mud bowl if it so much as sprinkled rain. The bleachers were half what you see here. But folks drove in from all over to watch us play. Stand right along the field in their coats and hats until the final whistle."

"So what happened to Warrior football?"

Hines jutted out his chin. "Got cocky. You start winning championships two or three times a decade, folks start expecting it. Demanding it. People moved to Colby so their boys could play for Coach Burke." The old coach squinted at Max. "How old are you?"

"Thirty-eight."

"Burke was your age when he took over," Hines said. "Twenty years later he was dead."

"Are you saying coaching killed him?" Max absently ran his hand over the spot on his back where his phantom stress pains lived. *Used* to live.

"In a manner, yeah. He retired. Was dead two months later. The stress took its toll. The game becomes about everyone but you and the boys. It becomes about the school, the boosters, the community, then the biggest sin of all sets in. Pride. And that one gets in your bones and don't let go. The more successful Burke became, the more stressed he got. Money poured into this place. I watched it all from my program in Georgia." Hines flashed Max a fat, white smile. "I won a few state championships myself."

"So why aren't you coach instead of me?"

Hines laughed. "I told you, I retired. I like helping out these days. Besides . . ." The old coach glanced over his shoulder. "They're . . . well . . . looking for a man like you, Max . . . Coach Benson."

Max stared toward the field house. What did Hines see? Or not see? "What kind of man is that, Hines? Exactly?"

"You." Hines widened his stance and folded his arms over his chest. He wore a red Warrior pullover and coach's shorts. "First year the wife and I were back in Colby," he said, "I enjoyed watching football from my easy chair. But then I got to itching to be around the boys, on the field, under the Friday night lights." He popped Max on the back. "Besides, volunteering keeps me out of the house. And a happy wife is a happy Hines." His chuckle rolled and billowed, and felt far away from Max.

"Tell me why we're the only two here, Hines. If you heard about it, why didn't the kids?"

"Would you come if you were in their shoes?"

"Yeah, I would . . . well . . . no, maybe not."

"These boys have been burned and bruised. Coaches come and go." Hines peered toward the field house again. "Five coaches in six years? What's to say you ain't number six?"

"So how do we build a program without kids?"

"Guess we roll up our sleeves and beat the bushes. Don't wait for the boys to come here, we got to go there."

"You'd go with me?" Max faced Hines head on.

"I know most of the kids. Been volunteering for three years now. I want to see you succeed, Coach. I'm tired of watching these kids suffer 'cause some eggheads back up in them offices are playing tug-of-war."

"Tug-of-war? What tug-of-war? Hines, do you know something?" Jade's voice echoed across Max's mind. *If it's too good to be true . . .*

"I only know what my heart sees. I'm not in the inner circles. Just an old retired volunteer. But something's not right when a program can't find a good coach and keep him. I mean, look at this place. I did ten times more in Georgia with ten times less. We should be funneling players all over the NCAA. But we're not." Hines edged his tone with frustration.

"You want a job, Hines?" If he was hired to build a program, might as well start from the ground up.

He regarded Max. "You offering?"

"I'm going to need coaches who can show up when I ask. You want offense or defense?"

"I know a great D coordinator so I'll take the O. Run it with you, then help out on special teams. We running the spread or the option?"

"If I can get Calvin Blue, the option."

Hines laughed. "You know ol' Cal? He's a good kid. Quick as a greased lightning but about as mule headed as they come. But surely he'd make our offense come alive."

"So let's convince his mule head to play for us." Max tugged his duffel off the field and started for the field house. Hines fell in step with him. "I could use some help getting set up, then we can call some boys."

Max liked Hines, sensed a kindred spirit. Not only a love for football but a love for the One who was true light. They'd make a good team.

Holding open the field house door for Hines, Max composed his dismissal speech for Lars Martin and Kevin Carroll.

Sixteen

When Jade arrived at 1207 Gallia Street in historic Colby, Kathy Carroll met her in the middle of the green lawn. A bright, rainless sky blanketed the day and a swelling heat kissed the early afternoon hours.

"So glad you could make it. Welcome, welcome." Kathy was petite and trim with mounds of coal-colored ringlets bouncing about her face and shoulders.

"What? Miss a playdate and a stroll through a vintage lover's candy store?" Jade laughed. "Not on your life." She let Asa slip to the ground, then took his hand.

"I thought that'd hook you." Kathy threaded her arm through Jade's and guided her up the walkway to the Victorian house. "I told Kevin on the way home last night, 'I've got to hang with that girl.' Our husbands will be absorbed by the game and we'll be football widows, comforting each other. We'll be the best of friends. This is the first time a head coach has had a wife." Kathy reached for the door. "Who knows, in twenty years or so, your son might just grow up to marry my daughter."

"Okay, sounds like a plan." A dig-deep-roots plan. The idea grounded Jade. Four days in Colby and she'd already made a few new friends and arranged a marriage for her son.

It'd been years since Jade had ventured out beyond Daphne and Margot, her college friends. But now she had her first *mom* friend, and a whole new luxurious world opened to her.

Jade paused in the foyer, a burst of glee on her lips. "Kathy, this is amazing." The high walls were textured, bordered by etched, gleaming trim and molding. Her eye landed on a Victrola and what appeared to be an original Tiffany lamp. Even the air seemed to be from the nineteenth century.

"When you said you sold vintage clothes and what all back in Tennessee, I said to myself, Jade has got to see Nana's house. You should see the clothes in her attic. I'm not sure they're worth anything, but when we were kids, my cousins and I used them for dress up. What a hoot."

Who knew the vintage mother ship had landed in Colby, Texas? Jade pressed her hand over her heart. "This is fabulous. Are you sure your nana doesn't mind?" She held Asa's hand tighter as she followed Kathy through the house. No way would she let him loose in this place.

"Nana and Gramps Vance moved here in '32. A year after they got married. This was the original house of the family's ranch. In the late '30s Gramps started selling off the land because he wanted to make more money and work less. He died in the early nineties, but Nana still lives here. She'll be a hundred on her next birthday." Kathy turned into a grand, sunny kitchen. "Nana, this is Jade Benson. The new coach's wife." Kathy bent down to the woman pressed into a brown mohair chair. She had a cloud of fluffy white hair and a teacup in her hand.

"Another coach? What are they doing down at that school?" She shoved her saucer toward Kathy. "We're never going to get our Warrior tradition back." She smoothed her hand over her flowered housecoat and peered at Jade with soft but determined eyes. "Well, are you her? The coach's wife? You're right pretty."

"Thank you. As are you." Jade bowed slightly. Mrs. Vance reminded her of Granny, with her white hair and forthright opinions. "Your home is lovely, Mrs. Vance."

"It's old, that's what it is. Got too much stuff and that dang girl who comes to clean . . . what's her name, Kathy? She didn't show again."

"Mariah Walberg, Nana." She rolled her eyes at Jade. "I'll check into it."

"Get me someone new." Mrs. Vance sat back, closing her eyes. "Some people just don't want to be helped."

"Listen, Nana, the kids are going to play out on the porch. Do you mind if Jade looks around? She owns a vintage shop in Tennessee. She might like some of the clothes in the attic."

"A vintage shop? What the blazes is a vintage shop?"

"Just a shop that values old things," Jade said.

Mrs. Vance peeked at her. "Or just loves junk." She chortled. "Up in the attic I got those flapper dresses my sister and I used to wear. There's some Johnny hats and some old western wear from our rodeo days. A few fancy dresses. Go on, take a look. Take what you want."

"I'll run you up to the attic," Kathy said, "then come down and watch the kids. They're okay in here, but I don't like to leave them alone long."

Jade glanced at Asa as Kathy made sure Nana didn't need anything. He and Lola were chatting in two-year-old speak at a toy kitchen setup. Her dark curls bounced as she talked and waved a plastic skillet. Asa glanced at Jade. She smiled. *It's okay.* He dropped to his bottom and putted the truck he took with him everywhere along the carpet pattern, crawling away from Lola. *Good boy.*

"Asa's so sweet, Jade. He looks like you." Kathy led Jade toward the stairs.

"Yeah, h-he's a cutie." She was going to say he looked like Max, but did he? He looked like Rice, but Jade wasn't about to say it out loud. She'd done enough by confessing her secret to Dr. Gelman yesterday.

Kathy rounded the second-floor landing and climbed to the third, talking about Colby and football, Nana and the house. Jade listened, ducking through the low attic door and twisting up the narrow stairs toward the house rafters.

". . . so I hired Mariah Walberg to be Nana's house cleaner . . ." Mariah? The woman with Dr. Gelman yesterday. ". . . known her forever, she got pregnant right after high school by Dex Walberg. One of those prom king and queen deals gone bad. Ha, like they all do. Dex was a talented wide receiver, but love makes some people really stupid and Dex was one of 'em. They got married."

Kathy and Jade emerged into a warm, bright dormer with dust swirling in the streams of light. The walls were lined with boxes. Jade's fingers tingled. She'd go through each one. Methodically. Kathy went on about Mariah and Dex, shoving boxes out of the way, on a path to the back corner.

"But he couldn't let go of his dream to play college ball. He got an opportunity right after Tucker was born. Off he went. Never came back. Mariah fell apart and . . . let's just say all the doctors in Colby couldn't put her back together again. I feel bad for her, but everyone but Mariah knew he'd leave. Here we are. *The* closet." Kathy opened an angled door tucked under the eaves and jerked on a light string. "Clothes from the last eight decades. Maybe more. I think my great grandma's wedding dress is in here."

Jade inhaled the fragrance of wonder, the scent of cedar. "A cedar closet? Cedar is perfect for clothes storage, Kathy. I may have just arrived in vintage heaven."

She moved aside with a smile. "All of Nana's daughters and granddaughters have come up here at one time or another, tried to find something we liked and wanted, but in the end we all curled our lips and said, 'What's on sale at Dillards?'"

"You're crazy. You just don't know what you're looking at, Kathy." Jade ran her hand over the wool coats hanging on her right while spying on the fringe of the flapper dresses.

"One woman's junk is another woman's dream-come-true." Kathy backed out of the closet. "Have at it, girl. I'll go down and check on the kids. If you're not out in an hour, I'll send up a rescue team."

"Oh no, just let me die in vintage." Jade inched farther in the closet, understanding how Alice fell into Wonderland.

The closet was a treasury. Jade had been to a lot of estate sales and auctions. She'd climbed through many a stuffed closet but not one of fragrant cedar. She breathed in. Then out. Cedar mixed with the scent of ancient sunbaked attic walls nearly made her giddy. She gathered the sleeve of a coat and pressed it against her face. It smelled of life, and time, and days gone by. Perhaps a wee bit of menthol from cigarettes.

Jade pulled out her phone in front of the flapper dresses, took a picture and sent it to Lillabeth. *Hello, heaven. I'm going to buy these.* But Lillabeth had to promise to find the perfect customer.

She texted back immediately. *Where are you? They're gorgeous.*

I know. At an old woman's house. Met her gdau last night. Just as Jade pressed Send, something in the back caught her eye. She leaned, squinting. A black dress. Her breath paused momentarily in anticipation.

Could it be? No, no, she'd never seen a vintage Coco Chanel little black dress. There were too many knockoffs. After all, fashion lived and died today by the little black dress. Jade had acquired and sold a few vintage Chanel suits—which were amazing finds. But an LBD? Only in her vintage dreams.

Shoving aside boxes, Jade worked her way toward the dress. She could see the tag, but part of it was turned up. Women in the '30s loved Chanel dresses. They were elegant and affordable. Electricity buzzed up Jade's fingers as she reached for the tag. Slowly, she turned down the edge. Her knees shimmied.

Chanel.

Jade wheezed out a stuttered gasp, snapping her hand back as if she'd touched an ancient, hallowed shrine. Vintage Chanel LBD. Her heart stuttered in homage. Nana Vance owned the dress that revolutionized evening wear for women in the Depression.

She had to have it. Simply put. She'd empty her accounts, and Max's, for the contents of this closet. For that one dress. Jade scouted the rest of the clothes and peered through two cedar chests that were filled with gorgeous costume jewelry.

This closet was a vintage shop all its own.

Her cell pinged. Lillabeth. *Well???*

Oh, this was going to be fun. Jade aimed her phone at the little black dress. She sent the picture with no text and barely drew a deep breath before Lillabeth answered. *Is that what I think it is? I nearly passed out. Deets, please.*

Details to come. Hang tight. Will make offer to buy. Whole closet is a vint shop.

Jade backed out of the closet into the cooler attic air. Perspiration beaded along her neck and back. More from the excitement than the heat. The flapper dresses, the coats, and the trunks of shoes and jewelry she'd purchase for the Blue Umbrella. But the little black dress? Would hang in her own closet for a special night with Max.

Running down the stairs, she calculated a fair purchase price, planning how and when she could retrieve the items. Max could trade Jade the truck for a day.

"Kathy," she called the moment she landed on the first floor. "That closet is amazing. I don't want to take anything but I'm willing to . . . pay . . ." What was Asa's diaper bag doing tossed against the front door. "Kathy?"

"Jade." Kathy appeared in the hall with Asa in her arms. "You need to leave."

"Why? What happened? Did Asa do something?" She examined him, listening for sounds of Lola crying in another room. Asa appeared fine. Bright-eyed. Unscathed.

"He's not hurt." Kathy jerked open the front door, kicking the diaper bag toward Jade. "I can't say the same for me. How could you come here, pretending to be my friend, knowing what your husband was about to do?"

"What?" Jade's face tingled as warm blood ran cold. "Kathy, I have no idea what you're talking about."

"Your husband fired mine this afternoon. Don't tell me he didn't talk to you about it. Coaches' wives always know."

"Excuse me?" Jade dribbled a small laugh. "He fired your husband? Max wouldn't do that, Kathy. He needs Kevin and Lars. I have a confession—he doesn't know what he's doing."

"Apparently, he thinks he does. He fired Kevin, Lars, and the rest of the coaching staff." Kathy kicked the door open wider. "You need to leave."

But the little black dress. "Okay . . . sure . . ." Jade bent for the diaper bag. "I'd like to buy the contents of the closet. There are quite a few amazing—"

"The contents are no longer for sale." Her icy words froze Jade to the floor.

"I see. Or just . . . not for sale to me?"

"Is there a difference?"

Jade held the sobs boiling in her chest until she got in the car and gunned the Mercedes down Gallia under gathering rain clouds.

She was humiliated. Sad. Embarrassed. How could Max fire coaches on his second day? Forget vintage heaven and the little black dress.

The red light flashed in her blurry, teary vision. A gust of wind butted against the car, driving early raindrops across the windshield. Waving tree branches exposed the pale underside of summer green leaves, warning of the coming storm.

"You fired the coaching staff?" Bobby moved like a locomotive toward Max's desk, shooting daggers at Hines. "Could you excuse us?"

"Max, I'll stay if you need me."

"It's okay. Go get your office set up." He'd bear Bobby's barrage for the both of them.

When the door clicked closed, Bobby spun toward Max with a face of fury. "Who do you think you are, coming in here, firing my coaches?"

"Yours? I thought they were my coaches. I'm head coach and can hire my own staff."

"Those men have been on the Warrior coaching staff for years. Between them they have more than twenty years' experience."

"And yet you still have a losing program. Did it ever occur to you that maybe it's not just the head coach that needs to go when a team is losing, but the assistants too?"

"Those men have something you don't. Or any other coach that's come in here. It's why they stayed. They bleed Warrior pride."

"They can still bleed Warrior pride, Bobby. From the classroom. From the stands. Not all over my season."

"I won't let you. Rehire them." Bobby smashed his hand down on the desk.

His intensity challenged Max's resolve. But the time he'd spent today with Hines, talking and planning, had fortified Max enough to fight for his right to have his own coaches.

"First day. All I wanted was a meeting at seven a.m. No coaches. No players. I don't need that kind of attitude to start off this season. We have a lot of work to do. Play-wise and heart-wise. I need coaches with a heart for me, the game, and above all the boys. Frankly, Bobby, I don't see that in the coaches. My contract says I can hire who I want."

"Since when?"

"Since I negotiated with Chevy. You didn't know?" A bit of revelation dawned. Chevy and Bobby had different agendas. "I wasn't planning on changing staff. Until they made it clear I had no choice."

"So this is how you want it? Coming in here and tipping over the applecart?" Bobby's frown suddenly bounced to a smile. "Okay, okay, I guess I can see it.

Next time, check with me first on the big changes. Just so I can be ready to field questions." Bobby patted his hand over his heart. "You scared your poor athletic director, Max."

"Fair enough," Max said.

Bobby started for the door. "By the way, I scheduled a little press conference next week. But I have a feeling the press will be on this story by the end of the day. Guess we're going to make the papers sooner than I thought. What's the saying? Any press is good press."

"So they say."

When the door closed, Max exhaled down to his chair. Bobby came in like a lion. Left like a lamb. It spoke volumes of his character. Max gazed toward Hines's office. The man knew something. But what? Max figured he'd have to watch his own back for a while. Keep it toward the wall, eyes peeled.

He flipped the bill of his hat around to the back and scooted up to his desk. He had work to do before the media descended. If they descended. The press was the least of Max's concerns. He'd managed them during high pro-file cases.

What concerned him the most at the moment was putting eleven men on the football field.

Seventeen

"So you fired them?" Jade cut Asa's peanut butter and jelly in half and set it on a paper plate. Since they had no furniture, Jade set him in the middle of the kitchen floor. "What happened to the great camaraderie from last night?"

The little guy frowned, pouting his bottom lip. "No, no. Don't like." He jammed his finger on the crust.

"Asa—" Jade sighed, her patience frail. "The crust is good for you. Eat it."

Max picked up the plate. "They were going to sabotage me, Jade." He tore the brown crusts off Asa's sandwich, eating them as he did. "Here, buddy."

Asa regarded him with big brown eyes that said *thank you*, then picked up the triangle closest to him and dove in.

"Based on what evidence? They didn't show up for your first seven a.m. meeting?"

136

"Yeah, Jade, because they didn't show up. Neither did any of the players. Those coaches have influence. If they wanted to be there, if they wanted the kids there, they would've been. Hines showed up, ready to work, ready to be on the team. But between you and me, something is going on. Something political, underhanded."

"Hines, the old coach you just met today."

"And hired as my assistant. Offensive coordinator."

Jade folded her arms and fell against the counter. "I was humiliated when Kathy asked me to leave. It was embarrassing. Just when I'd found an original Chanel little black dress, Max, an original. In all my years of vintage shopping and selling, I've never found an original. The contents of that closet were mine until you fired her husband."

Jade chewed the inside of her lip, her heart pressing hard to understand why she cared more about a little black dress than Max's defense for firing his coaches.

"I'm sorry, babe. I didn't know."

And now he was being all sweet.

"Kathy said we were going to spend so much time together as coaches' wives, we'd be the best of friends." Jade's eyes watered when she glanced at Max. "We even joked that Asa and Lola might fall in love and get married. Friends, Max. I was making new friends."

Without a word, he pulled her to him, kissing her cheek, then her hair, soothing her wound with masculine understanding.

"She probably has all the wives hating me by now." A dark gust of wind hit the house. More rain.

"I didn't even think of the wives' side. I'm sorry."

"Max, did you really consider any of this venture before you said yes? Before I said yes?"

"I thought I had." He released her and paced toward the empty dining room. "Maybe I just wanted to come so bad—"

"Hip-pocket dream?"

He moved to the window. "I thought God's will."

"Then we press ahead. Try not to offend any more wives so Asa and I can make a friend."

"Okay, I hear you, Jade. I understand today was hard, but there are other moms in this city who aren't going to care I fired the assistant coaches."

"You hope. Kathy Carroll's family is one of the oldest in the region. She could blackball me from the supermarket if she wanted."

"Jade," he said, low. "I'm sure that's not true, but let's just play this out and trust God for all things to work together for good."

"Easy for you to say." The first spatter of rain hit the window.

"Easy for me? No, it's not. I'm trying to see the big picture and it's not very clear. I've disappointed Warrior coaches and their wives, the athletic director, fans, and above all, you. I'm trying to make a go of this opportunity. I can't second-guess myself. So I go with what I think is right, what seems like wisdom, and if I'm wrong, I pray God has my back." He was the One Max could trust.

Jade's first run of tears were thin, like the rain draining down the window. She wiped them away with the back of her hand.

"What's wrong? Why are you crying?"

"Because . . ." She reached for the paper towels. "I lost a friend. I miss home. I miss Mama. And oh, it was the most beautiful little black dress. A vintage dream. The mother lode."

His quick grin tipped over her heart. She couldn't be mad at him. Not when he looked at her with those brown eyes. Not when he gathered her in his strong arms and whispered she was beautiful.

"We knew this would be a challenge, Jade."

"For you, yes. Not me." Her "me" was watered with emotion and a sniff. But she fought a smile. Couldn't she have a moment longer to be mad?

Max laughed and she broke. "Fine, it's tough for both of us." She peered at Asa who lifted his peanut buttered hand to her. "Yucky." He wrinkled his nose.

"I'll say." Jade tugged a paper towel from the roll and wet it. "Max, can you pour him some milk, please?"

Max moved the conversation to coaching and his new friend, Hines, who had forty years coaching experience but had retired.

"He knows Calvin too, and between the two of us, we think we can get him to come out and play."

A knock rattled the front door. "Coach Benson, you home?"

"Coach Hines. I'm always home for you." Max stood aside for him to enter and introduced Jade and Asa.

Hines entered the house wiping his feet and Jade liked him immediately. "Sorry to barge in on you, Mrs. Benson.'"

"It's Jade." She shook his hand. "Can I get you something to drink? I'd offer you a chair, but as you see our furniture hasn't arrived."

"I understand moving, ma'am. Moved a lot in my time. And nothing to drink for me. But I'd like to borrow your husband if you don't mind. Coach, I heard from the potential D coordinator. If you're game, we can ride on out to the house for a meet. See if it's a go."

Max glanced at Jade. "Do you mind?"

"No, of course not. Go."

"We'll finish talking when I get back." He reached for her—she thought to kiss her on the cheek. But Max pulled her to him and gave her a slow, gentle kiss while Coach Hines waited on the porch. "I won't be gone long."

Jade fanned herself as she watched him drive off in Coach Hines's truck. It sure was steamy in Texas tonight.

She tossed Asa in the bath and while he played, familiar words danced across her mind. *Don't let life lead you around. Don't shy away from trouble.* These elements were the old Jade.

Take charge. She'd call Kathy Carroll and make amends. And not just for the sake of the LBD.

Later, she'd research churches. Find a good one that also had a mom's group, and forge her way into Colby society.

Hines drove his old Ford west on Route 60 for about five miles, and Max saw nothing in the windshield but dark fields hiding in the dusk. Every now and then a silo silhouette hit the horizon. Max and Hines talked football until the golden glow of house lights popped into view and Hines downshifted to turn onto a gravel drive.

"You ready?" Hines said, cutting the engine.

"Better yet, is he ready?" Max stepped out of the truck and surveyed the land. The Porters were ranchers, Hines had told him.

As they walked toward the house, the front door opened and a passel of border collies charged down the steps. "Friends," a woman said from the edge of the porch. "They're friends."

Max bent to pet a soft, dark head. For a moment he missed his old pal Roscoe.

"*Friends* is my code word for them to not tear our guests apart." The woman laughed. "Hines, how are you?"

"Good, Haley, haven't seen you in a while."

"Ranching keeps us busy." She faced Max. "Haley Porter."

"Max Benson. Thanks for letting us come out at dinnertime." Haley appeared to be about Jade's age, athletic and commanding with expressive eyes and long red hair. Max liked her. Good sign. He'd probably like her husband and welcome him to the coaching staff.

"No worry, Dane is still out in the pasture. He'll be along soon."

The Porter home sat on a grassy knoll, like a pushpin against green felt, holding the prairie to the earth.

Inside made Max think of the old west. He'd stepped from the twenty-first century to the twentieth. The air smelled of grilled beef. The walls and ceiling were joined by thick timber beams.

Haley led Max and Hines into a large eat-in kitchen, also carved of timber and granite. They grabbed chairs at the center island.

"Max, Haley's daddy was Coach Burke."

"Yeah? I've heard good things about him."

"He was one of the best." Haley poured three tall glasses of tea. "A great man and a great coach, but the game wore him into the ground. They made it about everything but football and the boys."

"They?" Max said. "Who is they?"

Haley and Hines shared a private glance. Max wasn't sure but he thought he caught the slightest shake of Hines's head out the corner of his eye.

"Just the boosters, the fans, the kids even. Parents, the school. You know how it is."

"No, actually, I don't. I'm learning, though. So, what—Colby just lost sight of reality?"

"Some did, yes." Haley smoothed her hands over the island surface. "I'm glad Daddy's not around to see the destruction of the Warriors. Though I think he saw it coming." Haley sprouted a quick smile. "But that's old history. Max, you're making new history."

"Hopefully." Max took a long sip of tea. He liked Haley. She reminded him more and more of Jade. Strong with a tender thread. She'd be a good coach's wife. And, a-ha, a friend for Jade. "Do you have children?"

"No, not yet," Haley said. "We're thirty-two so we think we'll try soon, but not during the season. Even so, having a baby won't interrupt football. I assure you."

Max smiled. "Good. There's nothing much for Dane to do during those first few months of pregnancy anyway."

"Just hold your hair while you toss your cookies, Haley," Hines said, burying his comment behind his glass.

"Yeah . . . I guess." Haley made a face.

The conversation stalled. Max glanced toward the door, anxious to meet this football coach Hines was so excited about. Didn't she say Dane would be here soon?

"So, Max." Haley popped to life. "You have a son?"

"Yes, yes, I do. Asa. He's almost two," Max said.

"Ah, sweet. They're so cute at that age."

Where was Dane? Max finished his tea.

"Well?" Hines turned to Max. "Aren't you going to ask about football?"

He furrowed his brow. "When Dane gets here, yeah. Do you think he'll be here soon, Haley?"

"Hines, you didn't tell him?" Haley said, exasperated. "I told you, it's not funny."

"I told you it is." Hines chuckled low. "Meet Coach Porter, Max. Coach Haley Porter."

She jutted out her hand. "Pleased to meet you, Coach."

"A woman?" Max slid off his chair and turned a circle. "Hines, are you serious? It's bad enough I fired my coaches today—but to hire a woman? Haley, do you know anything about coaching football?"

"Funny question coming from you, Max." Haley fired him a look that almost burned the soles of his shoes to the tile floor. "I reckon I know more than you."

"She's right about that, Max."

"But—sorry, I've never heard of a woman football coach."

"She's one of the best defensive coaches in the region."

"How do you know?" Max spun toward Hines, then Haley. "Where have you coached? Don't say the sidelines with your dad."

Was Hines serious? Max still boiled in the hot water he'd created this afternoon. The media would skewer him—after Bobby got through with him.

"Dad taught me everything he knew, Max. I grew up on the sidelines with him and my brothers. Sunday afternoon, the whole family watched film and learned."

"That's not the same as coaching, Haley. It's enough that I'm a greenhorn."

"I coached at a small school in New Mexico for four years after I graduated from college with a degree in sports psychology. I only quit the job to move home and marry Dane."

Oh man, oh man, oh man. Max paced. *Lord, what do I do?* The churning in his chest robbed what little peace he had.

"If she were a man she'd be coaching college ball," Hines said.

"I can do the job, Max." Passion powered Haley's voice. "I can do it well. Plus, I don't know if it matters to you, but I believe in you. I thought Chevy was a loon for hiring a coach with no experience, but from what Hines tells me and the fact that you fired those jackal assistant coaches, I think you've got what it takes to turn this program around. I know the players, Max. I know their families. I know this town. I know Warrior football. And if it's all the same to you, I'd like to coach so I can honor my daddy's legacy. What those boys did to him . . . no matter. It would just be an honor."

"What boys? Who? What's going on?"

"Nothing, Max. Old history," Hines said. "The question on the table is, are you going to hire Haley."

"I don't know . . . you've never actually *played*." Max pressed his hands on the island counter and faced her.

"I've played a lot of football. Not on Friday nights, but with my brothers. I played powder-puff in college. Not the same, sounds wimpy, but I know what it's like to be on the field. We were champions two years running. Not being a guy didn't handicap me in New Mexico. My defense led the division in sacks and forced fumbles. I have an aggressive style and I'm *really* good at reading the offense."

Max cut a glance at Hines. "Are you trying to get me fired? You're in on this *thing* no one seems to want to talk about."

"Simmer down, Max. I'll assume that remark came from panic, and I won't hold it against you." Hines's eyes darkened. "I'm trying to help you pull together a good coaching staff. I got two more, *both men*, who can help with special teams and strength training. Now, what you going to do about Haley? I'd hire her in a Texas minute."

Max regarded her, dropping to his stool. "Do you have any questions for me?"

"When do I start?"

"In the morning. Seven a.m. At the field house. Might as well start working on our game."

Hines popped his hands together. "You won't regret this, Max."

Yeah? Too late. The sour knot in his gut told him he already did.

Eighteen

"We're going to do nothing, Rick." Bobby aimed the water hose at the roses blooming in the side yard. "Max is playing into our hands. Even better than I thought. He's going to get himself fired long before we could concoct a case against him. If not by Chevy, then by public opinion." Bobby moved his hose to the next rose bed. The summer heat brought out the richness of the flowers' bloom. "How's the research into his background going?"

"He had a pain med problem. Went to rehab a few times. The last one was the Outpost."

"Drug of choice?"

"Percocet." Rick's answers were clipped and dull.

"I think we can lay our hands on some Percs, don't you?"

"Bobby." Rick paused with a sigh. "Does coaching at Colby mean this much to you? You can't keep destroying men's careers."

"Men destroyed my father's career. Specifically, Stebbin Burke. RIP old man. But his daughter, not one of his sons, is assuming his Warrior legacy." Bobby looked at Rick. "Isn't there something in the Bible about when a woman takes a man's place? It's like a curse, not a blessing. Max is going to fail. In ways I never imagined. I doubted Chevy when he hired him. But this is a major coup. If I didn't know better, I'd think Chevy was on our side."

"Our side? Your side. Why do there have to be sides, Bob? We *all* want a winning Warrior program again."

"But *I* want to be the head coach. Assume *my* father's legacy before Stebbin Burke took it from him. I was to be the next Warrior football coach. Me."

"Then you should've watched yourself in Plano."

"Watched what? There were no charges. No evidence."

"Then why'd you resign?" Rick started for his truck. "Talk to you later, Bob."

"Thanks for the info, Rick. You're a fine booster."

The man waved him off. Ah, let him be a bit sore. Bobby had him in his back pocket. His plans to become head coach were finally blooming. Just like the roses in his garden. Plans, like roses, require time and tender care. But in the end came the sweet aroma of victory.

In his office, Max worked on a strength training schedule for the first week of practice. To mix things up, they were running across pastures and tossing bags of seed and bales of hay at the Porter ranch.

In the week since she'd joined the team, Haley had kicked Hines and Max to the curb with her recruiting skills. She charmed a bunch of ranch and farm boys into playing for her. Kids who didn't care about sports politics, who just wanted to legally smash a few heads on Friday night. Maybe along the way, impress a girl.

But Max and Hines struggled to enlist the skilled players like Noah Warren, a talented QB, and Calvin Blue. Max heard this morning that Carter Davis had indeed transferred to another school district. So Max would surely see him on the field this season—as an opponent.

Tucker Walberg came by and said he wanted to play. Tuck was the opposite of Carter. All heart and little skill. *Lord, couldn't he have a mix of both?*

"Max, turn on Channel 13." Hines burst into the office, reaching for the remote on the corner of the desk.

"Coach Benson has been stirring things up in Warrior country. First he cut wide receiver Carter Davis—"

"I didn't cut Carter. He never showed."

"Well, you said if the boys didn't show up for that first meeting . . ." Hines upped the volume while Max regretted his first day words.

"Davis was the one player in Colby who showed promise for the Warrior offense. Coach, we want to know how are you going to build a team around . . . no one?"

Another reporter moved onto the screen. Another slick-haired, perfect-toothed young buck who looked like he'd just left a fraternity party.

"That's not all, Chip. Coach Benson opened his season by firing his assistants. Stirred up quite a controversy in Warrior Country. Channel 13 Sports has learned that Benson brought in retired coach Howard Hines to run his offense, leaving Warrior fans scratching their heads. Insiders at the school tell us the phone lines have been lighting up ever since. It looks like the hope for the Warriors' return to glory will have to wait for another season."

Images flashed on the screen, a composite of past Warrior championships, winning touchdowns, and trophy ceremonies.

"As if things weren't hot enough in Colby, Coach Benson added fuel to the fire when he announced his coach to run the defense. This time, it's not a retiree. Or even a young coach out of college. This time he picked Coach Burke's daughter, Haley Porter."

Max sighed, rocking back in his chair, shoving off the elephant smashing down on his chest. A clip of Haley played. She ran across the screen in a powder-puff uniform. Max pressed his hand to his back. Haley appeared on the sidelines with the New Mexico team.

"This seems like a crazy decision to me, Chip. Haley can't know what it's like to get mowed over by a two-hundred-pound lineman. Coach Burke's daughter or not. And we all know New Mexico football is not Texas football."

Max's door burst open. "Chip Mack and that yahoo Wiley Snyder are idiots." Haley flared, red and hot. "You think I don't know what it's like to get mowed over by a two-hundred-pound lineman? Come on over here, I'll show you what it feels like to get mowed over by a hundred-and-twenty-pound woman." She steamed in a circle. "They make me so mad."

"Haley, you knew this would happen." Hines, always calm. Always wise.

Max massaged his fingers into his back. He knew what happened that night in his bunk—God healed him. But for the first time, his faith was being tested. Stressed mantled his shoulders. But so far . . . his back remained strong. His taste for pills, a bitter memory.

"Yeah, but it doesn't mean I have to like it." She hammered Max's desk. "Max, we're going to go out and kick some football butt this year."

"Okay, let's do it. But for now, how about watching some film. See what we got to work with." He liked Haley's intensity. Her feisty determination. A red-headed powder keg. "We need an offense to match your defense."

"Well, stop sitting in here moping and get out there. I've seen Calvin Blue shadowing the field all week." With that, Haley flew out of the room.

Hines peered down at Max. "She'll calm down as the season wears on."

"I hope not." He came round the desk. "Am I moping?"

"A bit."

"I didn't think it'd be this hard. I mean—I knew it'd be hard, but—"

"It's just beginning, brother. Listen, let's call it a night. It's only Tuesday. We got all week to work hard. Go home, spend time with that gorgeous wife you got. 'Cause once this machine gets going, you'll be lucky to get a few hours a week with her."

Max stared toward the field. "Good idea. I'll tell Haley I'm going."

Hines started out the door. "I'll tell her. I'm going that way. Hey—is Chevy doing okay with all of this?"

"So far. He sent me an e-mail confirming you and Haley were going on the payroll." Max gathered his gear. "He seems determined to let me do my job." An evening with Jade would be nice. They could have dinner, take a walk, play with Asa. He felt like he hadn't seen them in days. "Should I give Calvin another call, or will you?"

"This one's on you, Max. I think Calvin wants you to convince him. I'll give Noah another try."

"Good enough. See you tomorrow."

Max went to the window and studied the shadows of the field. So, Calvin had been lurking for a week? How long had Haley been keeping that tied up in her ponytail?

The sun moved behind a cloud and Max turned from the window as Jade stepped over the threshold, wild and disheveled, her fine-boned expression drawn and pale. Asa rode low on her hip. Her cheeks were heat-red and her eyes sported a dewy glaze.

"This whole town hates us." She trembled, right down to the trailing hiss of *us*.

"Not the *whole* town?"

"Yes, the whole town. I've been screamed at, honked at. People drive by our house in the middle of the night, blasting music and yelling obscenities. Women accost me in the grocery store."

"Women . . . what?" Max took a page from Hines's playbook and remained calm. "What do you mean accost? Like hit you?"

"One crashed into my grocery cart today and told me where you could go, Max. In front of Asa. I can endure the honking and yelling. It's stupid and immature. People need to get a life. But today"—Jade fumed and steamed like Haley—"was the last straw. This insane, outside-her-mind woman let her kid *spit* on your son."

"What?" Max scooted around the chairs and gripped Jade by the elbows, peering into her face. "Spit on Asa?"

"A big honking kid loogie. Right in front of me. His mother did nothing. Oh no, wait, she scolded him for spitting on Asa instead of *me*!" Jade shifted into overdrive.

"Did you deck her?"

"Oh, believe me, I wanted to—but no one in the store would've backed me other than Dr. Gelman. She saw the whole thing." Jade's arms twitched with each syllable. "But I yanked the kid up and told him to never come near my son again. Rotten little brat. And then, she, *monster-mom*, threatens me with assault charges."

"Whoa." He'd never signed up for this. "Jade, I am so sorry."

"Sorry? No, Max. That's not going to cut it. I thought about this the whole way here. If it's this bad now, what's it going to be like when you start losing games?"

"I don't think folks expect a winning season, Jade. They're just ticked about me firing the coaches and hiring Haley."

"So when you lose, they're going to be happy? No, they'll be livid. If you'd kept the old coaches, they'd have claimed you might have had a shot at winning one game." Jade gripped his arms. "Max, we can't stay here."

"What? Not stay?" Was she serious? But the pop-snap in her tone told him she wasn't joking around.

"We're in a no-win situation, Max. Our son was spit on today. Spit. On. My heart broke for him. You know what he did? Ran after the kid. He wanted to play. Is this what you want for him? For his kind, innocent heart to be ruined by crazy people? I love football, you know that, but I hate this. Asa's been through enough. We've been through enough. I was just starting to feel at peace. You might be able to weather all of this because you're focused on doing a job, but I'm not. I feel abandoned, like the prey left behind for the vultures."

Max captured her. Jade shivered against him. This wasn't a panic moment. Not even a decision in anger. She was serious about leaving.

"You want me to resign?"

"I'm not okay with our son being spit on, Max." Jade pushed free of his arms. "If this was a permanent job, something you felt called to do for the rest of your life, then maybe I'd fight to stick it out. But why should we endure this abuse for the next five months only to end up back in Whisper Hollow? This ship is sinking, babe, faster than we can bail the water. I don't want *us* to go down with it."

Max adjusted his cap, bill in the back. *If you felt called . . .* he didn't know it until now, but he *did* feel called. More every day. He couldn't explain it, but this job made a part of his heart beat that he never knew existed.

"So, I'm resigning . . ." Max fixed his attention on her. How could he deny this woman? She forgave him. She raised his son. "Then what do we do?"

"Go back home. Or go to Prairie City, check out the old farmhouse. Or . . . or . . . hike the Adirondacks."

"With a two-year-old?" Now she was talking crazy.

"Okay, then we go west. California. Hawaii," Jade argued, weak and weepy. "Please, Max. This is not worth it."

He exhaled, a lump in his chest. But it was worth it. He *knew* it. Even after Chip Mack's scathing report, Max wanted to dig in and work.

"Answer me this and I won't question you again. Did we miss God in coming here? Or have things just gotten a little hard and—"

"Dangerous."

"All right, but did we miss God?" He held Jade's gaze as she stood in a stiff stance. "I might renege on myself, on you even—but Jade, I'm not reneging on God. Done that too many times in the past. Life is too short to do it again."

Jade focused on fixing Asa's outfit. Adjusting his baby Nike sneakers.

"Babe?" Max studied her. "You want to go home. Or at least . . . leave here?"

She nodded. Once.

"Then I'll resign tomorrow."

"Max—" Hines ran into the office. "Say hey, Jade. Come on out, you got to see this."

"I thought you left."

"Oh, Haley got me all interested in watching film. I'm telling you, she's a football pied piper."

"Where are we going?"

"You'll see."

The music of their footsteps filled the hall. Hines, Max, Jade hoisting Asa. Just outside the field house, in the red and gold summer twilight, a dozen boys stood shoulder-to-shoulder on the edge of the field. The wind swept through the stadium, rattling the bleachers. *They're here. They're here.*

Max scanned their faces. Tucker. Brad. Colton. Dale and Sam. Noah. Excitement traveled through him. But his heart didn't light up until he identified the last man on the field. Calvin.

"Good evening, gentleman. What can I do for you?" Max moved forward, hands anchored on his hips. They dinked around with him for a week? He was going to make them earn admittance to the team.

Calvin stepped forward. "We came out to play, Coach."

"I see. You want to play Warrior ball for me, Coach Hines, and Coach Porter?"

"We do."

"Where have you been all week?"

"I didn't know about it." Tucker jumped forward, panicked.

"Tuck," Calvin reproved in a harsh whisper. "Be cool."

"What made you change your mind, Calvin?"

"You fired the assistant coaches." The others nodded agreement. "And we want to play."

"Then you know this is my team, my way."

"Yes, Coach."

"All right. Two-a-days start in ten days. Seven a.m. and four p.m. You don't show, you don't play." Max glanced at Jade, who stood transfixed.

Calvin nodded, gazing at his boys. "We in, Coach. We all in."

Nineteen

Jade rolled off the air mattress. Asa's sharp knees had drilled her for the last time. He'd crawled into bed sometime last night and curled against Max, raising his knees into her back.

She wanted a real bed. She wanted . . . she didn't know what she wanted. Jade wandered through the house, and gradually onto the porch steps, sitting in the pearlescent glow of the moon falling through the birch tree branches.

She'd dreamed of the events on the field tonight. Seeing the boys' faces and hearing Calvin's, "We all in, Coach."

The look on Max's face? Sheer joy. But she wanted to move. Get out of Dodge. Run. Because she always ran when circumstances squeezed.

In fact, her battle with fear and panic was just another form of running. Or even worse, the fear she *couldn't* outrun. Did she want to run from Colby because of a few rude rednecks? Did she want to wipe out the precious expression she saw on Max's face tonight?

But a kid spit on Asa. How could she reconcile that?

"Jade?" Max's voice drew her from her thoughts. "On the porch again?"

"No place to sit inside." He lowered down next to her. "Besides, it's nice out here. I feel like it's one big room. Grass carpet, starlight ceiling."

"Something on your mind?"

"Besides Asa kneeing me in the back?" She grabbed her hair away from her face.

"I know . . . he got me in the side." Max laughed softly, rubbing his hand right below his ribs.

"I always run, don't I?" Jade said.

"Is that what you think?" Max's eyes appeared like twin stars beneath his dark brow.

"How many games do you think you might have won?"

"I asked God for two wins. For the kids. Give them a spark of hope."

"Two games? That's one more than they won last year."

Max smiled. So white and perfect. So heart-melting. "I thought I'd start small, give God a chance to overcome our odds."

"You mean the God who turned water into wine, who calmed a storm, who walked on water. That God?"

"The God that sent us here."

"You don't want to go, do you?"

"No, I don't. But I can't choose football over you, Jade." Max ran his hand over her hair. "Since I was Asa's age, expectations were put on me. I was the prince of Benson Law. The heir apparent. I didn't mind, really, but I never even considered another career. A lawyer life is a good life. A privileged life. But this coaching job feels like a calling, Jade. It satisfies me in a deep place. I don't feel restless anymore. Today, when Channel 13 ripped me and the team, I felt the stress but my back didn't twinge or tighten once."

"Max." Jade laced her fingers through his. "I don't want to teach Asa to run. I don't want to subject him to my fears."

"But if you don't feel safe, Jade—"

"Earlier, you asked me if I believed God sent us here. I do believe He did, and if I ask you to leave, I'm telling God no. And I don't want to tell Him no."

"Jade." Max brushed his hand along the base of her neck so chills crept down her spine. "Don't mess with me. What are you saying?"

"That I'm going to believe God for two wins."

Max lunged for her and grabbed her in a massive hug, rolling her back on the porch boards. She buried her scream in his chest.

Max rose up on his elbows. "Are you sure?"

"Absolutely."

"Don't move." He scrambled up and into the house, his footsteps thundering. When he returned, something was gleaming in his hand. "I meant to give this to you today. But then we got distracted." A gold chain dangled from his fingertips, glinting in the mosaic light of the heavens. "It's an anklet made of two gold and one platinum braid. One for you, one for me—" Max's soft touch traced Jade's calf as he raised her leg to fasten on the anklet. Shivers fired beneath her skin. "And one for Jesus. The One who holds us together."

"When did you get this? It's beautiful."

"Before we left. I wanted to give it to you as a surprise." Max tenderly kissed the top of her foot, moving his lip to her ankle, then to her shin.

"Max . . ." Jade closed her eyes and let the weight of the chain and the softness of his kisses ease the burden from her heart. It was good to say yes to Jesus as the man she loved embraced her.

"Look, Jade, I'm not a perfect husband. A far from perfect coach. But I have to try."

"Maybe learning to trust God and each other is part of what this journey is all about."

Max brought her to her feet, and taking her in his arms, turned a slow, sexy sway, and sang a soft song in her ear.

you are in my arms
the nightingale tells his fairy tale

Jade closed her eyes and rested against his heartbeat.

When he lifted her chin and softly kissed her, she rose on her toes in response, free from reserve, free from fear. Trust had fully come home.

Twenty

"Offensive line, stay with your blocks." Max moved through the middle of the shredded play and grabbed Brad Schmidt by the shorts, driving him toward the *supposed* hole on the line. "This is where you're supposed to be."

"I know, Coach, but I couldn't get through."

"Exactly. You're supposed to make a way, Brad. You got a tailback coming behind you looking to get into the secondary."

Third week of practice and the boys remained disorganized and unfocused. School had started two days ago, and as much as Max would love to blame the broken plays and lack of energy on schoolwork, he couldn't.

The problem was his stupid coaching. He had no idea what he was doing. Hines offered ideas and advice but he worked too hard at being just an assistant. Well, that worked well if the head coach knew what the flip he was doing.

To compound matters, the boosters and parents sat in the stands every afternoon and watched.

Three weeks of summer practice, including a week of two-a-days, hadn't brought the boys together. He thought they were just feeling their oats, young bucks clashing with young bucks, adjusting to a new set of coaches. But the boys stayed in clusters of class and skill. Rich verses poor. Skill players verses linemen.

The boys came to a PE class Chevy let him have every afternoon during school. Then at four thirty for regular practice. But he had no team. He had nothing. During summer practice, he'd gathered a team of forty. But, only—what?—ten or so had any skill. On either side of the ball.

Max backed off the line. "Let's run it again, Coach Hines. Brad, you're lead tackle. Everyone stay with your assignment until the ball carrier is nothing but heels and elbows for the end zone."

Coach Hines blew his whistle. "On the line." The boys dropped with one hand on the ground. Noah called the play and handed off to Calvin, who ran into a brick wall of defense. Hines whistled the play dead.

Haley praised her defense. "There you go. Way to read the run."

"Do you think they're doing it on purpose?" Max lifted his hat, letting the air cool his head. "Not running the play?" He looked up as Haley joined the huddle. "They're not even trying. We're never going to be ready for our game next week."

Max blew his whistle to gather the team. "Everyone take a knee." He returned to Hines and Haley. "I'm open to any ideas. Our offense is sloppy. We have no kicking game. And that's the first time the D's read any of the plays right, Haley."

"No argument there, Max."

"Coach, do you want me to keep practicing?" Tucker Walberg ran over from the sideline where Max had him doing a hundred kicks off the tee into a net. So far, tripping over his own feet was proving to be Tucker's main athletic ability.

"Take a knee, Tuck." Max ruffled his hair as the teen ran past. "They look defeated and disinterested. Like they don't want to be here."

"They want to be here, Coach." Hines popped his hand on Max's shoulder. "They just don't want to give their hearts. It hurts to lose. It hurts to be laughed at."

"If they gave their hearts, we'd not lose or get laughed at."

"But that's not their experience."

"Yeah, I know. Let's take them in the film room, watch more film. Hines, go over the option again with Noah and Calvin." Max scanned his clipboard. Chevy wanted a report at the end of the week.

"You know what I think?" Haley said. "They've been working hard. Tell them you're proud of them, Max, and send them home."

He regarded her for a moment. She brought a soft touch to the program Max liked. "Listen up." He faced the kneeling team. "You boys have been working hard and we're proud of how hard you're working."

A rumble rose from deep in the group and Calvin Blue popped to his feet. Noah Warren jumped up to face him, hands fisted.

"Say that to me again, Noah," Calvin growled.

"Hines—" Max motioned for him to go left while he moved right.

"I said you're a show-off, Blue." Noah pushed the tailback in the chest. "You've got no team spirit."

"And you do? Ooh, look at me everyone." Calvin mimed a pass. "I can throw the ball a country mile. Great, you can throw a long bomb but you can't pitch it five yards."

"If you're so good, you QB, Blue."

"I can't. I have to run the ball 'cause all y'all girls are too slow. I can't be the *whole* team, Warren."

"Who you calling a girl?" Noah shoved Calvin again.

"You. Want to do something about it?"

Brad stood with Calvin. Colton lined up with Noah. Max stayed behind the circle. Top dogs duking it out. This was good. The underlying tension was finally erupting.

"Look, Noah, all you got to do is run the play Coach calls. Don't improvise and do something different. Simple, my granny could do it. She could pass better too."

Oh, Calvin, bad move. Max moved through the boys just as Noah threw the first punch. Hines blew his whistle. "Focus. Focus. Eyes on me."

He waded through the team, grabbing the boys by the pads and tossing them out of the way.

But the fight was on. The boys imploded and Max saw nothing but heels and elbows.

"Break it up." Max worked through the wall of smell and sweat. Tomorrow, a hygiene talk.

Hines whistled his way through, reaching in, grabbing a kid and tossing him out of the pile. But he jumped right back in. Unlocked tension was a frightening force.

Then the oddest sound arrested them all. A shrill whistle and the bass bellow of Haley. "Enough!" She surged through the pile, yanking boys by the collar and tossing them to the ground like they were paper. "Get on your feet and start running." The boys stared at her, panting. "I said run. Now! Don't stop until my whistle blows. If you do, you're giving me fifty push-ups. Better hope your mamas are keeping dinner warm—this is going to be a long run." Haley looked back at Max with a wink. "I said run."

The boys jumped together and started for the track.

Hines bent forward, hands on his knees, panting. "If you have any lingering regret about her, Max, you best give it up now."

Max watched Haley run alongside the boys, backward, striding in time with them, ordering them forward.

"Oh, it's gone, Hines. Completely gone."

Twenty-one

When the truck headlights fired through the living room window, Jade jumped up from the sofa. Sofa!

The furniture arrived a day after she'd surrendered her fears and welcomed trust into her heart. Then Ellen Feinberg, a woman she met at the church Mom's Meeting, called for a playdate. Her youngest was the same age as Asa. They had three playdates scheduled for the next week—and Ellen didn't seem to despise Max for firing the old coaches and hiring new.

Tonight, pasta for the Warriors' head coach. Anything Italian fit his favorite-food bill. Steam rose from the boiling water as Jade lifted the lid and dumped in a handful of whole wheat spaghetti. Snapping open the oven, she slid in the buttered bread to warm. Max loved Italian—she loved bread.

"Asa, Daddy's home." He jumped up from playing with his cars in the dining room and thundered into the living room, flopping belly-first on the ottoman. Jade shook her head. For that boy, it was critical to run fast and loud.

Jade tugged her phone from her pocket and aimed the camera at Asa's silhouette against the pink and purple twilight window.

"Asa." Max swept his son into his arms. "Were you watching me?" A tall someone trailed behind Max. Jade recognized Tucker Walberg. "Look who I found." Max hooked his arm around the teen. "The Warriors' future star kicker."

"Well, future star kicker, I hope you like spaghetti."

"Yes, ma'am." He stood kind of hunched together just inside the living room, a white Walmart shopping bag hanging from his fist. He appeared to be both terrified and uncomfortable.

"Make yourself at home. You can shower right in there." Max pointed to the hallway, then motioned for Jade to follow him to the bedroom.

"You know about his mom—Mariah?" Max kicked off his sneakers and pulled his shirt over his head, tossing it into the laundry basket.

"Yeah, I've heard things."

"I'm driving home from practice, going over the day." He made a face. "It was a doozy. The boys got in a fistfight."

"Max, no. What happened?" Jade perched on the edge of their new bed.

"Just a bunch of young bucks duking it out." He grinned. "Old Hines and I are weeding through the pile, trying to break things up when Haley comes out with this big booming voice. You've never seen teen boys move so fast. 'Run until I tell you to stop. Go. Now.'" Max imitated her, stamping his foot. "They must have gone three miles before she blew the whistle. Ran the fight right out of them. The boys went dragging home."

"Go, Haley."

"But as I start home, I see this kid walking down the road."

"Tucker." Jade said.

"You got it. I thought, why is he walking home? He's got to be beat. Didn't any of the boys give him a ride? I pulled over." Max joined Jade on the bed. "You should see where he lives."

"I heard from Dr. Gelman. A pretty bad part of town."

"A trailer park from the '70s. When I dropped him off, it was obvious no one was home. He pretended it was all good, but I could hear his stomach rumbling."

"Oh, Max."

"So as I'm leaving, I check on him through the rearview. Know what he was doing? Sitting on those metal front steps, you know the kind I'm talking about, pulling his books from his bag. He had to be starving and exhausted, and it hit me, he was locked out. So I backed up and told him I needed company for a Walmart run. I drove through McDonald's on the way. He ate two quarter-pounders with cheese and fries. Ten bucks says he eats three big help-ings of spaghetti."

"Sucker bet. I'm not taking it." Jade caressed Max's cheek. "You're a good man, Maxwell Benson."

"Not really. Just trying to do a few things right. When I was his age, I ate a whole large pepperoni pizza for snack after practice. And two or three help-ings of whatever Mom made for dinner."

"Speaking of dinner." Jade rolled off the bed. "Max, do you really think it's that bad for Tuck?"

"Yeah, I do. I bought him some toiletries and clothes at Walmart. You should've seen his face. He kept telling me he couldn't take the stuff, but he seemed so amazed, like no one had ever shopped for him before. I told him he was welcome here anytime. Is that okay?"

"You don't even have to ask."

"Good, because if his mom doesn't call him back, he's spending the night."

Jade finished prepping dinner while Max showered. When Tucker emerged from the guest bathroom, his face scrubbed, his wet hair combed in place, he had the Walmart bag in one hand and a wad of clothes in the other.

Jade reached for them. "I got a load of laundry to do. Mind if I throw these in?"

"No, ma'am." His sweet voice matched his expression. "I appreciate you letting me crash here. My mom must be working."

"You don't have a key to your house?"

"No, ma'am. There's only one and the lock is so old we can't find anyone to make us a new key. Not that we can afford one anyway."

"I see." Jade turned for the laundry room. "You're welcome here anytime, Tucker."

About dinner, Max was right. Kind of. Tucker ate three helpings of spaghetti, plus one. Four helpings. That'd feed Jade for a week.

Mariah never called, so Tucker left word with his granny that he was sleeping at Coach's house.

Jade watched him as he played with Asa until she put him in bed, then Tucker sat at the dining room table doing his homework, looking up from time to time to tell Jade how much he liked the house. She made up his bed on the couch, and at ten, he closed his books and said good night.

Wandering into Max's office—the third bedroom—Jade slipped her arms around his shoulders. He watched a DVD of yesterday's practice, frowning.

"He can move in as far as I'm concerned."

Max hit Pause and glanced up at her. "Tucker?"

"Who else? Of course, Tucker. He's so sweet, Max."

"He's a good kid. Can't kick a football worth a darn, but I'd love to have more boys with his heart and eagerness." He kept one eye on the video while he reached around and brought Jade to his lap.

She curled against him and rested her cheek in the strong curve of his neck. "He reminds me of me. How I felt all those lonely days when Mama took off, leaving Granny to watch us."

"Ah, come on, we can't get that play right." Max spoke to the screen, resting his hand on her hip and backing up the video again.

Jade loved the feel of his chest beneath her hand and how his soapy shower still lingered on his skin. His love, constant but flawed, lifted her out of fear, shining a light in the dark corners of her heart.

His love brought her here, to Texas, to a level place. Brought her Tucker. The moment she saw the boy standing behind Max, just inside the door, love had pinged between her ribs. It only took a second and four plates of spaghetti for her to fall in love, again, with another son from a different mother.

Until this moment, the whole head-coaching gig felt surreal—as if Max meandered through an Indiana Jones dream. The hours he'd spent with Hines and Haley designing plays, developing strategy, and watching film consumed him enough that he didn't have to think about *this* moment—the one where he took his place on the sidelines and realized he'd bet his, Asa's, and Jade's futures on a whim and a prayer.

Nerves twisted his gut so tight he couldn't draw a deep breath. Everything called his confidence into account. Opening game against the formidable Canyon Eagles . . . and Carter Davis. But the energy in the air? It was intoxicating.

The marching band boosted the excitement with their drumbeats and the braided sound of woodwinds and brass. Expectant Warrior fans flowed through the stadium like a red and gold river.

Max cinched his hand into a fist. Then released it, stretching his fingers. He paced, watching Hines and Haley warm up the team. Finally, *finally*, the team had started to jell. The offense clicked. The defense understood their strategy.

The Warriors were as ready for this opening game as they'd ever be this season. Max prayed. Max hoped. He brushed the perspiration from his brow. It was a *hot* Texas Friday night.

This wasn't goofing around with a few boys at the Outpost. This was real. Texas high school football. Game on.

He searched the stands for Jade and Asa. When the dark sheen of her hair glinted in the bright field lights, his heart rattled his ribs. He'd not be standing here without her. It'd take the rest of his life to prove his gratitude. Jade smiled and waved, pointing Max out to Asa. Max raised his hand to hers.

Dr. Julie Gelman squeezed in on Jade's right. She also caught Max looking and waved.

"Max! Oh Max!" Brenda Karlin stood on the other side of the fence with her sidekick, Bit Wyatt. They were decked from head to toe in Warrior wear.

Max acknowledged them with a wave, but Brenda insisted with a fanatical arm gesture that he meet her at the fence. He jogged over. If other fans saw this, he'd never get back to the sidelines. "Yeah, Brenda, I'm kind of busy."

She smacked her hand on his shoulder, closed her eyes, and tilted her head toward the sky. "Lord God in heaven, I know you love Max, I know you love Texas, and I know you love football because we love football. Give Max grace, wisdom and oh, dear Lord, if it's not too much, a win. This year." Brenda's sincere prayer warmed the chill off Max's nerves. "Now, go get 'em, Coach." Brenda shoved him back and walked off, calling out to another Warrior fan. Bit passed Max, smiling, and whispered, "Amen."

Back on the sideline, Max checked the scoreboard. Five minutes to kickoff. Hines and Haley had their starters huddled up for last-minute instructions. Then Max called the whole team together.

"This is our game. Our team. Our season. It's not your granddaddy's or daddy's, or your brother's or cousin's. *We* are the Warriors. Wins and losses of the past mean nothing. Warrior tradition starts over tonight. I'm proud of you boys. You worked hard all week. The coaches and I couldn't have asked for more." Max thrust his fist in the air with confidence. "Warriors on three." The boys raised their fists and leaned toward Max. "One, two, three . . ."

"Warriors!"

The huddle broke and Haley gathered her defense. They were on the field first.

When Brad Schmidt walked past, Max collared the boy by his shoulder pads. "Brad, who's your quarterback?"

"Noah Warren."

"What's your job?" A decent-size kid with strength and quickness, Brad lacked the killer instinct.

"Protect him."

"Right. You block and tackle like Coach Hines told you. Got it?"

Brad nodded. "Yes, Coach."

"All right, good job." Max released him and found Tucker, who was practicing for the kickoff. His weak, nervous kicks mocked Max's confidence. Hours of practice and drills boiled down to this—opening their first game with their weakest player.

"Tuck, remember what you've practiced. Plant your foot and follow through. Right?"

"Coach, I can't—"

"If you say you can't, then you won't. Be on the team, Tucker. You *can*. Focus on your job, not on your fear."

He swallowed a shallow breath, nodding.

"Go do your job." Max smacked Tucker on the back and watched him run onto the field, the reverberation of his tone vibrating in his chest. Gruff and terse. *Don't take your nerves out on the boys.* But some of them, Tucker, needed to man up a bit, didn't they? Max paced past Hines. "Think we have a snowball's chance of winning?"

"I'm praying for a snowball's chance of getting out of here alive."

Max stopped. "That's all the confidence you have?"

"I do have a lot of faith."

Max broke, grinning. "That'll do, Hines."

The ref's whistle blew and the Warrior kickoff squad lined up on the field, a jittery, bouncing Tucker waiting to kick the ball. Max hunched forward, hands on his thighs. *Come on, Tucker.* He struck his kicking pose, then stepped one, two, three, drawing back his leg . . .

Tuck's foot thumped the ball and it took a low, low arc down the field. Ten yards. Tucker barely booted it ten yards. Max dropped his chin to his chest.

The Eagles landed on the ball at their own forty-yard line.

Haley shoved her defenders onto the field, shouting last-minute encouragement, her red ponytail flipping around her shoulders.

"Let's go. Bring the D, Warriors." Max walked the sidelines. The boys kneeled, focused on the game, just like Hines taught them. Max appreciated the man who brought so much texture and discipline to the team. Things he never would have thought to do.

Max bent down to Tucker's ear. "What happened?"

"I don't know, Coach. I thought I—"

Max turned his head to face him. "You know how to do this. You've practiced for hours. This is your time to step up, Tucker. Focus."

"I don't think I can do it."

"Then you won't." Max exhaled as he stood. "And you'll let yourself and the team down. So you just decided what kind of Warrior football player you want to be."

The Eagles scored easily on their first possession. Max and Hines's Warrior offense went to work. When the Eagles punted, Calvin Blue caught the ball on the twenty and ran, juking and jiving for a twenty-five-yard return. The stadium went wild, everyone on their feet.

When he ran to the sidelines to huddle with Max for the offense call, Max peered at him through his helmet. "Tone it down, hotshot. But good job."

Noah led the O to the field and started the series on the Eagles forty-five yard line.

"Now just run the plays," Max called, pacing. "Focus. Keep your heads in the game. This is our time." Did he sound calm and in command? Because his knees bobbled and threatened to drop him to the field in a quivering puddle.

The Warriors and Eagles duked it out in a defensive battle, holding the score at seven zip, until late in the second quarter when Noah found Calvin for a touchdown.

The team exploded off the sideline and onto the field. The Warrior fans rocked the house as the pep band lit the night with a victory rhythm.

Max glanced at Tucker. Eyes ahead, the kid stood frozen, helmet in his hands, instead of prepping for the PAT. "Hines," Max said, "let's go for two."

"You're the coach." Hines called in the play.

Noah found Calvin again in the far corner of the end zone, and when the buzzer sounded for halftime, the Warriors went into the locker room ahead of the Eagles by one point.

They were on fire, lighting up the locker room with exuberance, slapping each other high- and low-fives. When Max faced them, the boys talked at once.

"Coach, we can win this. We can."

"Calvin is faster than their whole team put together."

"All right, all right. Good job. See, I told you. We can win. We're not losers. This is what *team* is about. See the power you have when you play as one? Now, we need to make some adjustments . . ."

Max let the boys talk, one at a time, to share what was happening on the field. Then he made adjustments and challenged the boys to stay with their assignments, not to get intimidated. He pointed out a few tactics of the Eagles, then let Hines and Haley have the floor.

"I tell you what," Hines said, stepping forward. "What I saw on that field the first half was every bit as good as the championship teams I coached. I'm proud of you boys."

During the half, the Eagles also made adjustments and in the third quarter, wore the Warriors out with their quick defense and no huddle offense. Yet as the fourth quarter wound down to the final two minutes, the Eagles only led the Warriors by two: 16–14.

The Warriors had the ball on their own fifty, and the boys in red and gold were ablaze with confidence. First down. Noah dropped the ball and barely recovered his own fumble.

Second down. Calvin broke a tackle and barreled into the Eagles' secondary, running for thirty yards before the Eagles safety popped him out of bounds.

Third down. Big play for the red zone. Noah faked to Billings, then swept left to find Calvin cutting across to a wide-open center field. The ball sailed toward him in a perfect spiral.

The fans roared. *Come on, come on . . .* Max's fingers dug into his palms. Calvin ate up the yards with his quick, long stride. The NFL should execute this good.

The Eagles' cornerback shot toward Calvin like a blue rocket and just as he did a Superman into the end zone, stretching for the catch, the Eagles' defender batted the ball away. *No, no, no!*

The boys slammed into each other and crashed onto the ground. Max thundered onto the field. "Ref, where's my flag? Where's my flag? Interference."

"Max, Max." Hines grabbed his shirt and dragged back. "The boys are watching. Come on now—that was a clean play. No interference."

"That kid was all over Calvin. Where's my flag, ref?" He hated missed calls. "The boys deserved that one, Hines. That was six. A beautiful play." Max jutted toward the refs. "Cheaters."

"You want to run a mile, Coach? Keep it up." Hines shoved him toward the sidelines and called a time-out. "What do you want to do? Try for six one last time or call in the kicking team? It's fourth down . . . our last chance to score." He advised Max with his tone. "A field goal puts us ahead by one. Haley's D's been doing its job all night." Hines regarded Max with expectation.

"Coach, did you see me?" Calvin jumped in front of Max, mimicking his jump for the ball. "It was right here." He made a T with his left palm on top of his right fingers. "Can we run that again? I'll get it next time."

"Coach." Noah joined the confab. "I hesitated. Calvin would've had it otherwise." Ah, the nectar of teamwork. "He had that corner beat. I know dead to rights he can outrun Cooper Fielding. I've seen them at track meets."

The stadium rumbled. The drums resounded. Shouts rained down from the fans:

"Go for it. Give it to Blue."

"You stink, Benson."

"Let's go, Warriors."

"Don't put the kicker in, he'll miss."

Max's blood pumped. He was fifty seconds and twenty yards from winning his first ever opening game and breaking the Warriors worst losing streak in their history. He glanced down the sidelines. Tucker hid at the end of the row, staring out over the field, knees locked, gripping his helmet by the face mask.

"Noah and Calvin have been clicking all night, Max," Hines said. "We should go for it."

Max studied their faces. He had no doubt Calvin and Noah could run it again. But . . . this was about building a team.

"It's our first game. Let's see what we're made of." Max twisted toward Tucker. "Walberg, warm up. You're going in. Haley, get your boys ready to hold down their offense for forty seconds."

Noah exhaled with a *doggone* expression. Calvin started to protest, but one glance from Max and he clamped shut. He sprinted toward Tucker.

"Come on, Walberg, you can do this. You must have kicked that ball into the net at least a thousand times."

"Hines, you think Tuck can kick it?" Max said.

"Doesn't matter what I think, Coach. It matters what Tucker thinks. Hines popped his hands as Tucker ran toward them. "Come on, Tuck, this is every kicker's dream."

Dread sank through Max's belly. He could feel Tucker's terror. He glanced over his shoulder. Jade was on her feet, balled up fists at her face, her intense gaze toward the field. Tucker had spent almost every evening of the last week at their house, and Jade quickly had become his surrogate mom.

Max peered through Tucker's face mask. "You can do this. Split the uprights. Plant your back foot, square your hips toward the goal, and follow through. You've done it a million times."

He nodded, swallowing, but terror buoyed in his eyes. "I'll try."

"Go *do.*"

The kicking team lined up. Channel 13's cameraman ran past. The ref blew his whistle. Max took a knee and watched. *Come on, Tucker. Come on.* Max's neck tensed. His back ached with the weight and expectation of every watching Warrior fan.

"What are you doing, Coach?"

"He can't kick, Benson. Put in Warren and Blue."

"Come on, Tucker."

The center hiked the ball. Noah caught and teed it. Tucker strode forward. His form looked good. He was long and lean. *Come on, come on . . . connect with the ball.*

Then it happened. So fast. Tucker's plant foot twisted and his kicking leg sailed high and wide over the ball, nearly hitting Noah in the head. On reflex he ducked and let go of the ball.

Tucker spun a complete circle, his legs twisting like a pretzel, and hit the ground flat on his back, a mournful *oomph* coming from his chest.

A collective *Oooooh* rose from the stands, followed by a barrage of laughter and boos. Max buried his face in his hands. *Good grief, Charlie Brown.*

When Tucker didn't get up, Max jogged onto the field and bent over him. "Are you all right?"

"Everyone's laughing at me, Coach." Tuck squeezed his eyes tight and leaked a tear to his cheek.

"Get up. Shake it off." Max tendered his tone and offered the boy a hand. Putting his arm around him, they walked in solidarity to the sidelines. The players cut a wide berth.

Forty seconds later, the buzzer ended his misery. The Eagles won by two. Max jogged toward the field house where the press and the boosters waited, most likely to demand an account of his final play.

Twenty-Two

The red digits on the bedside clock beamed two a.m. Jade rolled onto her side and burrowed under the covers. The first Sunday of October had arrived with nippy temperatures. She needed to sleep. She'd been so tired lately, keeping up with Asa, trying to work around Max's schedule.

Ever since losing the first game, Max left the house early and came home late. She stretched her hand to touch his back. But his side of the bed was vacant. Sitting up, she shoved her hair from her eyes. A weary wave washed over her and she felt queasy from sitting up too fast. It'd been happening lately with all the late nights and early mornings. "Max?"

After Asa turned two in August, he refused to take naps. It was a sad day when she gave up trying to make him. He was growing up too fast. Someday he'd long for the beauty and luxury of sleep. And Jade already knew she'd remind him of this. Meanwhile, she never seemed to have a moment's rest and she was beyond exhausted.

Slipping on her robe, Jade turned on the hall light and picked her way through the living room. Calvin, Noah, Brad, and Tucker had surprised them last night, showing up unannounced, piling out of Noah's truck. They spent the evening tossing the ball around with Max, talking over the game.

Jade baked two batches of brownies—last weekend United Stores had Betty Crocker on sale two for one—and invited them to crash at the house if their folks didn't mind. She certainly didn't. Calvin snoozed on the sofa. Brad curled up on the chaise and ottoman. Tucker and Noah were burrowed into sleeping bags on the floor.

Jade picked up an empty glass by Noah's head. She loved the melody of the boys' excited voices and boisterous laughter. How they paid attention to Asa, letting him play the game with them. He was so cute trying to run with the ball. He could barely grip it with both hands.

"Max?" She peered into his office. Empty. Jade shoved Asa's door open. He'd kicked off his covers so she straightened the blanket. His toes stretched the ends of his pajama feet. She'd have to get him new ones soon. Tomorrow. She checked his diaper. With the hubbub of the boys in the house, she'd missed how Asa connived each one of them to fill his juice cup over and over. The empty Juicy Juice bottle gave him away. "Sneaky stinker." She kissed his soft, puffy cheek.

Oh, Asa. Surely you are Max's son. Jade sat on the edge of the bed. It was so easy to put Taylor and Rice out of her head. Most days she completely forgot Asa was not born of her.

Aiden had e-mailed the other day. *Did you tell him? Tell him.*

But she couldn't devastate Max when she didn't know if there was an ounce of truth to Taylor's story. Obviously Taylor didn't find the paternity test among Rice's papers. Asa was two now. If Landon had wanted to challenge the birth certificate, he should've done it before the two-year window closed. He should've followed up on the paternity test he took when Asa was born.

Besides, Max had enough stress. After a promising season start against Canyon, the Warriors had their fifth loss in a row Friday night. Max didn't get home until after midnight. When he crawled into bed, she asked where he'd been.

"Talking to boosters and the A.D." His next sound was a deep snore.

The next morning, Jade watched him carefully and checked his eyes. He didn't appear to be falling into his old pain med ways. But the wear and tear of the season showed.

As Jade left Asa's room, cold air swirled in the living room and bit at her ankles. Cinching her robe tighter, she went to the front door. It stood slightly ajar.

"Max?" She stepped into the shadows. He sat on the steps, arms on his knees, staring into the dark. Jade shivered as she sat next to him. "Aren't you cold?" He wore his jeans and T-shirt from yesterday. No jacket. Clearly, he'd not even gone to bed.

"No," he said. "It feels good."

Jade snuggled against his broad back. "The boys are sleeping like logs."

"I bet. We work them hard through the week."

"You work hard too. Asa and I barely see you." She shivered when the wind hissed along the grass and over the porch boards.

"I have to make this team come together." The burden of winning football games weighed down his words.

"By yourself? What about the rest of the coaches? Isn't football about a team?"

"Until a losing season. Until the boosters and the school go bonkers and demand the head coach's head on a platter."

"Are they demanding your head on a platter?" Jade bent to see his face in the half moonlight. He was a different Max than the one who sat with her on this porch two months ago. "Brenda and Bit think you're aces." Jade imitated Brenda's high, cowgirl pitch. "We just love that coach."

"Yeah, well, they don't carry much weight against an oh-and-five team." Max shot off the steps, straining his words through a taut jaw. "I *need* to win. I can't figure out what I'm doing wrong."

"What makes you think you're doing anything wrong?"

He whirled around. "Five losses. Last week we didn't score until the fourth quarter. We couldn't convert the extra point. We miss field goal opportunities because we have no kicker."

"Shh, Max, Tucker will hear you."

"Good, he needs to man up and play the game. He does have the skill underneath all his clumsiness and insecurity."

"Then you help him believe in himself."

"I'm a coach, not a psychologist. That's Haley's territory. Bobby's in my office every Monday morning and every Friday afternoon, flipping through the playbook, wondering about running the spread more or suggesting trick plays. Trick plays? We can't execute simple, plain ol' ordinary, everyday plays."

"You're a new coach, Max. Bobby is just—"

"Up to something. That's what he is. Up to something. Meanwhile, Chevy just lets me be. Checks in once a week like a big brother. Why in the world did they hire me?"

"Stop asking that question. It's too late. They hired you and here you are. Here we are. In our house are four boys very much impacted by you. What if God sent you here to win hearts, not games?"

"Unfortunately, I don't get paid or earn respect because the boys like me. I'm expected to win games, Jade. The boys are here because it's Sunday night and they're bored." Max dismissed her with a wave. "Or looking to get out of homework."

"Is that what you think? Max, babe, they connect with you. Tucker worships you. He watches your every move. You just might be the first and only decent man in his life." Jade gripped Max by the shoulders, digging in her fingers. "You're winning with *them*. Doesn't that count?" She couldn't see his expression in the dark, but his cold silence and stiff stance reminded her of lawyer Max. Of the old Max. "Are you having back pain?"

His chest collapsed with an exhale and broke away from her. "No. Do I look like I'm having back pain?"

"No, but you're stressed. It's a trigger. The Max Benson I know—"

"You've never known this Max."

"Yeah? Well, I'd like to know him better but he's not around much."

He started for the steps. "It's late."

"You don't have to walk through this alone, Max." She paused at the door. "I'm here. Hines and Haley are here. Axel's only twenty minutes away."

He hooked his arm around her waist and led her into the yard. "Last Thursday, I'd left the field house to come home around nine or so. I got all the way out to the truck when I realized I'd left the game DVD in the player. I wanted to review it one more time. Amarillo's a good team and they have a lot of plays to track. Just as I get to the door, I see two people in the hallway. It's Hines and Bobby."

"Hines and Bobby?"

"They shook hands and walked to the film room. I turned around for the truck. Didn't even go back in."

"I don't understand. Bobby is the A.D. Hines is a coach. They've known each other a long time. What's the big deal?"

Max sighed. "I think Bobby is the reason this program has faltered. He says things about when his dad and granddad coached Warrior football. How legacies need to be kept. So, I did some digging and Bobby's dad, Coach Molnar, was fired and replaced with the great Coach Burke, Haley's dad. After he retired, there was some debate about hiring Bobby Molnar as head coach but something or someone kept it from happening. He stayed on as A.D., though, hiring coaches and getting them fired."

Jade snorted a snicker, popping her hand over her mouth. "What? This is crazy."

"Yeah, well, five coaches in six years is crazy. Come on."

"They were sane enough to hook and reel you in, Coach."

"Chevy did, yeah. But there's something . . ." Max bounced his fist in the air, thinking. "There's something going on. This program doesn't smell like manure just from losing seasons."

"But the program has the best of everything, Max."

"Of course, the A.D. signs off on the budget. Bobby has the wealthiest booster in his pocket. He's keeping the facility up for when he takes over."

"So you think Hines is conspiring with Bobby against you? Why? Hines loves you."

"Then why the clandestine meeting? Hines supposedly left hours earlier. He's a former Warrior champ just like Bobby. Maybe championship loyalty runs thicker than new coach loyalty? Maybe Hines bellied up to my term as coach, cheering me on as I fired the old assistants so he could help usher in Bobby's reign."

"Okay, now you've crossed over to conspiracy theory. I'm going back inside. I'm freezing." Jade paused in front of her husband. "You're not a lawyer working an angle for your client anymore, Max. You're a coach. For a season. Do your job. Who cares what Hines and Bobby do in the dark of night?"

"I want to win, Jade. I have to win. I can't win if my coaches are against me."

"You have to win? Max, no, you don't. You just have to do your best and love these boys. Isn't that why Chevy wanted you over any other coach? You care. What's this really about?"

"Because, Jade, I fail. Golden boy Benson is a myth. Sure, I can be dashing and charming, I can make an argument with the best of them. I can give the Democrats spin lessons. But at the end of the day, I'm a failure."

"Evidence, please."

"I failed my parents with getting addicted. Failed the firm, thus my father.

I failed Rice and Asa. Worse, I failed you." *Oh, not so much, Max.* "And I've failed the Lord."

"I'm not a biblical scholar, but I'm pretty sure God says He works things together for the good of those who love Him. The only way you fail is if you stop trusting Him. If you stop trying. Is that what you're doing?"

"No, but I sure as heck would like to know what Hines was doing talking to Bobby."

"Then ask him." Jade folded her arms across her shivering torso. In their four-year relationship, Max had been the strong one. Jade spoke her mind, but she rarely confronted him. Even when she suspected he was using. Then he confessed about Asa. Tonight, she had a new revelation. Her husband *needed* her.

"And tip him off? No way."

"So you'd rather live with this fantasy in your head? What if that handshake was nothing more than swapping usher duties on a Sunday morning?"

"That's a phone call, Jade. An oh-by-the-way after practice. That's not a dark meeting after hours. They are up to something. It's all starting to make sense now."

"Ooh, a conspiracy," Jade whispered in a low sleuth tone. "They're setting you up to fail."

Max snatched her up by her arms, raising her off the ground. "Is that what you think?"

Jade burst out laughing. "You can't be serious. No." Max let her go. "They are not conspiring. Babe, you're turning into me. A frightened worrier." She grabbed his hands and tugged him toward the house. "Come on, I'll make you forget your conspiracy theory."

"Yeah?" There. His saucy grin. "What do you have in mind?"

"I don't know, but it's under this robe."

Max charged her, lifting her into his arms so she laughed, a crisp melody in the cold night.

"Brenda, hey, it's Max Benson. Yeah, right. *Coach*." Max rolled his eyes as he took the chair behind his desk. He'd slept in, snuggled next to Jade, deciding to let his Monday morning warm up a bit before he faced it. "Listen, I was wondering if you could do me a favor?"

"Coach, anything for you."

"It's kind of a DL matter. Can you be discreet?"

"You have come to the right place. Discreet is my middle name. Lay it on me, shug."

Max grinned, peering at his office door, hearing the stirrings of Hines just down the hall. "I knew I could count on you."

There was a sliver of the afternoon left and Colby Grounds was quiet, with only a couple of walk-in customers. Steam hissed as the barista cleaned the cappuccino machine. At a table by the door, Jade drummed her fingers and watched for Brenda.

She'd called Ellen Feinberg to see if Asa could play with her son for a couple of hours. Ever gracious, Ellen said, "Why certainly." Jade sweetened the deal by offering to watch Ellen's three next time she wanted a spa day or date night.

Once that was set up, Jade called Brenda for a meeting. Sipping a hot cocoa, Jade watched the street. Colby's downtown reflected the old west with its wide streets. Fall already tipped the trees with a deep gold and brilliant red. Even the season favored the Warriors' colors.

More and more the days dawned cold. Today Jade had fixed all the boys a hot breakfast before sending them off to school. Asa ran to the window, charging the ottoman, and watched them leave.

Max had moved slow, called his dad to say hello. Barely talked football. All the more reason Jade needed to talk to Brenda Karlin.

Two o'clock. Brenda assured her she was never late. Jade turned to check on Asa before remembering he was with Ellen. She felt free yet out of balance without him. What did she do before he came into her world?

"Girl, I'm not late. I'm right on time." Brenda popped onto the high stool next to Jade with a huff. She wore her usual dark suit but today with a bright yellow silk blouse. She motioned to the barista. "Debbie, darling, I'll have a tall nonfat latte and a panini. Jade, what are you having?"

"Hot cocoa." She hugged her mug with both hands. Her stomach retched a bit. "I'm not hungry today." The pace of their life wore on her. She wondered today if she was getting the flu.

"Well," Brenda said and exhaled, "isn't this my day? First Max, then you."

"Max called you?" Jade leaned over her cocoa. He must have been thinking the same thing. *Great minds . . .*

"It was nothing." Brenda fussed with her wallet, a flush on her cheeks. "He was just asking for some . . . snacks . . . for the boys after practice. Maybe do a pancake breakfast this fall. We've not done one of those in so long."

"He didn't ask you about Bobby Molnar?" Jade got right to business.

"Bobby Molnar? No, shug. Why would he ask me about old Bobby?" She muffled her laugh. "You know, in high school the kids used to call him BM." She accented her laugh with a hand slap to the table.

"Did he ask you about Hines? Or Chevy?" Was she exposing her husband instead of helping him? A bit of dread swirled in her sour stomach.

"He surely didn't." The real estate mogul scowled. "Should he? What's on your mind, Jade, and don't tell me nothing."

Jade inhaled deep. She raised her cocoa for a drink, but the sweet fragrance made her lip curl.

"It's just . . ." She breathed deep.

"You okay, darling?" Brenda took her latte from Debbie and handed her a couple of bills.

"Thanks, Mrs. Karlin."

"Yeah, just tired," Jade said.

"You look it. Now, what's bothering you? Tell ol' Brenda."

"Do you think Bobby believes in Max as head coach?"

"Bobby believes in himself." Brenda sipped her latte and waved to someone out the window. "Helen Alba. I'll be. If that woman don't spend a thousand bucks a month on clothes. Hey, Helen, you clotheshorse. Your shoes don't match your dress, shug."

Jade pinched a grin. "You don't get along with Helen?"

"Oh sure, and don't worry, I've called her a clotheshorse to her face so many times she's starting to believe me. Now, Bobby. I wouldn't worry none about him. The boosters support Max."

"All of them?"

"Well, the ones I influence do. Principal Buchholz supports him. Chevy really wants Max to succeed. He cut everyone out of the hiring process, even BM." She snorted into her latte. "It takes time to build a team. We're not going to let Bobby run roughshod over him like he's done the other coaches. I reckon you don't know Bob's story, but he's always wanted to be the Warriors' head coach. Mercy, some dreams never die."

"Roughshod? Like how?"

"Oh, the usual stuff. Making life difficult. Riding the coaches so they quit. One coach Bobby hired knowing he had infractions against him."

"Why isn't Bobby coach?" The perfect motive to sabotage Max.

"Chevy won't let him. Neither will half the boosters." Brenda leaned over the table. "My half. Rick and his consort can stomp around all they want, but we're not going to cave." She smacked the table.

"Why can't he coach? Why doesn't he go to another school?"

"See, the Molnar men were Warrior coaches for three generations." Brenda leaned toward Jade, hand to the side of her face. "But Bobby's got that awful temper. Hit a kid down in Plano. Oh look, there's Lisa Webb, one more face-lift and her eyes will squirt right out her head."

"He hit a kid? Brenda, focus." Jade snapped her fingers.

"That's the scuttlebutt. Nothing came of it. Got kind of swept under the rug." She rolled her eyes. "Big surprise. Anyhoo, the Plano school released him or he resigned, another mystery, and Bobby pulled a few strings to get hired on here as athletic director. Which really is perfect for him, you know? He's involved but not *involllvved.*" Brenda rolled the word with her tongue.

"So, he doesn't want to coach anymore?" Jade blinked. A greasy mist floating in the coffee shop from the panini maker fogged her senses. She breathed back the sting of bile.

"Oh, he's dying to coach. Sure. He thinks Chevy will cave and see the wisdom of carrying on the Molnar coaching tradition. Chevy may look like a pointy-headed intellectual but he's got aces in places Bobby don't even have place." Wink. Nod. Brenda went on with the coaching history. Molnars to the Burkes to a string of failures.

To Max.

Oh, poor Max.

". . . biding his time until the Warriors called him up to head coach, but then he popped that kid in Plano and"—Brenda dusted her fingers together—"gave Chevy the perfect excuse. The Molnar style of coaching would never fly in today's culture." Debbie arrived with Brenda's panini. "Thank you, shugpie. I was about to pass out from hunger." Brenda passed over a couple more bills. "Keep the change."

"Do you think he'd sabotage Max so he could get the job? I mean, if he'd counted on Chevy to hire him . . . is there some condition or whatever that would give him the job?"

"Well, if the head coach gets fired in the middle of the season, then the A.D. can take over."

"Fire? They'd fire Max in the middle of the season?"

"Shug, don't worry about it. We won't let that happen." Brenda bit the corner of her sandwich. "This is fabulous. Are you sure you don't want a bite?"

"No." Oh no . . . Jade scooted her chair downwind. "Appreciate it, though."

Debbie dropped a quarter in the jukebox and a sultry voice filled the coffee shop.

"So what do you need me to do, hon?"

"Can you find out if Bobby is scheming to fire Max? Or set him up? Like, is he really in cahoots with anyone?"

Brenda wiped the corners of her mouth. "Now that would take some smarts and I'm not sure our dear A.D. is quite so clever. But you leave it to me." She winked, then rolled her eyes when her phone pinged. "Oh mercy, ain't no place to run and hide these days. It's Bit. Can't be late for a client meeting." She shoved away from the table. "I'll let you know what I find out."

"Please, keep this between us. I'd hate to cause trouble for Max."

"Between us. Never you fear." Brenda slung her purse over her shoulder. "As for you? Run on up to see Dr. Gelman. I do believe you're pregnant. Debbie, thanks for the latte."

Twenty-three

Noah's pass sliced through a shower of afternoon sun rays and hit Calvin right in the numbers. Max punched the air with his fist as Calvin spun away from the safety and crossed the goal line in three long strides.

"That's the way, Noah." Max ran toward his quarterback. "Right over his left shoulder. It couldn't have been more perfect."

Hines slapped Max on the back. "Son, we got us a football team."

"We're turning the tide, Hines." Max evaluated his assistant with his lawyer lenses. He'd been watching him since the clandestine meeting with Bobby and so far, nothing about the good ol' coach said *traitor*. In fact, the play they just ran was his design. Hines wanted to win football games.

"Max," Haley called across the field. "Run it again. We'll defend it."

"If you think you can." Max laughed. "You've been beating us all season, Hale. We're finally throwing you a few curves."

"Just run it, Max," Haley said. "D, on me."

Max set up the offense to run the pass play again. Haley was more than a good idea to run Warrior defense, she was a brilliant idea. Also, Hines's idea. The man had to be on Max's team. Had to be.

Noah and Calvin executed the play over and over, outwitting Haley's defense every time. Finally, on the last play, her brute linebacker Carpenter leveled Calvin, who bounced back up laughing and juking.

"Woo-hoo, Coach, we're going to kick butt Friday night."

When Max released the boys to go home, he caught up with Tucker. "Can you stay? Practice a bit more."

"I *been* practicing, Coach. I'm no good." Eight weeks. Tucker still had no confidence.

Max lassoed him in a hold. "Not if you keep declaring it, Tucker. Ever hear of self-fulfilling prophecy?"

He led Tucker to the tee on the ten yard line. Jade was right. Tucker needed him more to build his heart and soul than his kicking skills.

She was right about his conspiracy theory too. He was building a fantasy case against Hines and Bobby. It was probably nothing more than a friendly question. In the dark. At the field house. After nine o'clock. Nothing to call into suspicion.

Ha! He'd gotten jury convictions on less.

"Tucker. You've been hitting the weights, training, practicing. There's no reason you can't hit a field goal. Let's start on the ten and work our way back to the thirty."

"The thirty? That'd be a forty-seven-yard field goal."

"It's only a number. Let's go." As Max held the ball, he saw Jade running wild across the field. He motioned to Tuck. "Hold up."

"Max, Max . . ."

Was she crying? He sprinted to her, catching her on the fifty yard line. "Babe, are you okay? Where's Asa?"

"He's, he's—" Jade bent forward, catching her breath. "I'm so out of shape."

"Asa . . . Jade, is he all right?" Max bent over to see her face, his heart on alert. "Are you?"

"He's playing with the Feinberg boys." When Jade raised up, her clear eyes glistened. "Max, I—" Emotion quivered on her bottom lip.

"Babe, come on, you're scaring me. What is it?"

"Max. A word, please." Bobby marched across the field toward them. "I need to see you."

"I'm busy. Talking to my wife."

"It'll only take a moment." He marched in between their private huddle. "Afternoon, Jade."

"Bobby." She stepped back, still catching her breath, tucking her fingers into the pockets of her shorts. Her go-to stance when she had something to say but couldn't.

"Hurry up, Bob. What is it?" Tucker practiced kicking on his own. Max glimpsed the last kick. Tucker fired the ball *under* the goal post. But at least he had the distance. As much as Max wanted Tuck on the team, he might have to enlist one of the other boys to be the inept kicker. Brad Schmidt had put it through the uprights from the twenty yard line a couple of times. Okay, maybe once. On a fluke.

"Bad news. Noah Warren and Calvin Blue can't play this Friday."

Max snapped his attention to his A.D. "Come again?"

"They're both failing algebra."

"What? How? I check their grades every week. I saw their last test. They both had B minuses."

"But they didn't turn in their homework. No more practice until they get those missed assignments turned in, and no game on Friday." Bobby watched Tuck try to hit a field goal and shook his head. "Never saw a kid work so hard for so little gain."

"You're benching our star players? Just like that? Let me look into it, Bob." *Could the man be any more smug?*

"There's nothing to look into, Max. They're grounded until they get the work in and have a report from Mr. Parrish." He stood aloof now, hands on his waist, watching Tucker.

"Bobby, we have no offense without Noah and Calvin."

"Then you have your work cut out for you. I can't treat them different because they're your stars, Max. Rules are rules." Bobby cupped his hands around his lips. "Draw your leg back straight, Tuck. You're hooking it right."

"What are you doing, Bobby?" Jade charged him with a low, commanding accusation. "You want to sabotage Max and take over the team, don't you?"

Bobby glared at Jade, then Max. "Want to control your wife?"

"Want to not insult her? She just asked you a question, Molnar." When had Jade joined the conspiracy theory? He liked it.

"It's true, isn't it? You want to coach but Principal Buchholz won't hire you—something about a kid in Plano?" Jade's voice dropped to a fierce whisper. "You think this job is yours because your daddy and granddaddy were Warrior coaches before you."

"Who do you think made Warrior tradition great, Jade? Small-town southern lawyers?" He daggered Max with a glance. "No, it was made by men like my father and grandfather." He leaned over Jade. "Men like me."

Max shoved Bobby's chest. "Move on, Bobby."

"Tell your wife to mind her own business." Bobby pushed between them, heading off the field.

"Max is my business." Jade rushed him but Max grabbed her arm.

"Easy there, Annie Oakley."

"He's a rat fink."

"What's going on? Who have you been talking to, Jade?"

"Brenda Karlin." Jade recounted her Colby Grounds conversation with Brenda.

The small breeze tugged at Max's shirt. "Tuck, let's do some drills here in a second." He peered at Jade. "I can't go with 'Brenda Karlin said,' Jade. Rat fink or not, Bobby's the athletic director and he calls the shots."

"What? Last night you were sure there was something fishy going on, and here I am with the evidence. Talk to Chevy, Max. Don't just let Bobby sideline your best players."

Max regarded his wife for a moment, loving her passion. "Let me look into it. I do check their grades, but not their homework. If they're failing, then—"

"Sure, they're failing. Wink-wink."

"You think Bobby has that much power? To get a teacher to say two kids are failing when they're not—and deliberately undermine the head coach? He knows we'll lose Friday night. Conniving a way to bench Calvin and Noah is a bit drastic, don't you think?"

"If something happens to you, who takes over coaching?"

"Whoever Chevy picks. Most likely the A.D. I get it, Jade."

"He never denied he wants to coach, Max." Jade dog-boned this conspiracy notion and wasn't letting go. "Once he's in the job, he can leverage for a permanent position."

"I can't see how they'd fire me just for losing games. They've had twenty straight losses."

"Just watch your back." Jade leaned into him making sure her gaze locked with his.

He laughed. "Seems I got you pulling rear guard."

"You know you do." She tiptoed up to kiss him. "I'll see you at home."

"I won't be home early. I'm going to call Hines and Haley back." Max shrugged the weary weight from his shoulders. "We need a plan for Friday night."

"You'll win anyway, Max. Don't let him get to you."

"Win? I'll be happy if the score is less than fifty to nothing." He tugged on her belt loop and drew her back for a kiss. "Is this what had you running across the field like a crazy woman?"

"Um, yeah. Just thought you needed to know. See you at home."

Max watched her go. How he loved that woman. "Okay, Tucker, let's go. I might need you Friday night."

She was pregnant. With a Texas baby. But she was at the critical ten weeks mark. Dr. Gelman seemed undaunted by Jade's medical history—which Jade delivered in snatches as Dr. Gelman examined her between scheduled patients.

"It's still early, Jade, but everything looks good."

Dr. Gelman's voice resonated in her heart and sank deeper and deeper into Jade's soul. *Everything looks good.*

Everything certainly did.

Except for Bobby Molnar. She still hadn't recovered from her run-in on the field with him a couple of hours ago.

"Asa baby, come on. Let's go inside." Jade shivered as a cold wind snapped the trees and pressed the twilight ribbon across the fading blue sky. "It's getting cold."

Asa made his way up the steps, stretching to reach the rail. Dr. Gelman had reminded her today to let him do more on his own. *"He's going to be a big brother."*

Big brother. Jade loved hearing those words.

During her examination, Dr. Gelman seemed amused that Jade missed three periods without noticing. She laughed when Jade claimed she just thought her body was giving her a break for the summer. It'd happened to her a few years ago. Before she married Max.

Dr. Gelman had laughed. "Just the opposite. Your body's working hard."

Pregnant. Jade was pregnant. She couldn't meditate on those words enough. Every molecule in her body was smiling.

After her last miscarriage, Jade shoved all hope of having a baby of her own to the side of her heart. Asa's presence had eased much of the pain and yearning of being barren. Then Max decided to chase a hip-pocket dream and move them across the country.

Jade spent the last two months distracted, managing stress, thinking of everyone and everything but herself. Pregnancy was the last thing on her mind.

Asa jumped from the last step to the porch with a big "Whoa."

"Way to go, my little man." Jade stroked her hand over his head, brushing his bangs aside as she unlocked the front door. But something tucked up beside the brick porch posts caught her eye. A large box.

"Go on inside, baby." Jade helped Asa over the threshold before retrieving the package.

Southern Life. The fall issue. Jade hurried inside, setting the mail and groceries on the counter. Then back out to the porch. What a lovely surprise.

She cut the box open and pulled out the courtesy issues *Southern Life* had sent. On the front cover, with the gold and white lights of the Blue Umbrella blurred in the background, stood Jade, Max, and Asa. Laughing.

Eric's capture was perfect. Real. A prophetic image of days to come. Joy swirled with tears. Jade ran her finger over the caption.

"The Blue Umbrella is anything but blue for vintage princess Jade Benson."

She flipped to the center spread and images of the shop and swelled with tears. Her Blue Umbrella. It made a piece of her heart beat.

She sobbed at the picture of Asa sitting on the floor running his car along the edge of the sunspot. Oh, the Wall of Calendars. Lillabeth, laughing with customers. Jade at the maxi-dress display talking vintage with Raven.

Jade cradled the magazine to her chest and let the tears run, feeling proud and homesick at once. She'd call Lillabeth and read it with her over the phone after she got dinner started. Chili tonight.

If she had a calendar, she'd circle today. Putting the magazine on the dining table, Jade put away the groceries, then grabbed the mail. It was usually junk, but she checked each piece just in case.

She froze at the very last envelope. It did not flow into the trash with all the others. The return address pricked her nerves. Jade's cold fingers fumbled with the envelope. She couldn't get a hold of the flap's edge. Finally, a piece tore and she was able to rip open the letter.

She slipped out the single piece of paper and spread it on the counter. Taylor had written a note on a sticky.

Sorry this took so long. It took me forever to go through Rice's stuff. I started dating someone and he's way more interesting than going through documents. Taylor

Jade scanned the lab report. Landon Harcourt. Twenty-six.

Interpretation: Based on the DNA Analysis, the alleged Father, LANDON HARCOURT, cannot be excluded as the biological Father of the Child, ASA MCCLURE, because they share the same genetic markers. The probability of the stated relationship is indicated below, as compared to an untested, unrelated person of the same ethnicity.

Combined Direct Index: 17,446

Probability Percentage: 99.9942%

Landon was Asa's biological father. Jade collapsed against the counter, all her bubbles of joy sinking. The light in the room paled. *Oh, Max . . .*

Jade folded the report and stuffed it back into the envelope. Aiden's advice haunted her. Of course. *Secrets come back to bite you.*

Lies leaked. Secrets spoke.

In the bedroom, Jade crammed the envelope under the jeans in the bottom dresser drawer and slammed it shut. Composing herself, she returned to the kitchen.

"Lord, help me. I have to tell him."

She muttered prayers as she mixed up the chili, then stared absently at the directions for a box cake.

She prayed as she fed Asa. While she bathed him. As she tucked him in bed. When he was asleep, she wandered out to the porch, tugging on one of

Max's Duke sweatshirts. The air was scented with fall leaves and Indian summer grass.

Oh, Jesus. Squeezing her eyes shut, Jade listened to the night wind and the song of the redbird. Did he sing a dirge for her? Or a melody for joy? *I don't want to do this.*

The wind tangled her loose hair over her shoulders and the questions in her heart melted into the burnt amber hue of panic.

Max is going to lose all faith in you when you tell him how long you've suspected he wasn't Asa's father. You blew it, Jade.

She jumped up, stepping into the yard. The warm grass caressed her cold toes. *No. No fear.* She pressed her fingers to her temples.

Nothing, nothing, *nothing* was ever stable in her life. This was a disaster. Never mind the news about Asa—the stress of the football program was going to push Max back to his old ways, his phantom back pains. Which would lead to meds. Always did.

With his charm and smarts, he could doctor-shop for Percocet within a week. Who wouldn't want to help the new football coach?

And this baby? Jade pressed her hand over her womb. It would die like all of her babies. Jade wasn't favored enough to give birth. Only to raise the son of her husband's former lover.

A slow oozing sensation hit her head and slid down her scalp. Panic, a monster of fear, rose up in her soul. Jade paced, fingers digging into her palm. No. She could not run. She could not leave Asa. She could not give in. *Jesus, Jesus, Jesus. Peace. Perfect love . . . no fear.*

She pictured the words in her Bible. *Perfect love casts out all fear. Jesus, Your love is perfect toward me.*

Pacing, she battled. Fear had had its day. Time for love to rule the night. Throwing back her head, she flung wide her arms. "Peace! I say peace!"

Silence. In her heart. In her mind. Even the breeze settled at her feet. Peace. Jade breathed in. Then out. *Peace.* She waited. She listened, her heart a symphony of expectation.

The leaves over her head rustled and the first tweet of a bird was soft and low. Like a tentative invitation. The leaves rustled again and a second tweet came stronger. A redbird emerged.

He broke into a chorus, a guttural song of intricate twitters and tweets of harmony chasing melody.

"Hello, friend." Jade broke with a laugh, tears swimming in her eyes. "Life. You sing the song of life. That's what you were telling me that night in Iowa when you scolded me with your song. Choose life. Choose life."

Life was truth. She would tell Max tonight about Landon Harcourt.

With a shiver down to her toes, Jade ran inside. She checked on Asa, then made a cup of hot chocolate. *Truth wins. Truth wins. Max, I need to tell you something. Two somethings, really.*

But which did she tell first? Baby or paternity? Before she could decide and take her first hot sip, headlights bounced down the driveway, shining through the front window.

In a jolt of nerves, she ran to the master bath, splashed water on her face, and ran a brush through her hair. She really needed to find a stylist—she'd resorted to the ponytail look. Then smoothed a bit of color on her lips.

When she went to the door, the yard was full of voices. A car door slammed. Then another. Oh Max, did you bring the coaches home? She'd been prepared for Tucker, but not Hines and Haley.

"Hey, babe," she said, swinging wide the door.

"Hey, look who I found?" Max jumped the steps and kissed her. "The McClures." He stood aside for Jade to see their surprise guests. She gripped the doorknob as all the air left her lungs. "They brought a friend." Max leaned forward to see the man standing behind Gus. "I'm sorry, what did you say your name was again?"

"Landon." The man peered directly at Jade. "Landon Harcourt."

Twenty-four

What was the matter with Jade? Max invited the McClures and Landon into the house, listening as they told about their delayed flight and hassle with the rental car company.

"I'll tell you," Gus said, standing, surveying the living quarters. "Customer service is a thing of the past. With this stinking bad economy, I can't imagine any business treating their customers as if they don't care. I'll never fly on that airline again."

"Yeah, I hear you." Max shot a look at Jade. She hovered just inside the living room entrance, twisting her fingers in her hand. "Listen, let me get out of these clothes and we can visit. What made you decide to come out today? You should've called—Jade might have been able to keep Asa awake. Is that chili I smell? Y'all hungry?"

"Landon is why we came out on a whim, Max." Gus motioned to the man in designer slacks and starched button-down. Max recognized the outfit. He saw a bit of himself in the man's expression and posture—a twentysomething with big dreams and the fuel to make them come true.

"Babe." Jade's voice burst into the room. "Can I see you? In our room?" She whirled away.

"Sure." He backed toward her. "Y'all excuse us." Max closed the bedroom door behind him. Jade cowered against the far wall. Trembling. "What's going on?"

"I can't believe it. I was going to tell you tonight. I just found . . . the proof. Max." Her eyes were wild. "I needed the proof."

"What proof? What are you talking about? By the way, I took Tucker home tonight. Seems Mariah isn't too keen on you being a surrogate mom. Tucker said she's jealous. You might want to give her a call, invite her to coffee or dinner, let her know you're not—"

"Max, please, be quiet." Jade pressed her fist against her forehead.

Max glared at her. "What's up?" He was tired. Hungry. And frankly, thought a good ol' chat with folks from back home sounded like a good way to unwind from his day. Hines and Haley had helped him plan this weekend's game, but it was going to take every Warrior on the roster. And all the prayers of the saints. "It's the McClures, isn't it? Landon?"

"Yes." Jade stared at the floor.

"I'm all ears, Jade. If this has anything to do with Asa, you'd better tell me. I don't want to get blindsided by those two."

"Blindsided." Her angry whisper lifted her head. "I was blindsided by you, Max."

He regarded her. She'd thrown a few curves at him, but he wasn't interested in keeping score at the moment. He'd lose anyway.

"Tell me. Straight up. I can't deal with whatever's making you so nervous if you don't tell me. What proof are you talking about?"

"Max, you have to know I was going to tell you. But I didn't know for sure. How could I break your heart on a stranger's word?"

The slightest ping of dread echoed across his mind. "Spit it out, Jade."

She sighed. "I guess this is why they're here." She opened the bottom dresser drawer and retrieved an envelope from under her jeans. "I just got this today." But she didn't pass it over.

"Is it a paternity test?"

She gazed at him with surprised eyes. "How did you know?"

"The McClures. A strange man. You, panicked and fretting. A thin white envelope. I used to be a lawyer, remember. *That* in your hand is proof." He processed, emotionless. Rice had her paramours. Her flings. But she'd never lied to him. *He thought.* "How long have you known?"

"The end of June. Right before you came home. I mean, I never knew *for sure* until today—"

"And you didn't tell me . . . because?"

"I didn't know if it was true or not. I never met Taylor before—the woman who told me. She just . . . blindsided me with this crazy news. If it was all some horrible lie I didn't want to upset you for nothing. For me, it didn't matter. I love Asa either way."

"You thought it would send me into relapse?" Max realized the depth of the damage he'd done to her confidence and trust by the slow way she shook her head.

"I didn't know, Max, how you'd respond. I didn't know where we stood. How I felt about you, our marriage. Asa's been through so much, I couldn't tell his daddy that his mama had lied to him. If I had no proof, I could pretend it was all a big lie. Then this came today." Jade offered him the white envelope.

He scanned the front. Taylor Branch. Didn't recognize the name. He slipped out the contents and read the report.

He was not Asa's biological father. "Landon was only twenty-six? Rice . . ." He muttered a hot word and handed the envelope back to Jade, drawing in his emotions, steeling up. "This means nothing. I'm on his birth certificate. He's two years old. Landon waited too long if he wanted to claim Asa as his."

"That's what I said, Max. Why does this stupid report matter? You're his daddy, the one loving him and raising him."

Max perched on the edge of the bed, suddenly very tired. "Do you know how this happened?"

"Yeah, I do." Jade sat next to him and smoothed her hand down his back. "Landon denied it when she told him she was pregnant. Then you went to Vegas and—"

Max dropped his head into his hands. "I'd wondered why she came. When she and Kim decided to fly out with us, it just felt weird. Rice kept talking about old times and what a great relationship we had. I thought she wanted to hang out one last time before I got married. Then in Vegas, she went her way, I went mine. Until she knocked on my door." He stood. *Stupid, stupid, stupid.* "When I told Mom about Asa, she suggested a paternity test. But Dad said leave it be, it was a done deal. I never considered Rice had lied to me. If she said I was Asa's father, then it was true."

"She wanted you to be his father. I'm not sure she planned to seduce you in Vegas, but that trip sure gave her opportunity and motive."

Max rubbed his eyes, trying to make sense of it all. "So why did this Taylor come to you?" His head throbbed and his stomach protested.

"She said she wanted to clear her conscience. She hated that Rice lied to you."

"But Landon took the test and he just now find out?"

"He bolted after he took the test. Never returned for the results. I guess part of Taylor's emotional housecleaning included telling Landon he was Asa's father." Jade smoothed her hand over the made bed. "When you caught me burning something in the alley behind the Blue Umbrella, it was his business card. He showed up in Whisper Hollow. But I still had no proof and I didn't want to know if he did."

Max headed out of the bedroom. "So Landon, you're Asa's biological father." He glanced at Gus and Lorelai. "Did you two know about this?"

"Just this week. Landon came to us."

Landon stood, his fine-weave slacks shaking loose from his legs, the hem falling over his leather shoes.

"Taylor came to see me last June," he said. "I didn't believe her but I requested a copy of the test from the lab. When I saw the result, I called her. She gave me your name, Mrs. Benson. I was in Georgia on business so I drove up to Whisper Hollow to see you, but you were busy. Since then, I've been traveling out of the country on business and didn't have time to pursue this. Then I got a call from Taylor telling me she sent the results to you. I called the McClures and well, here we are."

"We want this thing right, Max." Gus stood. "Landon's his father. He should get the boy."

"Get the boy? He's not a possession, Gus. We're not arguing over money or land here. We're talking about a living, breathing, beautiful little boy. Who does not deserve one ounce of this."

"He's the rightful father." Lorelai fired to her feet. "Asa should be with his blood kin."

"Landon wanted nothing to do with him until Taylor showed up."

"Because Rice told me I wasn't the father."

"You didn't request your own test, Landon. You waited two years."

"You wanted nothing to do with him either, Max," Lorelai said, her accent refined and Whisper Hollowan.

"I was only twenty-six." Landon made his defense. "Just starting my career, when Rice told me she was pregnant. But we'd broken up and I was dating another woman. Actually, Rice seemed happy to let me off the hook."

"Good. I'm happy to let you off the hook too. Thank you for coming, but Asa stays right here. With Jade and me." He fired a glance at Lorelai. "As far as my relationship with Asa, Rice told me she wanted to raise him on her own and I was wrong to let her. I was a newlywed and afraid for my marriage."

"Excuses, Max." Lorelai, the mother bear.

"Let's talk about how Rice lied to me. Lied. Look at all the pain and confusion she's caused."

"Don't blame her, Max, you got in bed with her a week before your wedding."

He was two breaths away from firing out the door. Words—mad, harsh words swirled in his belly.

"Landon here wants to see the boy."

"We don't have to let you see him," Max said. "You have no legal authority."

Landon bent to his attaché. "I'm taking action, Max." He handed over a document. "Thanks to Gus, I was able to get a judge to grant me temporary visitation. Jade, since you knew, I could charge you with kidnapping."

"What?" Her voice sheered the tension in the room. "I heard a rumor. A story. I had no proof."

This was Gus's doing—the mountain thug—getting back at Max for besting him when he and Lorelai sued for custody. What a treat Landon turned out to be. Walking into Gus's lair.

"You sure you want to go up against Benson Law again, Gus?" Max understood the power of grief's voice speaking from the McClures' hearts.

He'd been a father for four months. If something happened to Asa, he had no idea how he'd manage. Rice had been the McClures' only daughter. She died tragically and suddenly at thirty-eight. The depths of their grief had to be profound and blinding.

"We just want what's right. For the boy. For Rice. Even Landon here."

"Since this case has legal ramifications, I'm going to have to ask you to leave. You'll be hearing from our lawyer." Max heard his calm response, but he remained on the verge of flying apart.

Lorelai wrung her hands. "Gus, please, we'll never get to see him if we keep this up. Max, we only want—"

In an instant, she'd changed her tone, ready to plead out and confess it was all a bluff. "Lorelai, it's best if you go. We'll work this out."

Gus tried to debate, but Lorelai shoved him out the door. "Do as he says, Gus, for pity's sake."

Landon lingered, the last to leave. He tried to give Max the eyeball-to-eyeball thing as he walked out, but Max had perfected that look. Landon softened and remarked, "This is only the beginning."

"Yeah, fine, whatever."

Max slammed the door, then turned to stare at Jade. "If you'd have told me, none of this would've happened. I could've done an end run on Landon and kept him from going to Gus."

"So this is my fault?"

"No fault. Just wish you would've told me." His fire flickered lower, fading.

"I didn't want to hurt you."

"Jade, I'm a big boy. I've handled lots of surprises and stresses over the years. Without pills. You can't avoid telling me things because you're afraid."

"Okay, then you tell me when and how to tell the difference between big boy Max and pill popping Max. Dang it, you have to think about what I went through with you. Here's what it was like: If it's Tuesday and the sun is shining, and you've had your coffee and won a case, I can lay the heaviest burden on you. But if it's Wednesday between ten and ten forty-five and your coffee is cold and the partners meeting went long, I can't tell you the toilet needs fixing or you'll pop a Perc."

"Oh nice . . . good, Jade, is that how you see me? A neurotic moron?"

"Well, Max, you tell me how I'm supposed to know for sure that you'll never pop pills again?" Hands on her hips, she leaned into him. "'Cause I trusted you before, and that didn't work out so well."

Max moved for the door. "I need to think." He jumped off the porch and started down the driveway, running, drawing in the cool night air, burning off the stress with each mounting and mourning stride.

Twenty-five

Midnight. Max rapped on Holiday Inn room 202. Landon Harcourt opened, his shirttail out, his collar open, limp and tired.

"Didn't expect to see you tonight. We do have a legal case pending."

"Can I come in?" Max said. He'd calmed down on his run. Formed a plan. Went home, showered, and kissed his wife.

"Suit yourself." Harcourt powered off the TV. "Can I offer you a cocktail?" He waved a mini liquor bottle.

"Don't drink. I came to find out what you want."

"I told you. I want to see the boy." Landon tossed the empty bottle in the trash.

"Just like that? Out of the blue? You decided to pop into Colby, Texas, and see about your kid? He's two years old, man, where you been?"

"Staying out of Rice's way. Living my own life. Same as you."

"You're not the same as me." Not anymore. But seeing Landon disturbed Max in the shadowy places of his soul. Was this how he looked ten years ago? It made him ill. "Have you ever seen him?"

"Right after he was born. See, you and I are exactly the same, Benson. Weak against Rice's charms." The sound of his laugh rattled Max's bones.

"How did you two meet?"

"Mutual friends on a ski trip. But I live in Denver and the long distance thing got old. Not that we were serious anyway."

"Why didn't you bother to check the lab reports for yourself?"

"You ask a lot of questions, Benson, for a *coach*. I'm not sure I should be talking to you."

"Cut to the chase, Harcourt. What do you want? It's not to see Asa." Max felt it. In his gut. Landon was up to something. "You're an intelligent man, you're educated. You don't waste time on things that don't benefit you."

"You think you know me, Benson?"

"I know I know you."

"My grandfather recently died and it made me aware of how . . . well, how fragile life can be. I took the paternity test in a moment of regret. Then Rice told me she'd been mistaken, you were the father and already on the birth certificate. So I let it go. To be honest, I was glad." Landon leaned against the desk. "But I'm two years wiser now. And with my grandfather's death, it got me thinking about my life and mortality."

"So you went looking for Rice's son?"

"My son. I called the McClures thinking they'd know why Rice lied. Why she named you father and told me I wasn't."

"Something about you must have spooked her."

"Maybe, but at least I didn't cheat on my pretty wife."

Max fired across the room. "I'm asking you again. What do you want, Harcourt? I'm not buying this newfound enlightenment. And I can check to see if your granddaddy died." Stay on offense. Execute. Read the D. Break him. Get his pride to speak. "Asa's not leaving this family. You should know that right now. I'll fight you tooth and nail. You got any money?"

"Yeah, I have some money." So cocky, this guy.

"You won't by the time I'm done with you."

Harcourt slowed the confrontation by moving to the minibar. This kid was a snake. Did Rice know before or after? "Ah, the rehabbed heir of the grand Benson Law firm bares his teeth." Harcourt feigned a shudder as he popped open a Coke. "I told you, all I want is to see my son."

"Then what?"

"I don't know." Harcourt moved as if he commanded the game. "Maybe file suit. Get my son back." He eyed Max over the edge of his Coke can. "Gus and Lorelai seem bent on raising their grandson."

Max lunged forward and slammed his hand against Harcourt's chest, gathering his collar in his fist. The soda dropped out of his hand and poured over the carpet. "You're lucky I don't break your face."

"Keen on assault charges, are you?"

"A night in jail would be worth it. Now you tell me exactly what you want." Max pressed against the base of Harcourt's throat.

"Five hundred."

Max shoved him back and stepped away. "Five hundred grand. That's what it'll take to get you out of our lives?"

"Make it a cool million. I'll sign whatever you want and you'll never hear from me again."

"A million? That's all? Just . . . one cool mil?" Max brought down his ire with deep breaths. And waited.

"I know you've got more, Benson, but I don't want to be greedy. Asa is my flesh and blood, after all. A cool million ought to make me disappear."

Max backed toward the door and pressed the handle. "Be gone by morning, Harcourt. If I see you anywhere near my family again, I'll sue you for blackmail, embezzlement, and harassment. You'll be up to your eyeballs in legal fees."

"You don't scare me, Benson."

"Then you show your foolishness," Max said, exhaling. "You think I want to look at my son and know I paid a million bucks to a scumbag like you just to get you out of our lives? For no reason? Because according to the birth certificate, I'm his father."

"But according to the paternity, I'm his father."

"No, you're the DNA donor. Crazy as it may seem, Harcourt, you're not always going to be a jerk wad, arrogant twenty-eight-year-old. Asa might want to meet you some day—shudder to think—and I'm not going to let you put a price on his head. Forget it. You're not worth it. Get out of town."

He laughed. "Or what, a showdown at the O.K. Corral? Benson, Benson, Benson, this isn't about me. It's about him. The boy. He's not worth everything you have?"

"He is worth my life. But you're not."

"Look at this deal as an insurance policy, Max. That's all. Insurance that Asa will forever be yours. Otherwise, I might just have to sue you for him."

"That'd be great." Max pulled his phone from his pocket. "Because I'd love to play this conversation in court for everyone to hear." He tapped the screen and Landon Harcourt's voice slipped through the speaker. *"Make it a cool million."*

Landon moved after him, a wild fire in his eye.

Max jerked open the door. "I don't want to see you again."

At the click of the door, Jade scrambled to sit up, reaching for the light. When Max came in, peeling off his shirt, she held her tongue.

Let him speak.

He hung up his shirt, popped off his sneakers, then slipped out of his shorts. "I went to see him. Landon. He wanted money. A *cool* million. If we paid, he'd go away, drop the lawsuit."

"He wanted money? Is he insane?"

"I told him to get out of Colby and if I ever saw him again, I'd charge him with extortion, harassment, and everything in between. My guess is he didn't care about Asa until he heard we had money. Probably tried to shake down Gus too." He crawled into bed, pressing the heels of his hands over his eyes, breathing out a long, weary breath. "I've got to figure out who we're putting on the field this Friday."

"That's it?"

He peered at her. "Yeah, well, I got the firm on it. I have a recording of Landon asking for payout . . . what?"

"Rice lied, that's what, Max. She lied." Jade stepped out of bed, a small steam rising in her head. "She nearly ruined our marriage."

"I nearly ruined our marriage, Jade. Rice lied. If she were alive, I'd be duking it out with her, but she's not. There's nothing I can do about it now. The damage *and* the blessing have been done."

"How can you be so cavalier?"

"What are my options?" He fluffed a pillow to stuff behind his back. "Stew over it? Get mad? Disown Asa? Not going to happen. It stinks. I wish it were different but it's not. He's not mine biologically but in my heart, he's all mine. I've only been with him for four months, but I've known about him since he was born. I've been supporting him. There's no way I'd give him up. No way. The boy deserves the best I have. The best we have. When I was running, thinking, trying to sort it out, I just had a peace over it. I could get mad, rail, sulk, ream you out, but to what end? My heart said *peace*. It's done. All this mess with Rice. Done."

She regarded him, testing his words against his body language. "Do you want to ream me out?"

He shook his head, watching her with tired but very clear eyes. Like honey-hued marbles. "I caused all this mess. I'd cash in every dime to my name and surrender my reputation to undo it. But I can't."

Jade crawled onto the bed and sat crossed-legged in front of him. "Now that we've met Landon, Max, I can see why Rice named you Asa's father. I can't imagine how she felt when she first saw Asa, so in love, so fierce to protect, all the while realizing Landon was his father. I might have done what she did. Not seduce another woman's fiancé, but—" The tears in her eyes were from forgiveness. "If I could choose between you or Landon? No question. You. And I wouldn't have cared whose marriage I hurt in the process."

His eyes brimmed. "I don't deserve you. Or that confession. Or all that God's doing here, with us." Max rubbed his eyes, flicking away the soft dew of tears. He cleared his throat. "I never thought any good could come from so much pain."

"All things work together for good. For those who love God." Jade shifted her position and curled next to Max, burrowing in next to his heart. "I've done plenty of bad things. Aborted a baby. Lied. Cheated. Fornicated. I'm no better than you. If Jesus is our standard, then we both fall way short."

Max slid down on the pillow and wrapped Jade in his arms, kissing her forehead. "I'm still so sorry, Jade."

"Yeah, me too. But"—she exhaled, pictured the song of the bird on the branch, the call to life—"let's move on. Forget the past, press forward to what lies ahead."

"No more secrets."

"Please, no more secrets." Except one. She smiled. She'd tell him when the weight of the word hadn't just fallen off their shoulders. Besides, another week or two and she could tell him with certainty they *were* having a baby. She'd passed the ten-week mark.

Max absently caressed her hair and a soft chuckle rumbled in his chest.

"What's so funny?"

"Asa. He slept through it all. He'll wake up tomorrow morning none the wiser."

Jade rolled to her back. "Man, you're so right. Ah, to be two."

Max propped on his elbow. "Do you have any memories from when you were two?"

Jade pinched her brow. "I don't think so. Do you? Who remembers being two?"

"I'll tell you who. My cousin Jeff." Max dropped to his back, locking his hands behind his head. "A few years ago we were at a family reunion and my Uncle Lake broke out the old slide projector. First slide up, Jeff starts talking. 'Oh, I remember this picnic.' I said, 'Jeff, you're like, what, a year old in this picture?' My Aunt Glo was holding him and Jeff had this long string of drool swinging from his chin. How could he remember? So what does he do? Starts describing the day and the details." Max laughed. "I mean, Jade, it was incredible. I swear, he was just repeating stories he'd heard from the grandparents and aunts and uncles over the years, but it sounded like he really remembered."

"Maybe he really did."

Max shot her a wry lip-twisted grin. "A one-year-old remembering a family picnic up on the ridge. No. Jeff just likes to hear the sound of his own voice."

"I hope Asa doesn't remember this spring. His mama suddenly ripped from his life, moving across the country, bunking in with a strange lady." Jade stared at the ceiling. How far away it all seemed. But tonight it came full circle in her living room.

"That makes two of us. I don't want to remember it either. You know that wall of calendars at the Blue Umbrella? Let's not pin up this year."

"Oh, I don't know." Jade peeked at him. "This year's not over yet."

"You think it can be redeemed to wall worthy? Everything we went through, then topped off with a crazy venture from Tennessee to Texas to . . . coach football." Max ran his hands over his face. "A losing season. What was I thinking?"

"The season's not over. The year's not over. Let's wait and see." They'd conceived this baby in Texas. That alone made this venture worth it. And this pregnancy different. She brushed her hand along the curve of his shoulder. "Don't worry, Max. If this doesn't work out, it's okay. Go back to talking about Jeff. I like hearing you laugh."

But his eyes were slipping closed. Maybe he'd tell her a story later. Jade reached for the lamp. When the room was dark, Max exhaled the sound of sleep.

Then he started laughing. "Did I tell you about the time Jeff tried to fly off Eventide Ridge?"

"Fly? Like an airplane?"

"Oh no, why use a machine when he had arms? He made his own wings." Max's laugh started in his belly and rolled up his chest. "It was the summer after tenth grade. Five of us ran around the Hollow together, three cousins and two other friends from school. One day, Jeff said, 'I'm going to fly off the ridge.' The rest of us packed a lunch and grabbed our cameras. We had to see this and . . ."

Jade closed her eyes, listening to her husband's heart. Smiling. Drifting to sleep on the peaceful texture of his voice and the current of his love.

Twenty-six

"Lorelai. What are you doing here?" Jade scanned the porch and yard for Gus and Landon. The blustery Tuesday morning threatened a cold rain.

"I'm alone, Jade."

"What do you want?" Jade blocked her view into the house, pulling the door against her.

"I, um . . ." She held her gaze down. "I'd like to see him, Jade."

"I'm not sure I can let you. There is still a restraining order against you and Gus. Pending lawsuits."

"I won't make trouble, Jade. You have my word." She raised her chin, displaying every bit of her Whisper Hollow aristocrat heritage, and the stubborn pride chiseled in her cheeks. But a bit of humility had replaced her smug look from last night.

Jade hesitated. Lorelai remained steadfast, the hem of her sage green skirt pressed to her knees by the chilled breezed. Jade stepped back, drawing the door wide.

"Asa, look who's here. Grandma Lorelai." Jade grabbed her arm as she crossed the threshold. "If this bites me, so help me, Lorelai—"

A mist coated her gray eyes. "There'll be no more trouble."

Jade fixed Asa's breakfast as Lorelai chatted with him, asking about his cars. He babbled away, a string of vowels and syllables that for the moment only made sense to him. He recognized Lorelai. Jade knew it. Of course, she and Gus were very much a part of his first eighteen months of life.

"He's growing so fast, Jade."

"He's in 4Ts already." Jade set Asa's eggs in front of him. Then a cup of coffee for Lorelai and the last cinnamon scone. "He looks like Rice, doesn't he?" she said, brushing aside his thick hair and taking the seat next to him.

Asa lost half of his first bite of eggs to his lap. He frowned, looking down, then retrieved the yellow piece and stuffed it in his mouth. He cracked her up.

"He does. Better than looking like that scoundrel." Lorelai covered her quivering lips with her slender, manicured hand. A sob ricocheted in her chest. "What was she thinking, Jade? That girl . . . she was so smart and intelligent, and beautiful. One of the ones who had it all. Gus and I made sure . . . we made sure."

"You can't blame yourself, Lorelai. Rice was a grown woman."

"Do you hate her, Jade?" The glossy sheen in Lorelai's eyes thickened. "I don't think I could bear it if you hated her."

Jade watched Asa for a moment, bonding with Lorelai's mother's heart. "No, I don't hate her. I wanted to, but it's hard to hold a vendetta against a dead woman. Besides, I'm not one to point fingers. I've made a few regretful decisions. I mostly felt betrayed by my husband. We've been through a lot in our three years of marriage and Lorelai"—Jade peered at her—"there's no room for hate."

"We miss her so much," she said, quivering, struggling to hold herself together.

"I can't imagine how hard this must be for you."

"When Landon called us, we thought for a moment, we'd get our girl back. He'd sue for custody, then give Asa to us. Gus had him all talked into it when he found out Benson had deep pockets. A million dollars . . . he's a fool. What was Rice thinking, going to bed with that man. My stars, you'd think she was raised in the hills by wolves. I taught her, Jade, to be discerning."

"My own mama died in the spring, Lorelai. I can't know what it feels like to lose a grown child, but I have lost four babies to abortion and miscarriage. I am far too acquainted with grief." And the child she loved now was not her own.

"A woman lives her whole life dreaming and hoping for her children. Rice was to marry well and have gorgeous, smart children. We'd have family vacations, celebrate Thanksgiving and Christmas. We'd be best of friends with the in-laws." She pulled a tissue from her purse. "When she was engaged to Max all the dreams were coming true. Then she found out he was addicted and bolted to Washington, D.C., so fast, it left us all spinning."

"Sounds to me like the pills were an excuse, Lorelai."

"I don't know, maybe you're right. She did tell me I could be a bit smothering. Trying to make her live life for me." She smoothed her hand over Asa's arm. "I was more prepared to be a widow than childless this stage in my life. Gus and I decided when one of us died the other would move to California to be with Rice. At least part of the year. We were looking into town houses when she died . . . in that stupid, stupid plane." Lorelai smacked the table with each "stupid." Asa jolted, eyes wide. "The mechanic told her it might not be safe, but Rice . . . never a fear."

"It's what made Rice . . . Rice." Jade smiled tentatively at Lorelai. Did she understand it was uncomfortable to talk so casually about Rice? No, probably not. Rice was her daughter, and right now she saw only through the narrow eyes of grief.

Jade preferred to never speak of Rice again. But since she lived on in Asa, Rice McClure would always be a part of their lives.

"Foolishness is not the same as fearlessness."

"More, Mama. More." Asa raised his juice cup, dropping it on the table. Jade scooted away from the table.

"He's all we have of her, Jade."

"I know." Jade filled the cup with juice, cutting it with water. "But you have to stop throwing punches, Lorelai."

"We'd decided to accept things until Landon came around." Tear chased tear down her cheek, carving a wide trace in her makeup. "We miss her so much. We used to talk every day. Then I saw her one morning, said good-bye, and she never came home. Gone so suddenly. Then Max banned us from Asa and . . ."

Her words . . . her tears . . . watered the dry soil of Jade's heart. The places where she'd patted over her own sorrows. She brushed the dampness from under her eyes. "I'll talk to Max, Lorelai."

"Jade, I promise." She regained her composure. "We'll not do anything like this again. We can't raise a two-year-old. We're seventy. Gus's diabetes is giving him problems and we long ago lost the energy to chase after a toddler. But we'd love to help you and Max."

"You are his grandparents." Jade smiled. "And my parents are out of the picture. I don't speak to my dad, and Mama died in March. I think it'd be lovely if you were in his life. In our lives."

Lorelai squared back, tugging on the hem of her suit jacket, straightening her composure. "I declare I've cried more tears this year than in my whole life."

"It's been a year for tears." And joy. "I was arranging with my brother and sister to spend Christmas together. I'd love it if you and Gus joined us. Wherever we are. Here or in Whisper Hollow. Depending on what Max and the lawyers say—"

"There will be no need for lawyers. I guarantee it. This ends now." Lorelai pressed her hand to her chest. "We'll be there for Christmas. If it's here or there or in Timbuktu. We'll be there." Her words faded, choked and thin. "Thank you."

Jade reached across the table and squeezed her hand. And for a long while, that was all the talking they needed to do.

"Do it, Rick. Just go in there and drop the pills in his desk."

"Where did you get these?" Rick pinched the bag between his thumb and forefinger.

"Doc Dooley." Long time Warrior booster, friend of Bobby's.

"Why am I doing this?" Rick's furrowed brow and quizzical gaze grated on Bobby's last nerve.

"Insurance. They'll help us with Benson."

"Forget it." Rick tossed the baggie to the desk. "I agreed to help you find a way to the head coaching job, but I'm not planting drugs to frame Max."

"You owe me." Bobby prowled toward him. He could almost taste the job, the sidelines, the cheers, the glare of the lights. No way was he spending one more year in this claustrophobic athletic director's office. He'd signed his last girls' softball and volleyball rec form. He was a football man. The only sport that mattered. Football and the Molnar legacy.

"I don't owe you anything worth this. You want to out me for my part in sabotaging the coaches for you, go ahead. But you'll go down with me."

Bobby glared at Rick.

"You're right." He tossed the pills into his trash can. "I just get riled up at times. I'm sorry, Rick. I've tested our friendship and overstepped propriety."

"Wise decision, Bob." Rick started for the door, then backed up and took the pills from the can. "Let this season play itself out. Wait and see what happens." Bobby followed his broad back as he went into the bathroom off his office. "Benson has a law career in Tennessee. Fifty bucks he'll go back on his own at the end of the season."

"I'll take that bet. Steaks at the Stampede." Bobby winced when the toilet flushed.

Rick came out holding up the empty baggie. "I'm in."

Rick left and Bobby dropped to his desk chair. Rick was a good friend. An idiot, but a good friend.

Twenty-seven

From the empty bleachers Friday night, Jade watched the Colby Warriors go down to the Palo Duro Dons 52–0. Her heart sobbed as Max tried to hold the team together, but when the Dons went ahead 38–0 at halftime, the Warriors imploded.

Without Noah and Calvin, the offense never found its rhythm. The Dons' offense ran all over Haley's defense. The Warriors moved like slow, sleeping babies compared to Palo Duro's quick backs.

Three times, Max sent Tucker out to kick. He missed—wide left, wide right, and way short. Jade watched Max hang his head each time the refs blew their whistles, swinging their arms, "no good." Then he'd meet Tucker on the sidelines and pop him on the shoulder pads. *Good try.*

Every time the Dons scored, Max searched the stands for her. She'd smile with thumbs up. But, oh, it was brutal.

She was glad only the faithful few remained when the clock wound down and the torture ended.

"At last, I can breathe." Brenda patted her chest. "Jade honey, how do you stand it?"

"Part of being coach's wife, I guess." How *did* she stand it? Jade reached down for Asa and landed him on her hip. Max jogged toward the field house, head down, his feet dragging the ground. What this team needed was a party. Something fun. "Say, Brenda." Jade pulled her close. "Have you heard anything? About Bobby?"

"Nothing, shug. No rumors of sabotage or wanting to fire Max. But I've got my ear tuned to Rick Lundy. He and Bobby are T-I-T-E tight, you know, and if anyone's going to cover Bob's shenanigans, it's Ricky. You know, any more games like this where there's no one to buy food and trinkets, the boosters will start crowing. Look, there's Lila Jane. Hey, Lila, is that a new hairdo? Love it. *Love* it." Brenda waved, smiling, then cut her lips sideways to Jade. "What was she thinking? She's sporting a Brillo pad."

"Brenda, did you see Lila Jane?" Bit scooted down the metal bleacher. "Hey, Lila Jane." She waved like Brenda. Then, "She looks like Lil' Orphan Annie."

"I said Brillo pad."

"Ooh, I like that better." Bit patted Brenda on the shoulders.

"You two frighten me." Jade shifted Asa to her other hip. He was heavy.

"What? We're just citizen observers. Now, Jade, forget ol' Brillo pad hair and Warrior football. What did Dr. Gelman say? And I know you had an appointment 'cause I ran into her at the grocery store the other day."

"I went. Yes." A crimson of heat spread across Jade's cheeks. "But it's sort of a personal matter, Brenda."

"What? Oh Bit, she hasn't told him."

Bit leaned to peer at Jade. Her blue eyes were accented with major green eye shadow and dollops of mascara on the edges of her lashes. "You're right, B. She's not told him."

"Why haven't you, Jade?" Brenda folded her arms.

"Told him what?"

"You're pregnant." Bold, unabashed. Nosy Brenda.

"Shhh." Jade looked around. Why? She didn't know. She'd sat alone on her side of the bleachers for the last half of the game. "It's been kind of hectic around our house." Football. Landon. "I'll tell him when it's right."

"When will it be right? You know what? You need to go out and do something fun." Oh, that sounded fabulous.

"The carnival," Bit said.

"The carnival. Bit, you are brilliant."

"That's what I keep telling you."

"Well, keep talking. Jade, do you like carnivals? There's one at the Randall Country Fairgrounds. You and Max should go, kick up your heels, cast off your cares. I'll watch Asa for you and you can *tell him*."

Tell him. A recurring theme in her life. "Brenda, thank you, but I can't ask you to do that."

"You didn't. I volunteered." Her phone buzzed. "Aw, what in the blazes? It's my husband. He's sitting in the car waiting." She squinted at her phone's screen. "Says, 'what's for dinner? Starved.' Mercy, the man has two healthy legs and two healthy arms but when it comes to feeding himself, he's a bawling baby. I knew it when I married him, though. His mama catered to him. Practically fork fed him our wedding cake." Brenda started down the bleachers. "Bit, I should've never taught him how to text. Jade, how about Sunday night? I'll come over around five."

"Five? Well, um, sure, okay. Five."

Bit paused in front of her. "She means well."

"I know she does."

"She's the best one to have on your side when the chips are down. I know." Bit's voice softened. "Have a good night, darling. See you, Asa."

"Night, Bit." Jade kissed Asa's forehead and started down the bleachers. The carnival. She hadn't been to one since she was a girl. Mama used to drive a truck for her friend Carlisle's carnival. But Jade had hated the carnival. It usually meant Mama would leave again for months on end and she'd have to help Granny care for Willow.

A carnival *would* be a fun date. Outdoors, under the lights. A great place to deliver the baby news. "Let's go find your daddy, Asa."

As she approached the field house, Hines passed her. "Jade, come on inside. Wait in Max's office."

"Do you think he'll be long? We just want to say hi, cheer him up. I can go on home if he's busy."

"Well, he's got to talk the boys off the ledge." He held up his hands for Asa and Jade let him go. "But this little guy will brighten the team right up. Tough night, eh?"

"Brutal night." Jade adjusted to having empty arms and walked toward Max's office with her hands in her pockets. Hines split off to the locker room with Asa.

In Max's office, Jade flipped on a light and took a seat on his sofa. The leather was thick and deep, but oh so comfortable. What else did he have in this office? Her gaze paused at the window. One, he had an amazing view of the field. Who wouldn't be inspired by this place? Grand field house. Manicured, custom field with all the bells and whistles.

But Brenda was right. If attendance remained low, the concession staff would make no money. The souvenir sellers would have to fold up shop. Warrior pride would not live, but die. Max was supposed to be a fresh spark.

Jade got up and moseyed to his desk. Nice chair. She pressed her palms on the arms. And he had the new iMac. Very classy. Absently she opened his desk drawers. So like him. Max the minimalist. Most of them were empty. She spun the chair around to the credenza. Books about football and strategy lined the top shelf. Playbooks and regulations were stacked neatly on the bottom.

Jade drew open a bottom drawer with her toe. Something rattled in the back. She flipped on the credenza lamp. Didn't Max ever dust? She reached inside the drawer. What one thing would he keep down here?

Her heart crashed the moment her fingertips shouted "baggie" to her brain. Jade pulled it out, dropping it on the desk like a hot rock.

Percocets. Hundreds of them.

Her face flashed cold and fear filled her veins. Anxiety charged her heart so its rhythm stole her deep breaths. Where did he get these? Why would he get these? Jade stood, then sat, running her hand over her forehead. *Think, think, think.*

His eyes had been clear ever since he got home. He wasn't distracted. Well, he was, but football-distracted, not sneaking-Percocet distracted. She couldn't remember the last time he pressed his hand to his back and said something about the constant ache.

He went running the other night. He confronted Landon and ended the ordeal laughing with her about goofy cousin Jeff.

The weariness in her bones compounded to dread, her own fears alighting. This would never end. The lies, the drama, the addictions. They'd never end.

How could he have told her the wild story of Jesus's healing and stash these in his credenza? Was this his just-in-case plan? Well, it stunk.

"Hey, there you are." Max came in, Asa in his arms, his Warrior cap on billbackward. He bent to her cheek but she backed away. He frowned with a fast visual scan. "Asa had a blast with the boys. He thinks he's one of them. Jade, you okay? Tuck's coming over with Noah and Calvin for pizza. Jade?"

"You're using again." She snapped her pointing finger to his desk where the baggie of pills lay in the spotlight of his desk lamp.

"What?" He paled. "Where did you get those? Were they on the desk when you came in?"

She pointed to the credenza drawer.

"Oh, Jade, come on. Those aren't mine."

"Then what are they doing in here? If they aren't yours, then whose?"

"I have no idea."

"So, the drug of your choice, Percocet, just happened to land in your office, in a lower drawer, without your knowledge."

"Yes. Jade, look at my eyes. I'm clean. Besides, a cheap plastic bag? Not my style. I used high-quality containers. I hid my junk in kiddie safes in my office closet, under mufflers and gloves. Not a bottom credenza drawer. So all of a sudden, I just drop them in a dime store baggie and leave them for anyone to find?"

"Maybe you forgot to hide them." Tremors zapped across her torso so she shivered without control.

"I'd never forget to hide them, Jade. I'm not an amateur. These are not mine."

"Then whose?"

"You tell me—you found them."

"What kind of crack is that, Max?" Jade reached for Asa. "Until you find out, they're yours."

"Except you know they're not."

"I trusted you before and was wrong almost every single time." Jade fired out of the office.

"Hey, Mrs. B. We're coming for pizza. Do you want Domino's or—"

"Not now, Tucker. Please . . ." The echo of her steps in the block and tile hall chimed in her ears. Her head pounded. She was too angry to let panic rise. What would it take to make him man up? How stupid. How very stupid. This . . . this would get him fired.

Wait . . . she drew up short and spun around. "Max—"

He was right behind her. "You're going to listen to me."

"No, you're going to listen to me." She rose up on her toes. "Max, what if Bobby put them there?"

About five feet away, the boys filed out. Noah. Calvin. Tucker.

"'Night, boys."

"'Night, coach."

"They're watching, Jade." Max held her elbow and steered her toward the parking lot. "We'll go to the ER, I'll pee in a cup, and you'll know for sure, I'm clean."

"But Max, I think Bobby put them there."

"And why would he do that?"

"To get you fired. Slow down, heavy kid in my arms here."

Max reached down for Asa. "I'm still peeing in a cup."

"You don't have to."

"Yes, I do. You thought they were mine."

"Well, Max . . . come on, can you blame me?"

He sighed. "I've been clean for half a year, and the first thing you did when you saw the pills was accuse me and call me a liar."

"A big bag of your old drug. Yes. But it makes no sense. Does Bobby or anyone else know about your Percocet problem?"

"Chevy."

"Ooh, do you think—"

"No, Jade. We have enough suspects." Max pulled up beside the car. "But it's not hard to find out my not-so-secret secrets. All you have to do is Google my name and find out I've been in rehab two times. For pain meds. The Chattanooga papers covered my first rehab and my stint at the Outpost. 'Heir to Benson Law Dynasty Kicking Drug Habit. Again.'"

"So Bobby did do it."

"Maybe. Open the car. You and I are going to the ER to pee in a cup."

"Max—" She was tired, hungry, and in no mood to spend an hour in the emergency room for a tox screen. "Just forget it. Someone put them there. I believe you."

"You don't. And even if you did, you need the proof for when those moments of doubt come. Wondering, 'Did he? He sure is gone a lot these days. Boy, the stress is sure getting to him. I wonder if . . .' Jade, I've failed you a lot.

I've failed myself and my family. God. But I'm not failing a drug test. You need to see that for yourself."

She regarded him for a long moment, the intensity in his voice vibrating through her thoughts. "I'll see you there."

Max walked beside Jade onto the carnival thoroughfare. The tinny sounds of ride music electrified the air as streams of carny fans flowed around them.

The ride lights flashed and blinked. Red. Blue. Yellow. Green.

Max folded the strip of tickets he'd purchased and stuffed them in his pocket. With the tense but cordial air between Jade and him, he doubted the intent of the outing. Fun?

He knew nothing of the planned date until Brenda Karlin showed up to babysit. He initially feared she was bringing an update to the task he'd assigned her. When she passed him at church earlier with a "See you tonight," he let it blow past him. She must be mistaken. Then she knocked on his door.

Jade confessed she'd planned a *fun* night out.

Max took a light hold of her elbow. "If you're not going to have fun, we can go home. I can always watch film. Review stats. I got lots to do."

"No, this is fine."

"The tox screen came back negative, Jade. You can look at me and see I'm not using."

"Then how did they get there? I can't stop thinking about it. What did you do with them? Just as bad is the idea that someone wants you out of a job so much they research you and set a booby trap."

"I flushed them." And flushed, and flushed, and flushed. "That guy is not me."

"Why don't we go and talk to Chevy."

"Jade, the carnival was a good idea. I need this. You need this. So let's forget Friday night, please, and have fun." He caught her waist and drew her to him, kissing her. "You look beautiful tonight."

She relaxed in his arms. "Thank you."

"Okay, what do you want to do first?" Max stepped ahead a few paces, surveying the rides. "We got your Screaming Swing."

Jade shook her head.

"The tilt-a-whirl."

Really shaking her head.

"The fun house."

Blech. She made a retching motion.

He laughed. "Come on. What do you want to do?" Jade lived with this lopsided kind of confidence—beautiful yet with a hint of frightened doe in her eyes.

"Eat."

"Eat? We have to ride something first." He motioned to the Ferris wheel. "One ride, then food."

Jade hip-checked him toward the food stands. Toward the aroma of grilling meat and sweet beignets. "How about the beignet-go-round and the big carniburger ride."

"Ride first, eat later. What happens if you get sick, lose your cookies?" He made a face.

"Good point. Ferris wheel it is."

As they made their way across the thoroughfare, Max caught a few "Evening, Coach" greetings. A man and woman passed with a wave and a nod. "Nice try Friday night. You'll get 'em next week."

Nice try? We were obliterated. "Go Warriors," Max said, smiling. Then he bent in Jade's ear, soothing his hand the length of her hair. "They must be from Palo Duro."

She laughed. "Come on, give yourself some credit. You played hard Friday night."

"It was like fielding peewee players against Ohio State or Texas."

Another couple passed with a "Go Warriors" shout-out. One man stopped to talk about the game for a few minutes, then moved on.

As they lined up for a ride on the Ferris wheel, Max caught a mass of red and gold moving through the crowd like a precision army.

His boys. His team. His chest swelled with a bit of pride.

"Coach and Mrs. Coach." Noah clapped his hand in Max's, then leaned into him for a shoulder bump. Calvin followed, then Tucker. One by one, Brad, Sam, Colton, Dale, Geller.

"Out on a Sunday night? Tell me your homework is done, Noah. Calvin?" The surrounding boys jeered. "All y'all better have it done too. I'm talking to Mr. Molnar in the morning and I want all my players eligible this week."

"It's done, Coach. It's done." Noah backed away, hands in the air. He was becoming the leader of the team with Calvin as a close second.

"Mine too, Coach. We thought we didn't have to turn it in. Mr. Parrish said we didn't have to 'cause he knew we practiced in the afternoon. As long as we passed the test and quizzes."

Max considered the teen. Noah nodded in agreement. "Are you sure? Did you talk to him about it when you got benched?"

"Yeah, but he said we misunderstood."

"How did you misunderstand?" Max said.

"Something about turning it in on Monday. After the weekend."

Max peered at Jade. She made a wry face. The conspiracy theory remained popular. "Look, we do all homework. No exceptions. Turn it in on time. Everyone clear?"

"Yes, Coach," the boys chorused with small head bobs.

"Good. See you boys tomorrow."

"'Night, Coach." The red and gold mass moved.

Except Tucker. His bangs flopped over his forehead and the back of his hair threaded the top of his collar. He was tall, good-looking, but always had a little bit of a lost look in his blue eyes.

"I'm sorry about trying to invite us over the other night for pizza, Mrs. Benson." He kicked the thoroughfare grass. "I didn't mean to bother you."

"No, Tucker, it's okay. You and the boys are always welcome. I snapped at you and I shouldn't have." Jade peered up at Max. "I was upset at something, but it had nothing to do with you."

"I know I hang around a lot." Tucker's voice faded. He wasn't willing to opt out of his nearly-nightly visits. Max felt it.

His boyish tone tugged Max's heart and his love grew a bit more each time Tuck came around. He was so hungry. So thirsty.

"We love having you hang around, Tuck." Max squeezed his shoulder. "Anytime. You are welcome and we mean it. If we yell at you, well, that just means you're really family."

"Asa would miss you terribly if you weren't around." Jade pressed her hand on his arm. "You are part of the family, Tuck. We love you."

His countenance lifted as he backed away, grinning. "Better catch up with the rest. Calvin will leave me here. See you tomorrow." He scurried to catch his teammates.

"Max, there's a good man waiting to break above all that pain and insecurity. Do you know his story other than Mariah being a single mom?"

"Dad left." Max shook his head. "Mariah kind of gets around."

"Next." The ride jockey called.

Max gave the man two tickets and settled in a bucket with Jade. When they were locked in, the wheel went round.

"Are you having fun?" Max slipped his arm around Jade as the wind blew her hair across her face. Sleek, darks wisps. He reached up to help her tuck them away, thinking it'd been awhile since she wore her hair down. He liked it.

"Yeah, we're having fun."

"Trusting me?"

"Max, I have to trust you. I . . . I . . ." She pinched her lips. Then grabbed his hand and curved it over his heart. "Do you promise me that those pills are not yours and you never plan to use them?"

The wheel rotated up. The carnival colors stretched beneath them. Sapphires, rubies, and emeralds flowing in a white river of light over western plains.

"I will never use them." He peered into her eyes, his voice firm with unwavering truth.

"Okay, then, I'll tell you why I have to trust you." The wheel lifted them higher. Jade stared out, then down. "Look, Max, we're sitting on top of the world."

"So we are, but Jade, why do you have to trust me? What's going on?"

She exhaled, turning toward him as best she could while locked in a metal bucket. "I'm pregnant."

He blinked. "W-what?"

"I'm eleven weeks pregnant. Dr. Gelman said everything looked good. I've been throwing up every morning after you leave."

"Y-you're pregnant?" His George Bailey stutter vibrated in his belly.

"Yes, babe, I'm pregnant."

His heart brimmed and spilled over. "But we weren't trying. I mean, we hadn't even talked about it."

"Well, I think we did a lot of talking, bucko. Nonverbal." She laughed. Soft. Without a care.

Max grabbed her and kissed her, sinking down in the bucket, sinking into her.

When he broke the passion, he sat back. "Ha, ha. We're having a baby." Max shot his hands over his head. "Look out, world. Jade and Max Benson are having a baby." He latched onto the crisscross bars and started rocking.

"Max, hey, wait." Jade fell against him laughing. "Woo-hoo, world, we're having a baby."

The couple below them applauded. "Congratulations."

The wheel spun down to the ground. Max shouted to passersby, "We're having a baby."

When they rode to the top, he shouted again, "We're having a baby." He punched the air. *Yes, yes, yes.* "Jade." He snatched her by the shoulders. "This one is different. This one will make it."

Tears slithered to the corner of her eyes. "I think so too. I do, Max."

"And Jade, guess what?"

She shook her head. "I don't know . . . what?"

"This is my first biological baby. And it's with you."

She dropped her gaze. "I know. It's what we wanted but now it feels so silly. Asa is mine. He's yours. He's our firstborn."

Max clipped his arm around her, kissing her temple, feeling the drop of the wheel as it spun around, then lifted them up. The circle of life. "We'll finalize Asa's adoption before this baby is born. Change his name to Benson. Call Cara. She's the lawyer on this. Tell her we want a December court date. The Warrior season will be over by then." Probably his career, too, if Bobby had his way.

"What about the McClures, Max?" She'd spoken to him about Lorelai's visit. But Max had encountered Gus's reputation enough times to doubt his sincerity. "Can they be in Asa's life? I don't think there is any other answer but yes. They must. They are his grandparents."

"I hear you. You're right. Let's talk to them when we go home for Christmas."

"Can I Skype with them?"

"Yeah, Skype." He grinned. "Your heart is reflected in all of this light beneath us." Max gestured to the white river. "God brought all the truth to light for us when we said 'yes' to Him and 'no' to our own fears and wills."

"I'm happy, Max." Jade leaned into him as the wheel rode around, the breeze cutting fresh and cool.

"Me too, Jade-o. Me too."

When the ride ended, Max passed the jockey two more tickets and a twenty, adding a hard glare for good measure. "We're not getting off."

The wheel started and Max rode again with Jade. Rising above the earth.

Then lowering to the ground. Rising. Lowering. Lights above. Lights below. This *was* the circle of life. Light and dark. Failures and successes. Triumph and sadness.

And love. Oh, love remained. And she rested in his arms tonight.

Twenty-eight

"Hey, Coach Mom." Tucker leaned over Jade's laptop, his beach-sand locks long and drifting down the sides of his face. Confidence finally resided in his gray-blue eyes. "We're going to play some ball." He spun the football in his hands. "Coach is going to teach us midnight football. Want to play?"

Jade paused from her e-mail. It'd been a week since she told Max about the baby so she figured she'd share the joy with Aiden and Willow too.

"Midnight football? First of all, it's only seven o'clock. Second of all, that's my game and what does Coach know about it?"

Tuck grinned. "That's what he said you'd say." He motioned for her to come on. "Teach us. The game works before midnight, doesn't it?"

"Har, har." It was a Saturday night and the boys, truck by truck, car by car, made their way to the house. "I'd love to teach you the game. Give me five minutes. Y'all set up a fifty-yard field and blast some tunes. Midnight football works best to The Boss, but y'all can listen to Chesney or Rascal Flatts, Johnny Mathis for all I care."

"Who?" He crinkled his lip.

"Johnny Mathis, you know, velvet voice, African American singer." Kids today had no culture. At all. The world's history began the day they were born. "After football season, all y'all are getting vintage music lessons from me."

"What for?"

"To make sure you don't repeat the past."

"Uh?"

"To humor me."

"Oh, okay." He raised his chin, eyes squinting with confusion. "See you out there?"

"On my way." She couldn't play, of course. Nothing, not even a reminiscent game of midnight football, was worth risking the baby's safety.

The door crashed and slammed. "Hey, Coach Mom is on her way. Get the cones. Fifty-yard field." Tuck's voice faded as he ran west of the house.

Jade stared at her computer screen, fingers poised over the keyboard. She reread the last line of her e-mail to Aiden and Willow.

Max and I are so excited about the baby. We are hopeful. For us, for the baby, for a new life in Colby.

"Coach Mom." Dylan dashed into the room. "Game's waiting on you." His bangs tangled above his hazel eyes and his ruddy cheeks popped with his smile.

"On my way."

He dashed out the same way he came in. *Bam. Slam.* "She's coming. Let's choose up sides."

Gotta run. Teaching the boys midnight football. Aiden, remember the time we snuck out to play and Granny was waiting for us on the porch at two a.m.? We were all tiptoeing and whispering. She said, loud as ever, "Where you kids been?" LOL. She had to peel us off the ceiling.

Miss you both. Write. Call. Something.

With love,
Jade-o

Tugging on her Tennessee Volunteers sweatshirt, Jade headed across the yard to where the boys waited, through a blast of October chill. The Boss sang "Born in the USA" from Noah's truck.

Max was positioned between two teams of three, Asa riding on his shoulders. The boys saw her and cheered.

"All right, Coach Mom."

Jade jogged toward the makeshift field. "Okay, it's three on three. These are the rules . . ." As she explained, Max caught her attention with his smile. Pearls of love drifted through her, warming her soul with its incandescent glow.

Max crouched with his hands on his knees, watching as Noah took the hike, dropping back, handing the ball to Calvin. Just four little yards and he'd be in the end zone. But the Lubbock Westerners blitzed. Hard. Unwilling to lose to the last-in-the-league Warriors.

Calvin tucked the ball away but ran into a wall of defenders, and instead of gaining four yards, he lost three. Driven back by a determined inside linebacker.

Max shoved his hat back on his head. "Time. Time."

The clock on the scoreboard stopped. The score blared red: 9–7.

Noah led the offense to the sideline. Hines and Haley huddled around Max. "What do you want to do?" Hines said, scanning his play card. "Option to the weak side?"

"Coach, pass." Noah pulled off his helmet. "I can see over their lineman a good two seconds before they blitz. Calvin will be in the end zone with the ball and all they think is blitz, blitz, blitz."

"Calvin has been running into the same linebacker all night."

Hines flipped his card over. "But their corner can run stride for stride with Calvin, Noah. He sees you set to pass, he's going to line up with Cal."

Max glanced down the line. "Walberg, front and center." He'd not called on Tucker since his three-field-goal-attempt calamity. But he'd been practicing. Hard. This was their next to the last game and he only had another four quarters to make a goal this year. And Max wasn't leaving this season—leaving this team, this town, this short career if God willed it to end—without Tucker putting three on the board.

"Coach, we can do it." Calvin jutted in front of Max. "I can cut around that corner. I know I can."

"Haley, get your boys ready to defend the last two minutes and forty seconds of the game like they've never defended before. With any luck, we'll get the ball back and run the clock out. Kicking team, let's go, on the field." Tucker jumped up, exchanging his bored expression for terror. "Walberg, let's go."

He jumped into action, moving on reflex instead of heart. But Max grabbed him by the pads as he ran past and peered through his face mask. "Get rid of that fear, Tucker. Missing is all in your head. How many did you hit in practice yesterday?"

"Twenty."

"So go out there and hit twenty-one."

"Y-yes, Coach."

"Concentrate. Follow through, head down. Keep those hips toward the goal. Kick that ball like you're a winner. Because, Tucker, this is for the win." Max shot his fist in the air and the team leaned into him. "Warriors on three. One, two, three."

"Warriors!"

The kicking team ran onto the field. Tucker brought up the rear, snapping on his chin strap. *Lift your head up, boy. Lift your head up.*

The fans stood with a mixed, mingling murmur of support. *Coach, what are you doing? Come on, Tucker.* Anticipation took the chill in the air down a degree or two.

Max scanned the stands for Jade. She watched with her hands balled at her cheeks, staring ahead. Mariah stood next to her, yelling, arms flailing, fingers pointing toward the field. *Sit down, Mariah. Cheer for your son.*

On the other side of Jade, Brenda bounced Asa on her hip. Then she moved, like a coiled snake, snatched Mariah's arm, gave it a twist and the irate mom melted down to the bleachers.

You go, Brenda.

Max faced the field. "Let's go, Tucker." Max stepped and leaned over the sideline, urging on his brave kicker. Whispering a prayer.

Haley lined up off his right shoulder. "Max, it's a twenty-four-yard kick."

"He can do it, Haley. We can't get much closer."

The ref whistled the play alive and Noah, the ball holder, encouraged Tuck by holding up his fist of solidarity. Then he called for the snap. The breeze landed on the field. The bleachers went silent.

Noah T'd the ball.

Tucker stepped, one, two, three, drawing back his kicking leg, his ankle straight, his plant foot pointed toward the goal. When he made contact, his hips rotated toward the posts and the ball arched end over end. High. Right . . . on . . . the . . . money.

Max's heart beat with each spiral. He was afraid to breathe.

The ball sailed through a bright wash of stadium light and for a second, Max lost sight of it. Then *whoosh*, it splashed into view and soared through the uprights. Smack down the middle.

The refs whistled and ran forward with their arms in the air. Good! The kick was good. The Warriors scored.

For a second, the earth stood still. Then the team erupted onto the field and the stands went wild. A stunned Tucker ended up buried under a pile of boys showing their undying gratitude.

Even Lubbock players applauded.

Finally pulled from the bottom of the pile, Tucker ran for Max, flying into him. "I did it, Coach. I did it."

Max wrapped his hand around his helmet, drew him in. "I told you, you could. I told you. How's it feel to be a football player?"

"It . . . it feels awesome." Tucker bucked back his emotion, but Max wouldn't blame him for bawling like a baby. A season's worth of tension and failure needed to be let out.

When Max let him go, Tucker ran to the fence, peered up at Jade who was jumping and waving. Mariah was nowhere to be seen.

"Defense, let's hold Tucker's lead." It was only by one. But it was their one.

Haley ran past Max. "I'm on it, Coach. Defense on me. This is what we've been working for all year."

He did it. Jade wiped away her tears. "Look at that, look at that," Brenda muttered over and over.

Tucker kicked a field goal. The Warriors were ahead. And the D was battling like their lives depended on it.

Jade glanced down the row where Mariah should've been, seeing her son win the game. But she was gone. When Max had called Tucker up, Mariah went ballistic, reaming Jade out because "your husband" put "my son" in the game just to humiliate him.

No, Mariah, you're doing that all by yourself.

"You think you can steal my son . . . Miss High and Mighty . . . Where were you when he had a fever and diarrhea?" She ranted. Railed. "Who do you think you are?"

Jade peered at her. "Just a woman who loves your son."

Fuel to her flame, those words. Mariah started back into it, growing louder, then Brenda reached around with some kind of scary kung fu grip and down she went. "Go clean yourself up, Mariah."

She steamed and stormed off. Just as Tucker made the kick. Women. Such a complicated species.

As the D ran onto the field, Jade winced. For the last few minutes, a discomfort settled in her lower abdomen. A second sharp pang awakened her senses. Something was wrong.

She'd had pain and cramping off and on for a couple of days. Dr. Gelman said, "The womb making room," and laughed at her own pun.

But this didn't feel like womb room. Another sharp pang fired up through Jade's abdomen and bent her forward. Then she felt it. The warm gush.

"Brenda, I'll be back." Jade tugged her jacket tight and moved down the bleachers.

"You all right, shug?" She bounced Asa. "Come on D, read the play. Get off the line."

Panic burped in Jade's mind and soured her heart. This wasn't happening. She was thirteen weeks. Past the old danger zone. The baby moved. Dr. Gelman verified the heartbeat.

Don't die on me, little one.

Following the signs to Warrior Women, Jade rounded the brick wall and ran into Mariah Walberg. "Mariah, I'm sorry, excuse me." She stepped around her. "You missed your son's kick. He scored." Jade shoved the door.

"Was that what all the cheering was about?" Was that remorse in her tone?

Jade held her next step forward. "I'm not trying to steal your son, Mariah." Jade winced with another cramping wave. Followed by another warm rush. "I'm sorry, but I need to go."

Barricading herself in the first stall, Jade realized her fears. Blood, soaking blood. "No, no, no." White spots paraded across her vision and her heart beat so frantically Jade lost control of her trembling hands and quivering legs.

The thin sheets of toilet paper shredded when she tried to rip them from the roll. "Oh, come on." Jade smashed the metal dispenser with her hand. "Jesus, Jesus, Jesus . . . please, please." Tears burned a hot trail down her cheeks.

"Hey in there, are you okay?" The tips of Mariah's boots barely showed beneath the stall.

"No . . . I'm not. Get Max, Max. Please."

"Coach? He's on the field."

"I . . . I'm bleeding, Mariah. Get him, please."

"Do you need a tampon?" Mariah's boot tips turned toward the opposite wall. "Oh, there's no machine."

"No, no, I'm pregnant." Jade held back a blue word. "Was pregnant."

"You're pregnant?" Mariah banged on the door. "Open up. I'm taking you to the hospital."

"Mariah, please, get Max." Jade collected herself as best she could and opened the stall door. The cramping came in small waves followed by purple swells of panic. "I need Max." She left her phone in the truck, but Max never took his phone onto the field. "Mariah, I need my husband." Jade lowered to the floor, stretching out on the cold, wet tile. *Please, God, this one was supposed to be different. Supposed to live.*

"What are you doing? You can't lie down on this floor, it's filthy." Mariah snapped a wad of paper towels from the dispenser and dropped to the floor, mopping up some of the grime.

"I'd lie on a mountain of mud to save this baby."

"Where's your car? I'll get it. Drive you." This stubborn woman was not the same insulting Mariah who'd dressed her down in the stands a few minutes ago.

"Go get Max. Get a deputy to help you."

"Are you sure? I can drive you to the ER, then come back to tell him."

"Mariah."

She bolted from the bathroom with a *click-clack* of her boot heels, then *click-clack*ed back. "I'm really sorry . . . about earlier."

"Mariah, it's okay. I understand."

"I was jealous is all. Tucker thinks you hung the moon. Oh, I'll shut up. Hold on, I'll be right back. Everything's going to be fine."

Lying on the cold, hard floor, eyes shut, heart wide open, Jade pleaded with the Lord of life to save her child.

~

"Coach." A sheriff deputy tapped him on the shoulder. "The woman at the fence says she needs you. Emergency."

Max turned. Jade? But it was Mariah. What? They had the ball back, a minute to go, and Noah was hitting Calvin in the numbers. They were down by two again. Lubbock had kicked a field goal but the Warriors were marching down the field.

"Coach." She waved him over.

Max checked down the line at Tucker. He watched, sheepish and distant.

"Coach." Again with the frantic arm wave. Max gazed up to the stands. Where was Jade?

He ran to the fence. "What?"

"Jade . . . in the bathroom. She's bleeding."

In one move, Max cleared the fence and raced for the low stone building by the concession stand, crashing shoulders, shoving bodies, hollering, "Out of my way."

Behind him, the crowd gasped. A whistle blew. He jerked open the bathroom door. "Jade." He dropped to one knee. "What's going on?" Her hair was soaked in a puddle of muddy water. Her eyes were red and raw.

"I'm losing the baby . . . I'm losing . . . it's never going to be right, is it? It'll always be almost but . . . never. Never." She shook with a sorrowful sob.

"Hush, you're not losing this baby." Max slipped his arms under her and lifted her off the floor. "The ambulance is right outside the door." Kicking his way out the bathroom door, he ran toward the red and white emergency vehicle. "Medic!"

The EMTs in the aisle watching the game bolted into action. "My wife might be miscarrying."

"Got you, Coach." The men in blue went into action, pulling out the stretcher, taking Jade from Max's arms.

Mariah danced and pranced off to the side.

"Mariah, where's Asa?" he said, turning to her.

"With Miss Brenda."

"After the game, get Tuck and take him to our house with Asa. Can you handle that? There's a spare key out on the carport. Under the flowerpot."

"Y-you'd trust . . . me?"

"Is there any reason I shouldn't?"

Her eyes grew wide and round. "No, sir." She swallowed and sobered. "Miss Brenda can come, too, help out."

"You probably can't stop her. But Tuck knows Asa's routine."

"Don't worry, Jade." Mariah reached for Jade's hand as the paramedics moved her into the wagon. "I'll take care of him."

"Just make sure he gets something to eat before he goes to bed. He likes applesauce or yogurt. Tuck knows."

Max climbed into the back and the medic clapped the doors closed. The engine fired up and the ambulance surged out of the parking lot. Jade gripped his hand so fiercely he couldn't feel his fingertips, but he held on to her.

Jade lay there, weeping, tears flowing with the speed of the vehicle. Max had no words. Only prayer. After a moment, he bent down to her face.

"Look at me, Jade. It's going to be all right. We didn't come this far by God's grace to fail."

"I can't do this again, Max. I can't lose another baby."

"We got to have faith, babe. What can we do—but believe?"

"I can't believe. I can't . . ." She winced, squeezing her eyes shut so water gushed from the corners. "Where are the lights of life now, Max? Where?"

Twenty-nine

Jade counted the ceiling tiles as the nurse pricked her arm to start an IV. Since she'd arrived at Baptist St. Anthony's, they'd put her in a gown, moved her to the OB wing, and drawn several tubes of blood.

Ten tiles down. Ten across. The window in the far left corner was dark save for the room's overhead lights bouncing off the glass.

Besides the number of the tiles, another number surfaced in her mind and demanded an account. Five. She'd been pregnant five times. Five times she'd lost.

Oh, Lord, another baby? A mournful moan sent a plea across her soul to her heart.

Max squeezed her hand. He'd not let go since the medics lowered her to the stretcher. The nurse bumped the bed and Jade moved her gaze to Max. He traced his finger along the curve of her cheek, smoothing away the residue of tears. Her eyes welled up again.

"Hey, babe," he whispered in her ear, "the baby is going to be fine. I feel it. Right here." He tapped his free hand to his chest. "Brenda's activated prayer meetings and prayer chains all over Colby." Max spoke low, tender and steady. "Dr. Gelman is on her way."

Jade nodded, crushing her fingers harder into his. "You have always been there for me. I ran and you chased me. I was so . . . so mad about Rice, but you are the one person in my life who never left me."

"We don't have to talk about this now, Jade." He kissed the back of her hand. His eyes searched hers, reflecting his heart. Jade knew. She had to let Max all the way in. Open up all of her heart's doors and windows, and trust. This beautiful man God gave her would never rob her soul.

"I trust you, Max."

"What's this all about, babe? I know you do."

"No, babe, I *trust* you. Trust. You. I see it now, so clearly." She struggled to sit up, a surge of passion and confidence overpowering her momentary sorrow. "You love me."

"You're just now figuring that out?" His smile was saucy and sexy.

"Yeah, I am."

If Jade had known at sixteen what she knew now, she'd have never let fear reign in her life. She'd never have lied to marry Dustin Colter, no matter how passionately he wooed her heart. She'd never have let her broken heart agree to Mama's "choice" for her baby—a Des Moines *women's* clinic. Don't get her started on the irony.

Remorse took a slow ride down her spine. She'd have never healed from the abortion without Jesus. Her heart condemned her, but in the end, He didn't. Kind God with kind eyes and a balm to heal the destruction of sin on her heart.

But now she lay in a hospital, again, losing the little life she already loved. Surely He did too. *Lord?*

A fresh wash of tears rode down her cheeks.

"More tears?" Max caught them with the curve of his finger. "What's going on behind your eyes?"

"Just realizing how blessed I am, Max. More than I deserve. But I don't want to lose this baby." Desperation filled every part of her. "Do you think unborn babies go to heaven, Max?"

"I'd bet my fortune they do." He brushed her hair with the tips of his fingers. "We have *four* babies there." He arched his brow. *Are you hearing me?* "But not this one. God didn't bring us to Texas to lose. Football games, yes, but not babies. Let's just trust Him to lead us to a level place. No matter what, we're together."

Max tapped his forehead to Jade's. "Jesus, we trust you to keep this baby. To heal, to redeem, to stop the bleeding."

Closing her eyes, Jade formed the words *heal* and *redeem* in her mind and made them her offering to the Lord. Peace, like a royal blue ribbon, swirled in her soul. It was then, when her mind cleared, she realized the pain had subsided. The blood flow had eased. "Max, the cramping . . . it's stopped."

"Babe, really?"

"Actually, I don't think it's happened since we got in the ambulance." Fear had robbed her reason. Turned her focus inside out.

"I told you." Max squeezed her hand.

She smiled. "Maybe it'll be okay." *Thank you, Jesus, thank you.* "Hey, how did the game go?"

"We lost." In an instant, they exchanged sorrows in their countenances. Max released her hand and walked toward the window. He wore his new red varsity jacket with a gold *W* on the back and black warm-up pants. He'd transformed himself this year. Exchanged addiction for freedom. Given up self for son.

"No, babe, no. You won. Those boys played like champs tonight. Did you see that kick? I mean *see* it? It was darn near perfect. Form and all. I've watched you all fall, Max. You've gone from privileged lawyer to redeemed cowboy to passionate football coach. From being fatherless to parenting a two-year-old and forty teen boys. All the while you chased me home. You never broke stride. You looked at yourself in the mirror and you said, 'Man up,' and you did."

"I'm not a hero, Jade."

"You are to me, Max. I never thought I'd have a true hero in my life and look, there he is, staring out a dark window with a loss on his mind but never once hinting that he needed to go, be with the team, talk to his coaches. Don't you see, you really love being selfless. As much as any man can."

"You think I'm all here mentally but I'm not. There's a big part of my brain right here"—he tapped his fingers to the back side of his head—"wondering why I seem to fail when I look like I'm succeeding."

"Because success always comes with a bit of failure—you know that, Max. You are succeeding. Look at the team. Babe, come on . . . they love you."

"I just wanted to do something for the boys. Something that was just me. Not my dad's or grandfather's. Not a life that was handed to me. Don't know why Bobby Molnar is so gangbusters to get his father's legacy when he could be out there making his own."

"Both are honorable, Max."

"Yeah, I know. When I was at the ranch I realized how much I loved being challenged. How much I needed to be challenged. How much I loved coaching and working with the boys, sowing into them."

"Don't look now, but you just described your goal for coming here. And you've accomplished it. Winning a game is the cherry on top." Jade folded her hands over her middle.

He adjusted his cap, settling it on his head with the bill in the back. "When you put it like that . . ." He grinned at her. "We make a good team, Benson."

"I think so."

The room door swung open. Dr. Gelman breezed in wearing an off-the-shoulder evening gown with her hair swept up, shining baubles swinging from her earlobes, a delicate strand of pearls jeweling her neck.

"Jade, what's going on?"

"You're dressed up . . . you were at a party . . . a date." Jade moaned. "Oh, I'm so sorry."

"Are you kidding me? It was a boring fund-raiser. My date abandoned me the first minute we walked in the room, completely oblivious to the pain and trauma I endured to look like a million bucks for his sorry self. Even worse, the filet mignon was overcooked. Who overcooks a filet?" She slipped into the white lab coat offered by the nurse. "Bring the ultrasound machine in, Linda. Let's get a look under the hood, see how this baby is doing." Dr. Gelman reviewed Jade's chart. "How's the cramping?"

"Stopped. The bleeding too. As far as I can tell."

"Well, that's good news." Dr. Gelman set up for an exam, talking the whole while about the fund-raiser, the music, the food, and the fashion. "I saw quite a few vintage gowns, Jade. You'd have been proud of those old ladies. And hats galore. Looked like a royal wedding. Remember that funky hat one of the princesses wore to Will and Kate's?" She raised the exam table stirrups. "Jade, scoot down for me just a bit. Perfect. Anyway, saw four of those monstrosities tonight. Unbelievable. On the heads of good ol' practical American cattle women. I almost wept."

Jade peeked at Max, grinning. He appeared appalled by the exam while amused by the stories. "You don't want to be a woman," Jade said.

"No."

"You're right, Jade, the bleeding has stopped," Dr. Gelman said. "Everything seems good. I'll wait for the lab results, but I bet the bleeding was from the placenta attaching to the uterine wall, maybe forcing older clots to dislodge and flush. But I want to do an ultrasound just to make sure we don't miss anything."

"So, the baby is all right?" Jade said.

"As far as I can tell. In fact, you're a lot more pregnant than I'd expect for thirteen weeks." Dr. Gelman warmed her stethoscope and listened to the baby, making a face with a throaty hum.

"What?" Jade peered at Max. He reached for her hand.

"I'm not sure. I'll know more with the ultrasound."

The nurse had rolled in the ultrasound machine during the exam. Dr. Gelman adjusted the monitor for Jade and Max to see. After she'd prepped Jade, the good doctor ran the wand over her abdomen.

The screen remained dark for a moment—a frightening moment—then an instant image filled the black-and-white screen. A wee form, lying in a womb cradle.

"There he is, Jade." Dr. Gelman pointed to the screen.

Jade caught her breath, hand over her mouth. Her eyes flooded. Dr. Gelman slid the wand to the other side of her belly and the baby kicked. She felt it. Then she saw it.

"He kicked. Max, we have a kicker in the family."

"One down, ten to go, and we have our own Benson football team."

Dr. Gelman pointed out the baby's head and body. Emotion scorched Jade's throat and burned her eyes.

"I can't believe it." Max held her hand so tight her fingers started to numb. But she didn't care. "Is it a boy? Can you tell? Am I further along than thirteen weeks?"

"I'll tell you what's interesting me, folks." Dr. Gelman moved the wand around to Jade's side, pressing, shoving. "This right here." She pointed to a round white image on the screen, beneath—or was it beside?—the baby.

Jade squinted. "Where?" She tipped her head to one side and angled for a closer look. "It looks like another . . . head."

"That's what I thought." Dr. Gelman moved the wand again, pressing on Jade's side. "When I was listening for the baby's heartbeat, I heard an echo. And unless you have a really big uterus with mountains and valleys, you have two babies in there."

Jade sat up, her heart careening. "Twins?" Jade said in perfect harmony with Max.

"Twins." Dr. Gelman gentled her back down. "It's probably why you were having trouble tonight, Jade. Your body's setting up to care for two babies instead of one." She slid the wand over Jade's abdomen. "Looks like one sack. So they're identical."

"Twins?" Her voice shook, her heart soared.

"Dr. Gelman, are you sure?" Max said.

"Well, 99 percent. Look, there's her hand." Dr. Gelman shifted her gaze from the monitor to Max, then Jade. "Can't tell for sure, but they're showing signs of being girls."

Jade peeked at her rounding belly glistening with gel. "Dr. Gelman, you wouldn't lie to me, would you?" Five minutes ago, she prayed one would survive. Now she had two—kicking and healthy.

"I don't lie about babies. And I *never* joke about twins." She maneuvered the wand for a better look, pressing Jade's sides to see if the babies would move. But baby B remained cloaked by baby A. "I guess we can tell which one takes after Max." Dr. Gelman grinned, tapping the image of baby A on the screen.

He laughed, a stunted, staccato sound followed by a cough and an *eek*. His summer tan had faded from his cheeks this fall, but this news made them instantly white. Ghostly white. His throat constricted with each breath and swallow.

"Two girls," he said, his voice wobbly but passionate. "And we have a house full of boys right now."

"Get used to it." Dr. Gelman put the wand away and cleaned the gel from Jade's belly. "If these two look like their mama, you're always going to have a house full of boys."

"I need to sit down."

Dr. Gelman's laugh chased Jade's. "Man up, Max. Coaching football will seem like a cakewalk compared to this."

"I know . . . and I'm not doing a great job as coach." He sobered, sitting straight, surprised by his vocal heart confession to the doctor.

"You are a great coach. And if you raise your kids with half the passion you've poured into those boys this year . . ." Dr. Gelman took a measurement and snapped the image. "You'll have a beautiful family."

Jade shot him an I-told-you-so look because she could. And it was fun.

Upon consultation and discussion, Dr. Gelman admitted Jade for the night. Just to be safe. Her long emerald gown swirled and swayed beneath her lab coat as she addressed the night nurse. A strand of her golden hair slipped free from the knot and looped about her neck.

"I'll see you tomorrow," she said, squeezing Jade's hand. "This is good news, isn't it? I'm thrilled for you. Max, good game against Lubbock. A bunch of us were hovered in a corner of this snoozer fund-raiser listening to the game on an iPad."

"Not one for the *W* column, but our best game yet."

"Against a good team. Be proud, Coach. Hold your head up. You're winning this town's heart. And that's not easy to do." Dr. Gelman headed out of the room. "'Night, darlings."

The sweet silence of good news lingered in the room long after she'd gone. The nurse checked Jade's IV, then showed her the call buttons in case she needed anything.

When she was alone again with Max, he bent his face to hers, nearly nose to nose. "Score, Mrs. Benson. Twins."

"Way to go, Mr. Benson."

He grabbed and kissed her hand. "I think my heart stopped beating when she said twins."

"Are you happy?"

"Delirious. Best news of my entire life." He kissed her, soft and sweet. "Twins."

"It's on now, Coach. We're going from one to three in six months."

"Bring it." A sober glint flashed in his eyes. "You want to go home? Be near the folks. The McClures? Our house in Whisper Hollow is big enough. All we have to do is fly home and unpack our suitcases. We're set with friends and community."

"You'd go back to Benson Law?"

"Yeah, of course. Got to earn a living, keep my chicas in the fine clothes and jewels to which my mother will make them accustomed."

"But you don't want to go back, really, do you?"

He twisted his lips. "This changes the game plan, Jade. Coaching is more than a full-time job. I can't help you much once the season starts. Some dreams just need to stay in the hip pocket."

"But if you could have any job you wanted. What would it be?"

He lowered his gaze to their clasped hands and ran his thumb over the back of her hand. "Coach."

"Then be a coach, Max. If they'll have you. Go for your dream."

"But what about you? Your dream? Your shop?"

"I have my dream, Max." The tears surged and overflowed the corner of her eyes. "Right here. Holding my hand."

Thirty

"It was quite a Friday night under the lights. Expected wins and a few upsets. But one near upset almost turned Randall County high school football upside down. Chip Mack is here to give us the story." The shot moved from Channel 13's newsroom to Chip Mack standing on the sidelines of Warrior Field.

Max aimed the remote to raise the volume a bit, careful not to wake Jade. She looked peaceful, breathing deep and even.

"That's right, DeeAnne, I'm standing on the sidelines of Warrior Field where the Colby High Warriors nearly knocked off the top ranked Lubbock Westerners. It was a brutal defensive battle all night. The talented Haley Porter's defense dominated and silenced all doubters."

"Yet your lips are still moving," Max muttered.

"Even though this is another L for Coach Max Benson, it's a W for the Warrior *spirit. The night's biggest win came when sixteen-year-old Tucker Walberg hit his first ever field goal to give the Warriors a one-point lead. Pay close attention, DeeAnne, because this is Sports Channel 13's Play of the Week."*

Play of the Week? Max sat up, eyes glued to the tube, watching the clip of Tucker lining up, making the kick. It was flawless. Hours and hours of practice formed him into the perfect kicker. If he got his head in the game, backed up his confidence with belief . . .

A thrill drummed Max's heart. He had a kicker. A darn good kicker.

The hospital room phone rang. Max frowned as he hurried around the bed to answer. Who would be calling here now?

"Hello?"

"Max, you seeing this?"

"Hines?"

"I called your phone but it went to voice mail."

"Yeah, it's at the field house."

"You see Channel 13?"

Max faced the mounted TV again. "The kick?"

"Woo-hoo, son, we got us a kicker. In forty years of coaching, I've never seen a high school kicker with that kind of form. We drill some confidence into the kid's head and we're going to state. Oh listen, they got man on the street interviews."

Max boosted the volume a touch. A man in Lubbock-wear was talking into a Channel 13 mike. *"It was a good game. Better than I thought. Scary when they went ahead."*

Flash to a man in Warrior attire. *"Coach Benson is doing a good job. I didn't know when he came in if he could do it. Who hires a coach with no experience, but he's really brought these boys together and created a team. I like him."*

A crowd shot of fans leaving the game generated a "Go Warriors" rally.

"Don't look now, Max, but you're winning. Got no Ws in the win column, but you're winning."

Max glanced back at Jade. "More than you know, Hines. More than you know."

To: Aiden, Willow
From: Jade
Subject: Twins!!!!!!! Girls!!!!! (We think)
Need I say more?
XO, Jade

Dear Lillabeth,

I've been thinking and praying all weekend, talking to Max, and I'm confident this e-mail to you is the right thing for me. For all of us.

As much as I'd like to think I'm superwoman enough to run the business with a toddler and twins, I've decided to let go of the shop. I know, just when the *Southern Life* cover hit the stands. Thank you for following up on that for me. You don't know how much I am at ease knowing you are covering the Blues.

I've heard nothing on the Blue Two. Not one nibble. Well, in this economy, what can I expect? But Max and I have really been putting it to prayer.

The football season is one game away from ending. We're not sure what the future holds. Max has meetings this week to see if the principal and boosters want to keep him for another year. Or two. Or five. Or twenty. He loves it, Lilla. Loves it. I've never seen him more stressed but so at peace. A win would be nice. Boost everyone's confidence.

All that to say, I want you to have the shop. You've been so generous and loyal to me, running the shop almost all year while taking classes, I am full of gratitude for you. I can't think of anyone more deserving of the business. You love vintage. You have a fabulous eye. You're studying business. You could take these shops where I never could.

I know it's a big commitment. And with Aaron being deployed, you can't know of your options or future, but I want you to know, the shops are yours, Lillabeth. My gift to you.

Think about it. Let me know when you're ready.

> With love and thankfulness,
> Jade

Monday morning Max unlocked his office with his thoughts already on Friday night's game. Amarillo. The best team in the district. 10–0.

Max didn't miss the irony. The best team in the district ending their regular season playing the worst. He'd started the Warrior season with the goal of winning one, maybe two games. Now all he wanted was to end with some dignity and self-respect. Not to let the Sandies pummel them into the field.

He dropped to his chair and powered up the iMac, stretching his legs, rubbing his eyes. First order of business when the season ended? Sleep.

Might be his last chance for the next twenty years. He may not coach football, but he'd be raising Asa, and twins, and prayerfully a baby or two more. If he could, he'd move Tucker in, but he and Jade had talked, concluding it would be the final straw for Mariah. Tucker was the one thing that kept her from flying off and going completely wild.

Instead, they'd fold both Tucker and Mariah into their extended family. Along with Gus and Lorelai. The notion popped a smile on his lips. Saturday night he and Jade made calls home.

Dad and Mom. Max's ear rang for an hour after Mom's scream. "Twins! I can't believe it. Oh my stars . . . Jade, I'm throwing you the biggest shower. Here . . . there . . . wherever you are. I have a million things to do."

Next Jade wanted to call the McClures. When she said they were going to be grandparents again, Lorelai burst into tears and left the call. Gus tried to carry on, stoic and hard like always, but his voice broke every other word with long, watery pauses.

Jade called Lillabeth. Max called his old friend and accountability partner, Tripp. Jade called her college roommates, Daphne and Margot. Max called Hines and Haley, and Chevy. His college roommates were party animals and partly responsible for his moral demise in Vegas. He'd distanced himself from them for a while. But next time he was in the Hollow, he'd grab a game of golf with them.

Last he called Axel. He owed the man for showing him the tools Max already possessed in Christ to overcome.

The bell rang for the first class to dismiss. Max logged into his e-mail, catching an immediate flood of congratulations and forwarded links from the local press.

He wasn't sure where he stood with Chevy or Bobby, but from what he was reading, Max was gaining favor with the community. One kid was quoted saying he planned to play for Coach Benson next year.

Footsteps echoed in the hall. Max looked up when they ceased at his door. Bobby Molnar stood in the doorway, Chevy Buchholz in tow.

"We need to talk." Bobby's tone and expression told Max this meeting wasn't about a good game on Friday night.

"Come in." Max rose, motioning for them to take a seat on the sofa.

Bobby's demeanor said confrontation. He kept his gaze steely and level, his chest puffed, his jaw taut. Chevy on the other hand looked beat down, defeated. His shoulders drooped and his eyes studied the floor as he took a seat on the sofa. When he sat, he exhaled weariness.

"Get to it, Bob. Might as well ruin everyone's Monday morning." Chevy slapped his hand on his leg, then absently brushed his fingers over his slacks. A nervous habit, Max knew, wishing today's issue could be brushed away like lint.

"Is this about me leaving the game Friday night?" Max straddled one of the chairs by his desk.

"No, but you might wish it was when I'm done."

"Bob, come on, just tell him why we're here." Chevy's pencil-thin expression twisted with frustration. He smoothed his solid blue tie. Ran his hand over his clipped gray hair.

The athletic director pulled a baggie from his pocket and shook it in front of Max. Percs. "Look familiar?"

"No, Bobby, they don't." The pills were in the same baggie Jade had found in Max's drawer. But he'd flushed them.

"Wasn't Percocet your drug of choice, Benson?" Bobby tossed them to the desk. "Why you spent three months at the Outpost?"

"Max, are you using?" Chevy asked the perfunctory question in monotone.

"I am not using. No, sir." Max stood to meet Bobby's challenge, hands propped on his belt. He was not ashamed. He had nothing to hide.

"There you go, Bob. He's not using. Good enough for me." Chevy smacked the leather cushion next to him and stood to go. "Great game Friday night, Max. Tucker's kick was the high school play of the week."

"Tucker's worked hard this season. His form was perfect."

"You made a kicker out of mere clay, Max." Chevy nodded. "Good job."

"Excuse me, Chevy, but kicker or not, I found a baggie of illegal prescription drugs in your head coach's office."

"Those aren't mine." Max corralled his temper. This was fourth down with goal to go and he needed his cool. Getting into his emotions would only fuel Bobby's fire. "But it does seem to me *Bobby* has a mighty large bag of Percs. Where'd you get them?"

"You can deny it all you want, but I found these in your office, Max."

"What were you doing in my office?" Max removed his coach's hat and donned his lawyer attire. "Did you have a reason to be in here?"

"I needed your compliance report. All of the other coaches submitted theirs on time, so I came in on a Saturday looking for you and the report. Found a baggie of pills instead. I have to tell you, I was shocked, Max. I expected way more of you."

Max inhaled. He needed to think. Saturday. He'd worked a few hours in the morning. Then came in for a few hours in the afternoon. He'd filed his report that morning—electronic and printed copy. So, when did Bobby come looking for his report?

"Trying to figure out your story?" Bobby said.

Trying to figure out yours.

Chevy dropped back down the couch, face in his hands.

"And where did you find these pills?" Was there another stash in here? How?

"Sitting right on top of your desk. Which also surprised me because your reputation hints you'd be a lot more crafty about hiding your habit."

"On my desk?" It made no sense.

"I'm calling you up on charges."

"Charges for what?"

"Illegally obtaining prescription drugs. Maybe planning to distribute to the boys."

Max reined in, jaw taut, fighting not to explode upside Bobby's feeble brain. "Chevy, are you just going to go along with him?"

"He's got the evidence, Max."

"I hardly call this evidence. How about witnesses? A confession from a dealer? From whom did I buy these? I'm the head coach of the football team. I can't hide very easily."

"You can buy anything you want," Bobby said. "Or find any dealer name you want."

"Who else is on your Bobby Molnar team? My coaches? Rick Lundy?"

"There's no team, Max. Except the Warriors. You seem a bit defensive."

Max appealed to his jury. "Chevy, those are not my pills. I'll take a drug test. Daily if you want. But I'm clean."

"Doesn't mean these aren't your pills, Max," Bobby interrupted.

"If they were, do you think I'm stupid enough to keep them here?"

"You're the drug addict. You tell me."

That's right, just keep saying it, thinking Chevy will believe it. Max knew this method of repetition, saying it over and over until the jury or the judge believed it.

Max lunged at Bobby, shoving him into the sofa. His head cracked the wall. "You want me out of the way so you can coach this team? You do it fair and aboveboard. But don't you dare try to frame me or hurt my family or these boys in any way." He jerked Bobby by the collar as he stepped back. "Get out."

"Are you going to let him treat me like this, Chevy? He assaulted your A.D."

Chevy stood. "Get out, Bob, I need to talk to Max."

Bobby hesitated, silently refusing. Then, "I'm calling a press conference for this afternoon. You'll resign due to . . . whatever you want. You're needed at the law firm. Family obligations. I don't care. But resign. I'll take over as coach for this last game and post season. Chevy?"

"I'll talk to you upstairs."

"See you at four o'clock, Max. On the field."

The door closed and Max faced Chevy. "You're going to let him walk over you, me, the entire program like this?"

"I called Axel when Bobby came to me. He vouches for you, Max. I believe you're clean, but illegal drug use, prescription or otherwise, won't fly. The mere accusation dirties your name and reputation as well as me, the school, and the program."

"What about innocent until proven guilty?" Max wanted to blurt the truth, that Jade had found an identical bag of pills a few days ago. But he wasn't a hundred percent sure of Chevy's loyalties—to his new coach, or to his school, his A.D. and longtime friend.

There was something real and sticky about friendships in Colby, Texas.

"Court of public opinion has its own rules. Even if you're exonerated, Max, the black mark is there. It will show up in every news story, in every report. This program doesn't need any more trash—I think you understand that. We need to keep the boys together and confident. I'd like you to resign so you can go out as much a hero as when you came in."

"If I don't resign?"

"Bobby will announce this afternoon you're being investigated for illegal possession of prescription drugs, that you're suspended. How are we going to explain that to the boys?"

"That I'm innocent. That I never purchased or obtained a baggie of Percs. Those drugs are not mine."

"Then it becomes your word against the athletic director's. The team will choose sides. The parents will get riled up. Question your integrity, mine. We're divided before we get fully united."

"Chevy, you fear the people more than doing what's right?" Max shook his head.

"If you've ever spent a weekend taking call after call about how the coach violated this regulation and that code of conduct, you'd fear the people too."

"But I'm innocent and you know it." Max saw a reflection of himself in Chevy. Fearing men more than God. "Why not fire Molnar instead?"

Chevy pinched his lips. "I can't do that, Max."

"Can't or won't? Chevy, what does Bobby have on you? You've resisted hiring him as head coach but you won't fire him. Now he's primed to take over the team and you're letting him. What's changed?"

"See you at four." The principal opened the door. "I'm sorry. I wanted this to work out for both of us. You might want to talk to your wife before this goes down." He started out, then paused. "I hear she's pregnant. Congratulations."

"Twins."

"Really. How nice. Does Brenda Karlin know?"

"Yeah, she was at the house when we came home from the hospital."

"If she don't beat all. We have a running bet to see who can find out news first. In fifteen years, I've never beaten her once."

"Until now. With this bit of drug *news*."

He sighed. "Until now."

Thirty-one

Talking kindly to folks went along with any good Realtor's job. Brenda considered herself quite versed in the art of schmoozing, but boy howdy, she hated plying her earned talent to the likes of cranky ol' Polly Vance.

But she'd promised Max she'd do a favor for him and darn it, she was going to see it through. Finally, after months of Sunday afternoons sitting in the hot, stale Vance house, with all the dust-ridden furniture, drinking Polly's bitter tea, the old woman made the offer Brenda had been longing to hear.

"Brenda, what do you want?" Polly said. "We like each other all right, but I'm tired of having you come around once a week for tea. Gets on my nerves."

"I want a black dress from your attic." Brenda set down her saucer and cup, wadding up her napkin.

"What? You been coming here every Sunday for months to get at a dress?

Land amighty, girl, you should've asked right off and saved us both." But her words were tender, kind. Grateful. "Ain't nothing up there worth a plug quarter. Take it. You can have the whole lot of clothes. Heaven knows the girls don't want any of it."

"I'll pay." Brenda snatched up her purse, kissed the old battle-ax on the cheeks, and ran for the doorway.

"Take it and don't come back until spring. That'll pay me plenty."

"Then Happy Thanksgiving, Merry Christmas, and Happy New Year, Polly." Brenda jogged up the stairs, gasping for air by the time she rounded to the third-floor landing. She spied the attic door. *Oh, mercy, no. One more flight?* She flopped over the end of the banister, catching her breath.

Know what? She was going to get that dress, but then Jade wouldn't even be able to wear it because of the two babies growing in her belly. Never mind, Max said to get the dress, and she was going to get it. Brenda opened the attic door and ascended.

Warm and dusty, a bit of the November light peeking through the portal just under the front eave . . . the attic felt a bit magical. As if stepping back in time five, six decades. Boxes lined the walls along with the odd piece of furniture. Brenda didn't see any clothes at first but then spotted the far closet.

What did Jade see in all of this old stuff? Turning on the closet light, Brenda ran her fingers over the fringe of the flapper dresses, spying the little black dress hanging on the back wall.

She examined it in the light. Sure enough, Coco Chanel. It was rather nice. Classy. *Hmm* . . . the coats were stylish. And a pillbox hat. Pink too.

With catlike motions, Brenda filled her arms with clothes from the closet, turned off the light, and scurried downstairs.

"Thanks, Polly. See you in the spring." Brenda reached for the front doorknob, trying not to drop the clothes. "Lovely having tea with you."

"Wish I could say the same. See you in the spring."

Out to her car, Brenda settled the clothes in the trunk, an urgency in her spirit. She'd learned to obey that prickly sensation. The wind gusted cold, fragrant with possible snow.

As she drove down Gallia, passing under craggy, barren tree limbs, Kathy Carroll drove by in her car.

Brenda gripped the wheel and glanced in her rearview mirror. Thank goodness! She got out of the house with the dress, just in time. If Brenda had met Kathy on her way out . . .

She peered at the little black dress lying over the passenger seat. Jade sure would look pretty wearing that thing.

Brenda was almost to her office when her phone rang. Rick Lundy's number flashed on her screen.

How do, if Brenda Karlin wasn't accomplishing all of her Benson duties today. She tapped her earpiece to answer. "Rick, sugar, tell me what you know." She listened, a bit of her hot blood running cold. "He what? Stay put, I'm coming over."

"Come on, catch it." Jade bent low and tossed Asa the small plastic Warrior football. His pudgy little hands, outstretched, beat the breeze but missed the ball. It floated through his arms and bounced on the ground.

He gasped, eyes wide, and stooped to pick it up. "I got it." The flash of his white grin sparked in his brown eyes.

"You did. Run for the touchdown. I'm coming after you."

Delight switched to shock and dismay. Asa placed the ball under his arm, just like Tuck taught him, and ran. Toward no particular goal. He just ran, his dark bangs flying.

Jade called the play. "He's at the thirty, the twenty, the ten, oh, ladies and gentleman, Asa Benson is going to score a touchdown. He crossed the five and—"

She turned toward the melody of tires crackling over the gravel driveway.

The last thing she expected was Max and her old pickup rocking toward the house this time of day. It wasn't even eleven.

With a glance at Asa, who was just running in circles now, Jade walked toward the truck, concern swirling under her thoughts.

"What is it?" Jade grabbed hold of the door as Max stepped out, pain in his eyes, his angular face drawn with deep lines of frustration.

"Bobby claims he found Percocet in my office." Max fell against the truck door. "Came in this morning with Chevy, accused me, and asked for my resignation. He's calling a press conference this afternoon."

"What? He makes a claim out of nowhere and snap, he fires you? No proof, no investigation or inquiry?"

"Chevy is backing him, Jade. Doesn't want it to go to the press. Doesn't want the bad publicity. Bobby will line up his greased-palm witnesses while I repeat the same mantra. 'They're not mine. I'm not using.'"

"Can't you take a drug test?"

"A drug test won't help—they'd still want me out," Max said, shrugging off his disappointment. But Jade felt his burden. "Even if I'm clean the story will change from suspicion of using to intent to distribute. Maybe pep up the boys before a game."

"So that's it? You're out and Bobby is in?"

"Chevy's letting it happen. I can't figure out what's going on between those two. Chevy refused to hire him. Goes out on a limb to hire me, then Bobby works up a frame on me and Chevy caves. Something isn't right—but I walked out without much of a fight. I can't keep working for these people."

"But how can you let them get away with accusing you like that? Those pills aren't yours and you're not using. I live with you. I can tell."

He grinned and reached for her, pulling her against him. "Don't look now, Mrs. Benson, but you're making an argument for your husband's defense." His kiss was sweet. Grateful.

She smoothed her hand over his chest. "I can't stand the idea of letting Bobby get away with framing you."

"But proving it is another story." He released her, letting his fingers slip under her palm. "There's no time to prep a defense."

"Why don't they just fire you?"

"'Cause that's too easy. Bobby wants a show. He's going to make a big deal out of stepping into his coaching shoes Friday night. He's restoring the Molnar legacy. He's rescuing, *finally*, the Warriors."

"But why the frame when he could just convince Chevy not to rehire you?"

"Chevy wants me to stay. And in case you haven't noticed, your dashing, brilliant husband is gaining popularity."

"Yes, I've noticed. Not surprised."

"If they fire me for no reason, the boosters, the players, and the parents would ask too many questions. Another coach? Seven in six? What gives? But if I'm a bad guy, like my past sets me up to be, then Bobby's the justified hero."

"That scheming, lying snake."

"He's good. Did a little research, found out what pills I popped. Now he's finally leveraged something against Chevy to get the job he's always wanted."

"Didn't you tell Chevy I found pills planted in a drawer?" Jade peered over the yard to check on Asa. Now he was rolling around in the grass.

"No, I didn't want to tip our hand, let on that we know anything about pills in my office."

"Okay, let's think." Jade paced a small circle with a glance toward her son. "Asa, baby, come back this way." She waved him toward the house. More and more, he tested his courage and independence, pressing his parents' and his yard's boundaries. It was going to be interesting as he got older. Jade planned on having Lorelai on speed dial. "Come see, Daddy."

Tires crunched against the gravel. Max moved to the back of the truck, staring at Haley's big F350 barreling down the driveway. Hines road shotgun.

"We can't let him get away with this, Max." Haley slammed her door shut. "He's pulling something."

"I'm open to ideas."

"I knew it, I knew it." Hines fumed in circular fashion, his broad hands on his hips, ire in his full dark features. "He's scared, Max, if he's calling for the resignation today. Doesn't think he can hold up the façade long enough for a real inquiry."

"Yeah, and what do you know, Hines?" Max regarded him. "I saw you talking to him in the field house one night. About nine o'clock. Sure you weren't cooking up something with Bobby?"

"Max!" Haley said.

"It's all right, Haley." Hines stopped wearing down the grass. "He asked if I'd be on his team. Keep an eye on you, let him know if you were using. He pretended to be concerned for you, your well-being, knowing you'd just left the Outpost and how stressful coaching could be. I was onto him—I thought, now's my chance to get in the inner circle. Find out *his* game plan. But he kept me way at the end of his arm."

"Did you tell him about my history with Percocet?"

"He told me. You and I never talked about it, Max. I figured it was over and done." Hines absently reached down for Asa and swung him into his arms.

Remorse flooded Max's expression. Jade related. If he'd known when he started abusing pills what he knew now . . .

"Lord, give us wisdom," she said, low, steady. "Max, if the Lord has truly called us here and if you are truly innocent—"

"If?"

"You know what I mean. You are innocent. The Lord will take care of you. Of us."

"Joseph was innocent and ended up in prison for fifteen years," Hines said.

"But eventually he got released and became a head football coach," Jade countered, offering her interpretation of the ancient Egypt events. "Max, let's trust God. Isn't that what this whole venture was about? I'm tired of being chained to our circumstances and our feelings. Tired of being in park. I want to be in drive. We've seen what man can do, let's see what God can do. If all you have at this press conference is your hat in your hand and your profession of innocence, then so be it. But do not resign. Do not."

"I'm with Jade on this, Max." Hines dotted the air with his finger.

"Me too. In fact, you might let Jade speak for you. Nice speech, woman." Haley popped Jade a low five.

Then Jade remembered Brenda. *Of course.* "Actually, Max, I've already put a dog onto this trail."

"What? Who? I was thinking we could get—"

"Brenda Karlin." Max's and Jade's voices bumped together.

"I'm thinking the same thing." Hines. Faithful Hines.

"If there's any chance of making this go away before four o'clock, I agree," Haley said. "It's Brenda Karlin."

Max tugged his phone from his pocket and dialed. "Jade, I'm starved. Got anything for lunch?"

"Come on in. Saving a career does make a body hungry." She started up the porch but Max snatched her by the arm, lowering the phone away from his head. Hines and Haley passed on inside.

"What'd you say? Just now?"

"I said, saving a career makes a body hungry."

"That's what I thought." Max hooked her waist with his arm and kissed her, a seal on the deal of this venture. "Thank you," he whispered, tapping his forehead to hers.

"I decided I like Texas. I like being the coach's wife."

Bobby's office door opened after a knock. He glanced up to see Chevy poke his head around. The man had no spine. Hallelujah. Worked in his favor.

"Got a sec?" Chevy invited himself in. "Let's get our story straight before this press conference."

"Story. Chevy, come on, you make it sound like a conspiracy." Bobby came around his desk, kicking out a chair to sit Chevy at the mini conference table. "We found the pills in Max's office. We don't need the scandal."

"Who put them there?" Chevy sat, paper and pencil in hand. Ever since high school, the man carried around something to write with.

"Don't bother yourself with the details, friend. But you know what they say, if you want something done right, you have to do it yourself."

"I've been chewing on that notion myself these days." Chevy looked up, and Bobby flinched at the courage he saw in his principal's beady eyes.

"Is Benson ready? All he has to do is resign and thank all the appropriate people. Blah, blah and everyone's happy."

"You know, you can't live a good life chasing the ghost of your dead daddy."

"Don't get all pop-psych on me, Chevy. This is my time. Coaching Warrior football has always been my destiny. And I finally found my way in." He arched his brow. Dumb Chevy.

"You're not a good coach, Bob. Plano didn't teach you anything?"

"It was my word against his."

"You're rigid. You don't like change. You're too controlling. Boys fear you but they don't respect you."

"They will when we start winning games."

"Remember when we went out this summer, after school let out?"

Where was he going with this? Bobby grinned. "You had one too many and decided to drive home? Got pulled over by a cop who called me instead of hauling you in. Yeah, I remember."

"Yeah, that was one time. I mean, the week before when I drove you home because you had more than a few too many."

Bobby furrowed his brow. "You helped me inside to the couch so Fiona wouldn't know how bad I was. Or so you told me." Where was this line of questioning going? "What does this have to do with the press conference?"

"You told me you hit the kid in Plano because he ticked you off. Provoked you."

"He was a crybaby. A whiner." Bobby pictured the skinny kid trying to make the varsity cut. "Had no athletic ability. For a black boy, you'd think he could at least run."

"That's why I can't let you coach, Bob."

"You have no choice. If Benson doesn't resign, I'm outing him and implicating you for hiring him. And if I need to, I'll put out my principal-got-pulled-over-for-DUI card."

"Either way, we're going to end this, Bobby. I should've sat on you a long time ago but I wanted to give credence to our friendship." Chevy held up an iPhone. "Benson lent this to me. Here's my insurance policy. Some of the folks might like to know how you really feel about kids trying to learn football. Especially young black kids. In your own words, of course. It's the twenty-first century, Bobby. Not the sixties of your granddaddy's day. And I have Rick on here telling me how you gave him the pills to plant in Max's office."

"You can't do this to me, Chevy." Bobby launched out of his chair. "That job is mine. Mine. The Molnar legacy. This is my last chance."

"No, this is your last chance. You can resign or I can fire you. Rick's waiting outside to corroborate everything if I need it."

Bobby shook, his hand clinching and releasing. "You two are supposed to be my friends."

"We are. Consider this an intervention. Now, we're going to go out there and have a press conference. I'm going to keep this quiet, and you're going to shut up about my DUI."

"Why have a press conference? There's nothing to say."

"I'll be naming Max Benson our head football coach for the next year with ongoing conversations the next five years. I'm also announcing my search for a new athletic director."

"Just like that, you're firing me?"

"No, Bobby, I'm actually setting you free. Go, get out of Colby, away from the ghost of your daddy. Your memories of him are far more glorious than the truth. He's gone. You don't need his approval anymore."

"You fire me, I'm taking you down with me. I'll report the DUI."

"I figured as much. I already have a call into the district supervisor. I'm tired of living in fear someone will find out." Chevy moved toward the door. "Now, do you want me to say you're leaving to pursue other opportunities or because you tried to frame Max?"

Thirty-two

Under the lights of the Amarillo Sandies stadium, the Warriors played their last and best game. The stands rocked with red and gold Warrior fans. The pep band beat the air with their rhythms.

Noah and Calvin clicked on play after play. Max's weaker skill players found their stride, especially sophomore tight end Grant Strickland, who broke free on his first play and ran forty-two yards for the Warriors' first six.

Tucker easily made the point after. The grin on his face and the power in his stride as he came off the field would live in Max's memory for a long time.

But it was fourth quarter. Two minutes to go, 23–21. The Sandies led by two.

Second down, Calvin caught a pass that led the Warriors to the Sandies' six yard line. The stands rocked and waved. Air horns blasted. Drumbeats sounded.

Max signaled in a run. The Sandies were weak on the left side and he was going to send Calvin through into the end zone.

The ref's whistle blew and Noah took the snap, handing off to Calvin. Max's pulse surged. Just six yards . . . six little yards.

Fumble. Max jerked upright. Calvin . . . *dropped the ball*. Every player on the field was scrambling. Black and gold tussling against red and gold. An anxious knot weaved through Max as he waited for the refs to clear the pile. When they did, a lone Warrior guard lay on the ground, curled around the ball.

"Yes. Way to hustle." Max ran down the sideline. "Haywood, way to go. Now, let's hang on to it this time."

"My heart darn near stopped beating," Hines mumbled as he walked past.

"I think mine did," Max said, shoving his hat back on his head. "Twice."

The boys ran toward the sideline, defeated under their helmets.

"Let's go, run, shake it off." Max stepped onto the field. "There's still a minute forty to play. We're not done yet."

"What do you want to do, Max?" Coach Hines scanned his play card. "Tucker's been hitting all night."

Now it was fourth and twelve. Tuck stood next to Max, ready to go. But there was more than enough time for the best team in the district to defeat the worst.

It was a repeat of last week against Lubbock. Except . . .

"I say we go for six. The Sandies won't be able to beat us with a field goal." Max looked at Tucker. "Want to give Calvin and Noah another shot?"

"Let's go for six."

"We can do it, Coach." Calvin clapped Tucker on the shoulder pads and snapped on his helmet. "I won't drop it. I won't."

"I know you won't." Max scanned his play card. He called a pass. "Calvin, you run straight for that flag just inside the goal line. Noah, you put it right over his shoulder. Warriors on three. One, two, three."

"Warriors!"

Max glanced back at Jade—she gave him two thumbs-up—then he scanned down the row for Asa. Dr. Gelman held him, helping him wave his Warrior flag. Asa already had a way with the ladies.

On the field, the offense lined up. The whistles blew. The clock started ticking. Expectation weighted the air. Noah called for the snap. The Sandies defense shifted.

"Blitz," Max called. "They're blitzing."

But Noah was poised and perfect, undaunted by the swell of black and gold coming toward him. Calvin blew past their cornerback and cut toward the left end zone marker. Noah released the ball. A beautiful, spinning spiral.

Calvin looked back. Max dropped to one knee. Eyes fixed on the left end zone flag. *Come on, Calvin, come on.* Calvin stretched for the ball.

It hit his fingertips and bounced, twirling end over end above his hands. Max dropped his head as Calvin tripped and stumbled.

The throw couldn't have been any better. It just didn't hit.

When he looked up, the Sandies' defenders were closing in. Calvin caught his stride and remained upright. Just before the ball hit the ground, he reached one-handed and pulled it in. By the time he hit the field, he had control of the football and his right foot anchored in bounds.

The ref's arms shot into the air. Touchdown. Touch! Down! Max launched out of his crouched position, firing onto the field, racing arms wide toward Calvin. The stands exploded with Warrior pride—a deafening noise.

"Coach, coach—" Calvin jumped into Max, nearly knocking him over. But Max held on, amid the throng of celebrating players, yelling from the bottom of his being.

"That's the way to play Warrior football."

The Sandies' offense didn't have a chance. Quick and accurate, they'd lost their momentum. No way would Haley's D let the team down.

When the clock ran out, the score said it all. Home: 23. Visitors: 28.

The Warriors had won their first game in two seasons with greenhorn

Maxwell Benson as their head coach. Even the Sandies had to celebrate with them. The stadium shook and shimmied. Both teams knelt to say the Lord's Prayer. Then the Warriors ran, celebrating, to their buses for home.

Max was pretty sure none of their feet touched the ground.

~

Sleep. What sleep?

"You awake?" Jade rolled on her side, resting her hand on her growing middle. Baby girl B had stopped being submissive to baby girl A about a week ago and it was an all-out war in there.

"Who can sleep?"

"You won, Max. You won."

"I keep going over everything in my mind. I know how it feels to lose. I've relived those moments, on and off the field, plenty of times. But this . . ." His smiled parted the darkness in the room. "Is amazing."

"I knew tonight was going to be different. Chevy stood up to Bobby. He got rid of the bad seed. These last few years Bobby brought the whole program down, Max. When Chevy let him run amuck, no one succeeded."

"Run amuck?"

Jade shoved him. "You know what I mean."

"Yeah, I do. After the press conference it felt different. Did it to you?" Max reached over, finding Jade's hand in the dark.

"Yeah, but I felt bad for him. He's just trying to fulfill his dreams."

"Chevy said his old man was pretty hard on him. He thinks leaving Colby High is the best thing for him."

"Where's he going?"

"Not sure. But I've been praying about getting a lunch with him, checking in, seeing how he's doing."

"I can't imagine how he feels, Max. In his mind, his friends Chevy and Rick betrayed him. Just when he thought they were in his corner. Instead of being coach, he's unemployed."

"I feel for him too, but he made the decisions that got him in trouble. Just like I did, Jade. I had to live out the consequences and it made me get on my knees before the Lord and get real. If Bobby runs headlong into Jesus, he'll look back on this day with gratitude."

"Are you happy, Max?"

"Yeah. Very. You?"

"Isn't it obvious? I can't stop smiling. I go to sleep smiling, I wake up smiling."

"How do you feel about living in Colby for the rest of your life? Or the next twenty years, anyway."

"I love Colby, Max. It's where we found each other, where the girls were conceived. Where we met Tucker. Did I tell you Brenda Karlin somehow got into Polly Vance's attic with all her vintage clothes?"

"R-really? How'd you find out?"

"She told me. She's been having tea with Mrs. Vance for months. Every Sunday. The old lady asked her what she wanted and she said a peek at the closet. So she told her she could have whatever she wanted."

"Wow, babe." Max squeezed her hand. "Didn't you want something from that closet?"

"Ha, I did." *Ppffllbbttt.* "I can't wear it now. A little black dress? Even if I could fit into it, these two would fight over it, calling dibs. Listen, I think we need to write out rules and discipline for these two. They're going to be terrors."

"They're going to be beautiful," Max said. "Perfect angels."

"Sure, okay, hold on to that fantasy."

"So, Brenda . . . ?"

"She found a storefront and wants to open a vintage shop. She asked me to help get it started. Guess who will be her main employee?"

"Bit?"

"No, but good try. Mariah Walberg."

Max hummed. "Good for Brenda. Mariah needs someone to believe in her. So, you don't want the little black dress? You won't always be pregnant."

"I asked her about it and she said she promised it to someone already." Jade sighed. She would've loved that little black dress. "Maybe I can convince Brenda I need the dress more. Or ask who she promised it to and see if they'll sell it."

Max turned on the light.

"What are you doing?" Jade squinted as her eyes adjusted from dark to light.

"I was saving it for a surprise, but since you can't wear it—" He ducked into the closet. "Of course, you weren't pregnant when I had the idea." Max emerged with the little black dress swinging from a pink satin hanger. "Happy late anniversary. I've been so busy with football we never got to celebrate."

"Oh, Max." Jade scrambled out of bed, prancing across the cold floor. "How did you . . . you? You're the one Brenda promised it to?"

"You talked about it like, I don't know, it was the holy grail. I felt bad I cost you the chance to own the dress, so I asked Brenda if she could look into it."

"Max, she went to Mrs. Vance's for Sunday tea all fall. Awful tea according to her too. Just for a chance at the closet."

"She did it for you, Jade."

"She did it for you, Max." Jade slipped her hand the length of the dress. "I love it. Simply love it." She thanked Max with a tender kiss. "I think this is about the nicest thing anyone's ever done for me."

"Better than the diamond wedding bracelet I gave you?"

"Okay, the second best thing . . ." Jade held up the dress. "A real Coco Chanel." Joy bubbled in her chest. "What a great end to a great day. Hey, this will motivate me to get back into shape after the girls are . . ." She cocked her ear. "Do you hear music?" She hung the dress in the closet and slipped on her robe and slippers.

"As a matter of fact, I do." Max tugged on a sweatshirt and worked his feet into his sneakers.

From the shadows of the living room, Jade watched the lawn fill with flickering firelight—torches and lamps. "Oh, Max, you have to see this."

"I'm seeing it."

Cars streamed down the road, turning into the drive, parking askew on the lawn. Players, parents, faculty, boosters, fans swarmed the house.

The pep band gathered to one side. But lining the front was the entire Warrior starting team.

As the music started, soft and brassy, Max grabbed Jade's hand and led her to the porch. The November air was thick with frost and emotion. It had to be nearly midnight.

The tiki torch brigade grew wider. More cars. More grateful fans.

"Coach, Coach, Coach, Coach, Coach . . ." The chant chased and echoed, rising loud, bold.

"Give it up for Coach Benson." Cheers, whistles, and applause.

Max moved to the first step. "Evening, all. What's going on?"

Jade leaned against him. A yard full of red and gold birds. Only the kind that played football on Friday nights.

"We just want to say thanks, Coach." Calvin stepped forward. "For chasing us all down, especially me, and giving us a chance."

"You believed in us, Coach," a voice called.

"You boys did it. You worked hard. And I couldn't have done it without Hines and Haley." He motioned for the coaches to join him on the steps. "And all the volunteers."

The volume from the band rose. Trumpets sounded a low, lingering note. The players linked arms and began to sing, gently swaying back and forth.

In hallowed halls, we remember you
Colby High, beacon of learned truth.

Chills skirted over Jade's skin, and not from the nip in the breeze. From the voices. From the hearts. Gathered on her lawn.

Max drew her close, the alma mater song vibrating in his chest.

> *In red and gold, we'll fight to win,*
> *Return to your teachings, again and again.*
> *So we sing to you, Colby High,*
> *You're in our memories dear and nigh.*
> *To you our loyalty we give,*
> *To your victory, we'll always live.*

As the last note rang out, Jade peered toward the stars, almost imagining that heaven paused to sing along. *Thank you, Jesus.*

Days and nights would come and go. Football seasons dawn and fade. But for these forty Warrior players, for the town, the school, Max and Jade, Hines and Haley, tonight would live in hearts forever.

Max's cheeks glistened in the firelight.

"Max?"

"Yeah?"

"I think we're looking at what God can do."

Thirty-Three

December 23rd
Whisper Hollow

The only sounds in the Blue Umbrella were Jade's breathing and the tapping echo of Lillabeth's footsteps on the hardwood as she came out of the storeroom.

Emptiness did that—caught the hollow sounds and echoed them across barren valley, barren rooms. Barren hearts. That's why valleys, hearts, and rooms needed to be filled with love.

"I guess that's everything." Lillabeth slowed her progress through the empty shop. "Are you okay with all of this?" She adjusted the box in her arm and walked to where Jade waited in the center of the room. Where the sunspot always fell.

Today the spot was a pale winter white with Main Street Christmas lights falling across the hardwood in long colorful lines.

"Remember the Halloween we built a pumpkin display right here?" Jade tapped her booted foot against the floor.

"How could I forget? We had that great big pumpkin and we couldn't keep the kids from sitting on it."

Jade surveyed the shop, hand resting on her rounding belly. "Lots of memories in these walls."

"I grew up here, Jade. You helped me—" Lillabeth set the box on the floor and gathered Jade in a gripping, sobbing hug. "I'm going . . . to miss you. What am I going to do without you?"

"Oh, what am I going to do without you? My beautiful Lilla. You've been with me through it all. My right arm." Jade cuddled her cheek against Lillabeth's silky hair and the scent of strawberries. "I love you so much."

"I love you too."

For a long while, Jade held her friend, their affection speaking louder than words. Funny, this wise twenty-one-year-old was as much a mentor to her as she was a baby sister and a friend.

Lillabeth had turned down the gift of the shop. Aaron was finally being assigned stateside, and they were driving across the country to California in the New Year.

"You are a jewel and a joy to me, Lillabeth." Jade's voice quivered. Her eyes welled up. "I don't know what I would've done without you this year. You were such a rock."

"No, Jade, I owe you. I learned so much watching you." Lilla brushed her hand across her cheeks. "About running a business, yes, but about running a life. I am in awe of how you took in Asa, forgave Max." She shook her head, gazing toward the gray day outside the window. "How you embraced faith and love, let them change you. I'll never forget this year."

"That makes two of us." It was healing to share a laugh.

"I pray I never face a trial like you did, but if I do—"

"Don't model yourself after me, model yourself after Jesus. He's the only pure way."

"I'm figuring that out. Aaron and I have been talking about church and faith, not wanting to just say we're Christians but actually *be* Christians."

Jade brushed her fingers along the sleek strands of Lillabeth's hair, smoothing them over her shoulder. "You have so much life waiting for you. Put it in drive and go."

"Preferably in a pink Cadillac?" She laughed and dried her cheeks again.

"With the top down, broken, and it snowing outside."

Jade stepped back, her heart taut with ebbing and flowing emotions. But it'd been like that all month. Since she came back to the Hollow to put the Blue Umbrella up for sale and begin the process of bidding adieu to her old life in order to embrace her new one. "I'll see you tonight? Up at Max's parents'. You would not believe the party June has planned. It's fit for kings."

"And queens?" Lillabeth stooped to pick up the box. "The queen of vintage."

"No, the *Southern Life* headline said princess. I'm not a queen. Yet." Jade curtseyed. "Did you get the antique jewel box?" She peered into the box.

"Yes, and your Christmas present. Thank you." Lillabeth kissed Jade's cheek. "I'll be sure to wear it tonight. Whatever it is. Jade, what is it? Tell me." Lilla squeezed Jade's arm.

"Forget it. Go home, open it. You'll see soon enough."

"Is it something—"

"Go. Open it. You'll see." Jade walked Lillabeth to the front door as Aaron pulled along the curb. "See you at eight."

"I almost forgot how bossy you are. Hmmm . . ." Lillabeth started out the door, but paused. "It's snowing." So it was. A light snow whispered from a covering of clouds and salted Main Street with wintery goodness. "Bye, Jade."

Jade raised her hand. "See you, Lillabeth." She would be the belle of the ball tonight in a vintage and oh-so-chic Chanel little black dress—accented by her sleek blond locks and porcelain skin.

She watched Aaron drive off. Jade stood alone in the Blue Umbrella. Max would be there soon.

When Jade had moved to Whisper Hollow, she came seeking peace. To find her place in the world, to discover her dreams. Had she known it would require charging through the gauntlet of life, unearthing shameful secrets and her painful past, she'd have never driven up the side of the mountain.

But, oh, she was so glad she did. Look what God had done. Gave her beauty for ashes. Exchanged her sorrows for joy, her fears for love.

For five years, she'd hovered under the protection of the Blue Umbrella. But now it was time to fold it up and move on. The rain had finally stopped.

One last time, Jade inhaled the warm, woodsy scent of the shop, the lingering wooly scent of vintage clothes, the tinge of fresh paint touch-up, the aroma of pine cleaner, and she listened for the final and last chords of her memories.

"I'll never forget you, Blue."

The hinges of the shop's back door moaned and a drop of light hit the floor. Max rounded the corner, dashing in his tailored, black wool coat and soft weave trousers. Snow dusted his dark hair.

"You ready, Jade-o?"

"I do believe I am."

"Asa's in the car with Mom." Max scouted out the shop, then regarded her. "Is it hard?"

"If it wasn't, then my years here wouldn't have meant anything, would they?"

Max paced farther inside, the *clip-clap* of his shoes skirting over the hardwood. He looked like lawyer Max tonight. "I suppose not."

"But better days are ahead. Is the judge ready?" Jade picked up her bag from the sales counter.

"He is. Are you?"

She grinned, nodding. "As I'll ever be."

Once they'd decided to stay in Colby, she'd put both shops on the market and spread the word across her vintage network that she was liquidating inventory. Within a week, both shops sold. A week later, all her inventory was gone. Except for the choice pieces she shipped to Brenda and the things she needed to keep.

Mama's show prints from her hippie days. Her picture with George Harrison. Her jade engagement ring. In her desk drawer, Jade found Pap's praying hands medallion. She cupped them in her palm, realizing she didn't need them around her neck anymore because they lived inside her heart.

"Did you give Lillabeth the dress?" Max said.

"She's going to be so surprised. I gave her the check too." Proceeds from the sale of the shop and the inventory. If anyone deserved a cut of the profits, it was Lilla.

"I'm so proud you're my wife." Max kissed Jade's forehead, then started for the door. "She'll have a nice down payment for a California house. But we'd better get going. Don't know how this snow will impact traffic."

"Okay, one more second." Jade took a final spin around the room. She flipped the Open sign to Closed. On the storeroom wall, she'd tacked this year's calendar. Every day was circled. Every single day.

Especially today. Three years ago at Christmas she'd told Max she was pregnant with their honeymoon baby. But he didn't live. Today they were driving down to the city for a judge to pronounce Asa as hers. Forever.

Max waited outside the door. When Jade came out, his eyes greeted her with love and compassion. She shut the door and turned the key.

It was like Max said the time they rode the Ferris wheel. It's the circle of life. Jade would embrace it all, enjoy the journey, and get a little bit stronger every day.

Joy! A Child Is Born

Emily June Benson, five pounds seven ounces eighteen inches

Elaine Beryl Benson, five pounds two ounces, eighteen inches

Born April 21st at 4:16 p.m. & 4:18 p.m.

We're tickled pink!

Celebrate with us, pray for us, drop by and change a diaper.

With love,

Max, Jade, and Asa Benson

Epilogue

August

Warrior Stadium

The summer heat hung over the stadium as Max glared across the field watching Hines, in the first Red v. Gold game in ten years.

"Bring it, Hines. Show me what you got."

Hines crouched down, his hard gaze aimed for Max. *He's thinking the same thing. "Bring it, Max . . ."*

The up-and-coming Warrior fall football team was on the field, duking it out.

Hines whispered to new assistant Carmen Maas, a friend of Haley's, and yes, a woman. She was a mirror of the defensive coordinator, only on offense.

Beside Max, Haley bent over, hands on her thighs. "He's going right, Max."

"You bet he is."

Max peeked over his shoulder. Jade juked in the bleachers with the new athletic director's wife, Ilene Maher, a Western Tech professor and mother of two.

Greg Maher was Max's age. Aggressive, eager to return to Colby's football tradition. He was the one who resurrected the red and gold game.

Chevy walked the sidelines, proud, a whole new man once he got rid of Bobby.

The pep band drums rolled, rocking and ticking. Hines's offense executed but ran into Max's defense.

As the boys ran off the field, Max gazed back at Jade. She was strangely unencumbered. The girls were . . . Max scanned down the row. With Brenda and Bit. They already had more grandparents than any pink, beautiful, melt-their-daddy's-heart twins should have.

But Max loved that they were loved.

Asa stepped into being a big brother with his usual forthrightness and bravery. Came out the other day trying to carry one of them. Jade moved so fast he considered getting her to sign up for the team.

The hardest part of becoming a head coach was saying good-bye to Benson Law. Dad's face had reddened and he choked on the emotion of his words, but he was Reb Benson, strong and decisive to the end.

"You have to do what you have to do, son. Your grandfathers never intended for the firm to be a prison."

But Max still retained his partnership and one day, if Asa chose the law, the firm would go to him. Or, even better, Elaine or Emily.

Four months old, Em already showed signs of being a good litigator. Elaine displayed more of Jade's refined, tender qualities. And love for clothes.

Max's parents were coming to Colby for the first game of the season, along with the McClures.

Brenda caught his eye and waved.

Wasn't she a blessing. Opened a vintage shop and handed it over to Mariah. Belief was a powerful tool.

"Coach . . . Max!" Haley waved her hand in front of him. "Did I lose you?"

"No, no." Max turned around, pressing his hand to his chest, almost expecting to feel the plump of the love filling his heart. "What's up?"

"Fourth down. We're on the fifteen."

No-brainer. "Send in Tucker."

"My thoughts exactly. Tuck." Haley ran down the line, but the kicker was already on the field.

His talent would get him to a major college.

When the whistle blew the end of the game, Max's Red team had bested the Gold by three. Everyone gathered on the fifty, talking at once. Jade squeezed through to stand by Max.

"Bonfire at our place. Everyone bring something to eat *and* to share."

The team scattered. Brenda shoved the twins' stroller toward them. Bit came along holding Asa's hand.

"We'd better go or we'll never get our car up the driveway," Jade said. "The kids will beat us there." She grabbed onto the stroller, talking food strategies with Bit and Brenda.

Max swung Asa up on his shoulders as the Channel 13 reporter Chip Mack approached.

"Got a second, Coach?"

Max stopped and faced the camera. Chip held up his microphone.

"They're already calling you the next great Warrior coach. How'd you rebuild this team, Coach? So fast?"

"We have a saying at my house. We've seen what man can do. Let's see what God can do." He gave Chip a second for it to sink in but it didn't, so he headed off. "See you on the sidelines, Chip."

Max carried Asa to the truck, talking, listening. He buckled him in, then walked around to the driver's side, tapping his hip pocket with his hand. It was empty.

His hip-pocket dream came true. All it took was complete surrender.

Acknowledgments

Ami McConnell for your insight and courage to say, "Write it again." You definitely made this a better book.

Rachelle Gardner for your fine eye in the small details. Thank your for your work and encouragement.

Kevin Mays, Defensive Coordinator at Bayside High School, Palm Bay, Florida, for taking time out of your day to talk high school football.

David Cisar at winningyouthfootball.com for the phone chat on how to coach young men.

Tony Hauck for the details of play-calling and enduring a lot of questions.

Ellen Tarver for reading and editing this story in its original draft.

Reading Group Guide

1. In chapter one, Jade discovers Asa is not Max's son. How did you feel about this? Did you suspect such foul play from Rice?

2. If you were in Jade's situation, how would you handle the news of your husband's son not being his?

3. Max came to a greater understanding of his life before God while at the Outpost Ranch. Was there a time in your life when the Lord revealed Himself in the midst of your pain?

4. Max takes on a huge challenge to become a high-school football coach. It's life changing. Have you faced a life-changing challenge?

5. Moving to Texas uproots Jade and Max and all they know. It's hard to move away from family. Discuss how this bold move impacted Max and Jade. Was it for the good? For the bad? Would you do the same if God opened the door?

6. Jade's first get-together with a friend in Colby quickly turns sour. Discuss how we can be better friends to one another even in adversity.

7. Max shows integrity by staying with the coaching job even though he was deceived about the condition of the football program. How important is it to have honor in your job, relationships, actions? Even when you've been wronged. Discuss.

8. Jade is surprised by her pregnancy. What does this event symbolize in her and Max's life, and in the story? Discuss a time in your life when the Lord brought good from a difficult situation.

9. Tucker is a sweet character in the story. What was your reaction when he finally scored the field goal? Is there something going on in your life that mirrors Tucker's desire to make a goal?

10. Sports often reflect life, especially in our spiritual journeys. Pressing in against the defense, against the odds. Playing hard even when we are losing. Playing to the end without giving up. Is there a situation in your life where you need a team to help you press in? Are you utilizing your team? Are you on the verge of giving up? Don't! Press on. Discuss ways to press on in a hard situation.

11. Max shows love to his enemy, Bobby Molnar. How about you? Can you love someone who's determined to take you down?

12. Joy! Jade and Max have twin girls. Discuss an area of joy in your life!

Also from Rachel Hauck, co-author of

The Sweet By & By

Visit
RachelHauck.com

One dress.
Four women.
An amazing destiny.

RACHEL HAUCK

The
WEDDING
DRESS

"All my songs tell a story. But this one is special. It's about looking backward while moving forward. About chasing dreams. Endless country roads, and tender faith."

—Mutli-Platinum Recording Artist Sara Evans

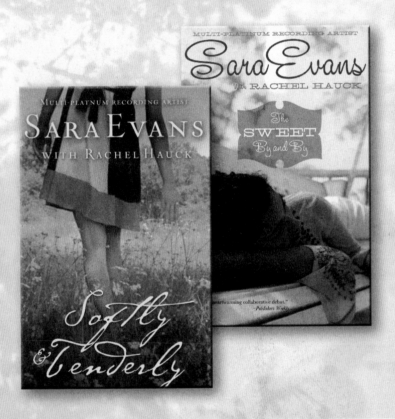

The Songbird Novels: An enchanting series of grace, redemption, and love by Sara Evans with Rachel Hauck.

Also from Rachel Hauck, co-author of *The Sweet By and By*

Discover Romance
in the Big City,
Southern Style . . .

Discover
NashVegas

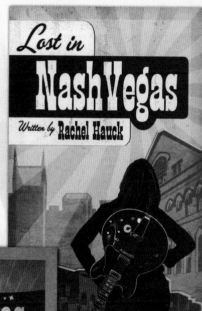

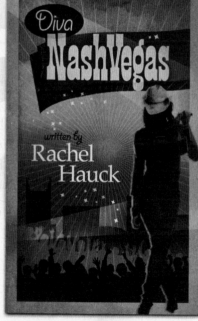

Author Bios

Multi-platinum recording artist Sara Evans has been honored with numerous accolades, among them the 2006 Academy of Country Music's Female Vocalist of the Year and the Country Music Association's Video of the Year for "Born to Fly." Evans has been named one of *People Magazine*'s "50 Most Beautiful People" and won the hearts of television viewers as the first-ever country star to compete in ABC's *Dancing with the Stars*. Sara is a Cabinet Member of the American Red Cross.

Best-selling and award-winning author Rachel Hauck lives in Florida with her husband, Tony, a pastor. A graduate of Ohio State University, she left the corporate software marketplace in '04 to write full time.